Shutterbug

Buz Sawyers

Savant Books
Honolulu, HI, USA
2013

Published in the USA by Savant Books and Publications
2630 Kapiolani Blvd #1601
Honolulu, HI 96826
http://www.savantbooksandpublications.com

Printed in the USA

Edited by Chunghea Oliver
Cover by Dennis Krull
Author Photo by Brian Braun

13 digit ISBN: 9780983286172
10-digit ISBN: 0983286175

Dedication

This book is for my many friends and associates at The Classical Center of Brandenburg Middle School, where I taught for twenty years. My thanks to Carra, our principal, who never forgot what it was like to be a teacher; Radona and Erin my best buds; Cheri,who supplied me with books to read and helped me to find my first publisher; Heather, who always made me feel like the best writer since Mark Twain; and Berkey.

Acknowledgements

Even though *Shutterbug* is a work of fiction, as in all cases with my writing, accuracy in real-life facts included within the fictional portion of the plot, is essential for me. First, I must thank Brian Braun, a friend and local photographer who allowed me to use his name and personality for my main character, and of course, for allowing me to probe into his unbelievable knowledge and expertise behind the lens. My dilemma for this novel was to find someone with the FBI that could give me counsel concerning undercover work and FBI protocol. This introduction came via Michael Hatfield, the Garland SRO officer at Brandenburg Middle School, where I taught for twenty years.

His contacts led me to Lupe Gonzales, who retired as the Special-Agent-in-Charge of the Dallas Division of the FBI six months before I met him. He was never shy about informing me, "...that only happens in the movies, Buz." He did his best and succeeded in keeping my literary privilege to a minimum. And a special thanks to *K*.

And lastly, none of this would have ever come together as a viable, working piece of fiction fit for the mainstream without the efforts of two important people: my editor, Chunghea Oliver and Zachary Oliver, the man behind the scenes that made all of this come together. Chunghea showed me the difference between *my* final draft of a manuscript, which I thought was untouchable, and hers, which was more streamlined and to the point without all the *fluff*. Zach was the man who decided to take a chance on a raw manuscript and idea and run with it. Thanks to both of you for your patience, diligent work, and new friendship that came about from working on the *Shutterbug* project.

Prologue

Thursday, July 29, 2009
Washington, D. C.

U. S. Senator "Jimmy" Fagan sat in his Cadillac with the air conditioner blowing full force, attempting to repel the sweat that beaded on his forehead like a rash. The sweltering, blanketing humidity of D. C. and the clandestine meeting in the middle of the night seemed to entice his sweat glands to empty their bladders. His car was backed into the parking spot so that he had a full view of the private parking garage. What if something went wrong? How could he explain his presence here at two o'clock in the morning? He tried to block such thoughts from his mind, instead relishing the Congressional summer recess that started tomorrow. Relieved that he wouldn't have to return to this God-forsaken town until after Labor Day, he'd have almost a month to envelope himself in the peace and tranquility of his ranch in Rusk.

An unexpected and loud rap of knuckles on the passenger side window made him jerk violently. He peered across the seat and saw his appointment's stoic face framed by the window's glass. The senator fumbled for the switch and unlocked the door. In spite of his bulk, the man slid easily into the front seat.

Visibly shaken, the senator exclaimed, "Jesus H. Christ, Freeman! You scared the shit out of me! Where'd you come from?"

Mark Freeman shrugged silently.

Fagan gathered himself and said, "Well? What's so damn important that you couldn't just call and give me this so-called good news? I'm headed for Texas tomorrow, you know."

"I'm surprised you even have to ask that, Senator. You mean, you'd feel comfortable with me calling you at the office?"

Fagan shook his head. "No, no, of course not," he said, correcting himself. "So what is it? What's the good news?"

Freeman didn't mince words. "I have a reliable source that says your friend has a new hit job scheduled."

The senator straightened up in his seat. This *was* good news. "Really? Well—that's great, isn't it? I mean, is there a way to use this? Do you have some kind of plan in mind?"

Freeman nodded. "Oh, I've got a plan alright."

"Well? Do we know the target and when it's going to take place? Details, man, give me details."

"Yeah, we know all that," stated Freeman.

"Dammit-all man, tell me! Who's the target?"

"You are," Freeman said simply.

A fresh blanket of sweat broke out on Fagan's forehead. "Me? And you consider this *good* news?"

Freeman finally allowed himself a tight grin for the senator's benefit and said, "Of course. Don't you?"

"Not really, Mr. Freeman. Why don't you enlighten me?"

"Think about it," Freeman stated. "With the summer recess you're looking so forward to, it'll give us a full month to arrange your assassination."

Shutterbug

DAY 1

Saturday, September 5, 2009

Shutterbug

Chapter 1

At first, it was a brief, quick squeal. Sharp stalks of old stale hay poked into his flesh, leftovers from a time when this place had still been in use. His body jerked alert. The slight noise of opening doors squeaking directly below him was definitely not an accidental groan from the old barn. His eyes strained in the early morning light. Then, as quick as the metallic sound started, it stopped.

He looked around the deeply shadowed hay loft and out into the clearing, adrenaline wiping clear the exhaustion lingering from a lack of sleep. Outside, the dim light revealed an overcast ceiling. A light mist covered the ground. His mind struggled to catch up.

The shooter? Have I located myself in the shooter's nest? If this is such a great spot for me, it might be the same for the assassin!

Then, the faint squeaking started again, this time lasting just a bit longer. He wanted to move, to get out. Lying prone for almost two hours had taken its toll, though; the stiffness that had crept into his joints and muscles held him back. There was no way of even shifting his position without being heard. So, the young man remained motionless, paralyzed, his mind racing. Cradled in his hand was his weapon: a camera prepped with a 24-70 mid-range zoom, the shutter set at 1/250th of a second. He had but to tighten his finger and the camera would begin firing eleven frames per second.

A swish of cloth brushing against ragged wood below in the belly of this old barn suggested that someone was squeezing through a barely open barn door.

Think. Don't move...just wait.

He heard the door squeak briefly again and everything became quiet. His aching mind and cramped muscles remained poised, straining towards the singular moment, which, at least for him, had been shaped by the more or less honorable Senator Fagan.

Photography used to be nothing more than a cover for Brian Braun during his previous life as a thief. Now it was a necessity to keep him away from temptation...and, better yet, jail. Five years ago, if someone predicted that he'd be working on a coffee-table book of photographs instead of planning a new heist in Monaco or Paris, he'd have laughed in their face and asked them what kind of drugs they were on. In fact, his past notoriety was actually helping him get sports figures, local wanna-be politicians, gang-bangers, homeless, and everyday Joes to jump at the chance to be in his *Faces of Texas*.

Nonetheless, he longed for his adrenaline rush from the past. Life on the edge. Instead, here he was taking pictures of faces, faces of the known, the unknown, the prominent, the downtrodden. In the past six months, he'd photographed countless people from the canyons and ranches of the Northern Panhandle, the Great Plains farmlands, and the oil fields of West Texas.

Now, laying awkwardly in the cold, straining to be quiet, he thought back on what had brought him here—the phone ring, the strange conversation that ensued. He had snatched the phone off the desk, checking the name of the caller, but all it said was UNKNOWN. During the brief moment it took to lift the receiver from cradle to ear, he had hoped that it wasn't one of his former netherworld associates proposing a new heist together.

"This is Brian," he had answered simply.

"Brian? Senator Jimmy Fagan, here, calling from Rusk. How're you doing this fine morning, son?"

Hearing the location, a small rural town in Texas, and the Senator's cheerful introduction, he had perked up. The old codger had been dodging Brian's calls for over a month. He would make a great addition to his book. "Well, I'm good, Senator. I'll have to admit, though, I'm a little surprised, but I…"

The senator's booming voice cut him off in mid-sentence. "I know. You've been tryin' to get through to me while we've been on our little summer recess, but you've got to understand, I need down time before going back to face those devils in D. C. Things to get worked out. Know what I mean, Brian?"

"Sure, of course, Senator," Brian responded. "What can I do for you?" *A photo-shoot, I hope.*

"Well, Brian, I've been thinking about that book thing you've been doggin' me to do for the past month."

"Well, that's great, Senator," he said, "I'm glad. But, I had the impression…"

The older man cut Brian off again, as though he hadn't said anything at all. "As you can understand," the Senator went on, "I had you checked out before deciding to do this thing. Hope you don't mind.

9

Gotta be careful about who I associate with, you know," he chuckled. "There were a few bumps in the road from your past, but we can't let a little obsession to steal other people's belongings and some bad PR keep a man from bettering himself…now can we?"

"Uh, no, of course not, however, I..."

"Your work is good, son…uh, the photography work, that is," he chuckled, again. "That's what's important to me, getting the right person for the job, you know.

"Yeah, I know."

"I do surf the net myself, you know. Checked out your website and that nasty stuff about you in the paper. Dug up that stuff about you and those Highland Park capers." His voice lowered to a conspiratorial tone, "And just between you and me, I can't think of a finer bunch of crooks that deserve to be fleeced. Since they're not in my neck of the woods, you know," he added with another chuckle.

"It's nice that you're the forgiving kind, Senator." Brian wasn't sure anymore if he wanted to deal with this egotistical asshole or not.

"Anyway, I'm not a complete computer illiterate like some people my age. Gotta keep up with the times. Stay on top of things. Right? Anyway, I think your project is very worthy. It'll be good for Texas and all…if you like that kind of thing. But, I've got an alternate project that's a little more pressing and immediate, you might say. And there's something I'd like to propose to you. Something that'll possibly put your name on the map quicker than any picture-book you're tryin' to put together now."

Does this guy ever take a breath? "I've already been on the map, Senator. I prefer low-key, if you know what I mean."

"Of course I do, Brian, but just hear me out, and I think you'll find me hard to resist."

"That's part of your reputation, isn't it, Senator? A man who's hard to say 'no' to?"

A slight change in the senator's tone indicated he was finally going to get down to business. "Listen, Brian, if you do *ex-actly* what I tell you to do and everything goes according to plan, you'll end up shelving that silly book. I'm offering you the opportunity of a lifetime. You can trust me on that one."

"That'd be your alternate plan you're talking about. Right, Senator? An alternative to my 'silly' book?"

"Brian, you just have to trust me. And yeah, Plan B, if you like. One thing I will tell you though…there might be…or could be a *lit-tle* risk involved on your part, but that shouldn't bother a man like you with your…professional background. Right? Anyway, you game?"

"M-m-m, I…sure, Senator. A little confused maybe, but game…at least I'll listen to what you've got to say." Brian was sure, at this point, that this idea the senator was pitching had nothing to do with coffee tables.

"Are you sitting down for this?"

"Yes, sir," Brian said, standing up.

"Son," Senator Fagan said, his voice dropping to a low whisper, "I'm going to be…well…assassinated. Tomorrow. And I'd like for you to catch it on film." Senator Fagan paused. "Now what do you think about that, Brian?"

And, if he had known then what it would be like in this barn on this gray morning frozen in place poised to witness the death of that man, then Brian was sure he would've found something smarter to say.

"Sir…" all the young thief-turned-photographer could think to say was, "…we don't use film anymore."

Chapter 2

Maxwell Edison leaned back in the swivel chair, slowly twirled around in a half circle, and took in a Friday afternoon view of the Dallas skyline through his office window. His company occupied the entire sixty-fifth floor in the Bank of America Plaza Building, the tallest in Big D. That's the way he did things, bigger and better than anybody else. That's why he decided to locate his corporate headquarters in Texas. Access to an international airport that connected him to anywhere in the world, international corporations equal to his own, four major sports franchises and the luxury boxes he owned for each team; and unlimited opportunities. For Edison, Dallas was the epicenter of the universe.

Edison was the founder and CEO of Elite Securities, Inc., currently the largest private military security/protection agency worldwide. His company even surpassed the lucrative contracts of his main competitor and nemesis from Houston, Zeta Corp, Inc. Edison savored his competitor's current shortfalls. And, he was right to enjoy his moment, since he was the one that instigated the investigations that led to the current federal indictments plaguing Zeta.

Zeta's one billion dollar, non-bid, five-year Iraq contract with the

Department of Defense was now null and void, due to accusations against its employees for murder, gunrunning, kidnapping, and other sordid criminal activity while on the job in Iraq. Edison was more than happy to pick up the slack left over from the contract and was now embedded deeply within the DOD in Afghanistan. There was no other security company in the world except his that had the capability and resources to assume Zeta's contracts in addition to their own.

For the time being, Edison looked to be soaring ahead. He was successful and had drawn that success around him, the axis of Elite Securities Inc. and all of the power that could spin off from its machinations.

But, all was not well in his universe, either. Edison's problems were looming even deeper than Zeta's at the moment and had the potential to be far more crippling. These were problems that hadn't gone public yet, but the stew would soon come to a boil.

For the past year, Senator Jimmy Fagan had dogged his tail. Not only to prevent Edison from doing business with the government, but to shut him down completely. Put him in jail and throw away the key. The clock was ticking. Congress was scheduled to reconvene, and the following week, the Committee on Oversight and Government Reform, chaired by none other than Senator Fagan, was scheduled to begin its witch-hunt.

He had forty-eight hours to stop the old codger, to stop the hearings. The hearings were intended to expose the innermost secrets and dealings of Elite Security, Inc., stories which included accusations of hit squads dispersed worldwide which were capable of taking on targets no other private enterprise or government entity would even dare consider, accusations of sanctioned eliminations of government and opposition leaders, accusations of cold, calculated, and deadly professional assassination.

The Senator was right, of course; it was all true, but that was beside the point. The point was simple and primary to his firm's survival: to stop these accusations from ever coming to light.

Edison grinned. It was going to be a very good day. There was no reason not to believe his own strategy wouldn't work to foil Fagan's well-planned hatchet job. He methodically pondered the two obstacles that stood between him and a clear, unfettered path to the future, obstacles which were essential for him to remove. No obstacles. No evidence. No charges. No hearings. There'd be damage control to implement, of course, but his pockets were deep; his anger was a bottomless pit; and, his drive pushed away any doubt that he wouldn't succeed.

Problem number one was the Senator. Fagan had unbridled power in Congress. He was a ruthless son-of-a-bitch who was known for his notorious grandstanding antics, which had earned him a reputation as the nation's overseer of evil corporate corruption. Senator Fagan always came out on top; his targets, dishonored, all left under the soles of his well-worn cowboy boots.

Problem number two was the source of Fagan's inside information. He knew he had a leak, a fucking rat that turned Benedict Arnold on him. Fagan's source was somebody that was part of Elite Security, someone that had to be a trusted member of Elite Squad One. Tomorrow's operation would eliminate problem number one permanently and drastically shorten the list of suspects for problem number two.

Interrupting his thoughts, a light on his desk phone blinked and hummed softly twice, signaling that it was time for his meeting with the members of Elite Squad One. He reached for the suit jacket hanging on the back of his chair and retrieved a set of keys from the side pocket. He unlocked the bottom right drawer to the desk, opened it, flipped off the video/audio controls to his office, and relocked the drawer.

No record. No meeting. This is my world and I will control it.

Edison pressed the intercom button and spoke crisply, "Send them in, Sandy."

Almost immediately, the office door swung open. Sandy, Edison's executive secretary, held back the door and motioned three men through, and then closed the door behind her without a word as she exited.

Three hulks dressed in suits sat silently across the desk from Maxwell Edison. No one spoke until the boss did. That was understood. He looked at each in the eye with his fingers together as if in prayer and let the question hang between them, unspoken.

Are you my rat?

Michael Hatfield, or "Hat" as he was called, was his first choice. He was the newest member of the squad and things had started going south after he came on board almost six months ago; he'd been employed with the company for almost a year, but was only recently advanced to the Elite Squad. It was unusual for someone to move up the ranks so quickly to such a secret post, but his credentials and past exploits in the security division, especially the Argentina affair, had made him a standout candidate.

16

Are you FBI, Hat? If you are, then I'll know.

Edison knew the only organizations that could even remotely have a chance at infiltrating his employment screening processes were the CIA or the FBI. He was ex-CIA himself and knew his own domestic dealings wouldn't fall under their jurisdiction. CIA was not allowed to interfere in domestic affairs, only foreign. He knew the rules. He knew the gray lines, the rules they knew they had to follow. He knew the lines that couldn't be crossed by either organization.

Edison had confided his suspicions about an informant only to his closest confidant and friend, William Duvall, the commander of all existent special squads within the corporation. They were both former CIA. Duvall had been an instructor at the CIA's training center, The Farm, in Virginia, when Edison came through as a rookie recruit. Duvall was the only man Edison trusted.

"Gentlemen," Edison started, as he removed a Cuban cigar from an elaborately carved container on his desk, "are we ready for tomorrow's operation?" He nodded at Duvall first, who sat on the end to his left. He knew how it was going to go down, of course, but he wanted to hear it word for word from those involved. Plus, he had his own surprise to spring.

"Yes sir," stated Duvall. "We've stepped things up and had 24/7 surveillance on the target for the past week. Nothing suspicious, no unusual activity, no one coming or going to the house that shouldn't be there. Matter of fact, the target hasn't deviated from his normal routine at all. Makes it easier for us." Duvall leaned forward in his chair and nodded to the squad member at the opposite end. "Hasan can fill you in on tomorrow's schedule."

Hasan Eldawoody was a native Egyptian, born and raised in Cairo. He was fluent in four languages even before he went stateside and enrolled at UCLA, attaining double degrees in economics and political science. After graduating, Eldawoody returned to Egypt and literally dropped off the radar screen as far as any background checks could verify. Edison knew all too well in what activities Eldawoody had participated. Those activities were the primary reasons why this Egyptian was a longtime member of the Elite Squad.

"The target is highly predictable, sir. He rarely strays from his daily routine," Eldawoody briefed them smoothly. "He leaves the house every morning at 7:25 a.m. in an old '72 Ford pickup and goes directly to the barn."

"What does he do there?"

"Smokes. Guess the old lady won't let him fire up his cigars in the house."

Edison smiled tightly, and continued to roll his own cigar between his fingers. "Continue."

Eldawoody's body posture relaxed a bit. "Well, sir, he drives up to the barn, stops about thirty meters short of the barn doors, steps out, lights up, and strolls around the property. Rain or shine. Doesn't matter."

"And the terrain?"

"Flat. The barn is situated about two hundred meters from the ranch house; however, it's completely isolated from view from the house or the road and in the middle of a clearing surrounded by dense woods."

Edison turned to Hatfield, "And the plan of action, Hat?"

Hatfield appeared relaxed and comfortable. "We'll be ready for action by 5:00 a.m. I'm the spotter for Hasan, Mr. Edison. I'll be positioned along the edge of the woods approximately fifty meters due east of the barn. No obstructions. A clear view of everything. I give the 'all clear' to Hasan. He exits the barn, approaches the target on foot, and completes the assignment at close range."

"Exit strategy?" Edison asked, moving forward in his chair, placing his elbows on the desk, his chin on his folded hands.

Hatfield continued. "Once done, we calmly walk away. There's a dirt road separating his property from his nearest neighbor's. There's been no traffic reported on the road in the past week by our surveillance teams. We've all got separate vehicles. We leave in opposite directions." Hatfield wiped the palms of his hands as though dusting them off, looked at Edison, and punctuated his gesture with one word: "Done."

Edison leaned back in his chair and gazed at the ceiling, clenching his cigar between his teeth and balling his hands into a single tight fist. He waited almost a full minute before speaking, before looking at them, before even exhaling. Then, catching their eyes, he spoke slowly and clearly, carefully reading each's response. "I know this is last minute, but I've decided to make a change." Edison's squinting eyes took in all three men. "I want Hat to do the execution instead of Hasan."

Hasan frowned, his shoulders visibly drooping.

Disappointment.

Duvall flicked the tip of his nose with a finger; the corners of his mouth turned downward.

Concern.

Hatfield didn't twitch or blink.

Approval?

The last minute switch was a necessity. Edison suspected his traitor would be FBI, and, being ex-CIA, Edison knew the rules for the Bureau as well as he did those of his former employer. He'd made it his job to know. If it was Hatfield and he was FBI, there were limits to what a federal undercover agent could do on an assignment, and committing murder was one of them. *Are you my rat, Hat?* thought Edison waiting to hear what Hatfield would say.

"Good," said Hatfield, "I'm tired of sitting on the sidelines."

"It's a big first assignment," said Edison staring directly at him.

"And a good opportunity for me."

Edison paused, as if reconsidering, then continued. "Your weapon of choice?"

"I prefer a Browning Buck Mark .22. Virtually untraceable, and our man has just finished one fitted with a silencer."

"And?" Edison asked, continuing to probe.

Hatfield didn't hesitate, but shrugged. "One in the head. Two in the chest. Walk away."

Edison seemed satisfied. "So, Duvall?"

He shrugged. "It's your party, Maxwell. Anyway, damage control. There's an old schoolhouse that serves occasionally as a community center. It's perfectly positioned on the other side of the main road from the Senator's barn, making it our common point of entry and exit. Plenty of cover. I'll make sure everyone leaves clean," he answered, and, after a pause, "and handle any unexpected problems."

Edison stood up from behind the desk, removed his jacket from the back of the chair, and put it on.

The meeting was over.

"Gentlemen, I don't have to tell you how important this operation is. It's our first domestic contract. 'We don't ask why. We just do it.' Don't fuck up." Turning to his squad leader, Duvall, he ended with, "William…lunch at the club tomorrow."

It wasn't a question. "Yes sir. Should be done and back by then," Duvall said, standing up, "I'll be there."

Edison opened the door and offered a hand to each of the squad members as they exited. When the last filed out, he closed the office door, waited five minutes, and punched a single speed-dial button on his cell phone. The call connected on the first ring. "Make sure Hat follows through with the job," Edison said, then hit the END button.

Shutterbug

Chapter 3

Frozen in place in the hay loft, Brian tried to recall as much of his phone conversation with Fagan as possible. It was hard, though, to remember anything while his brain was going into overload.

"Look," the senator had finally told him, "I know what I'm doing here. I've got things covered. You pull this off, my friend, and we'll both come out smelling like an East Texas Tyler rose. Can you spell Pulitzer, Brian?"

How can a dead man come out smelling like a rose?

"I can spell it alright, but I don't get it. According to you, I get the Pulitzer and you get dead? Is that the deal, Senator? Aren't you getting the short end of the stick here?"

"I never end up with the short end of the stick, boy. Remember that."

The Senator's assurances, however, didn't seem grounded. "You fuckin' with me, Senator?" Brian asked, suspiciously.

"Fuckin' with you? Who the hell's getting shot here? This is an opportunity for you, boy. In the end, for both of us." Then, as though there was no more need for discussion, the Senator began giving Brian specific instructions to his farmhouse in Rusk; where to park, when to be there. Over and over, he warned the young man to follow his instructions explicitly. No changes. No ad-libbing. It was Fagan who had sent Brian to this hayloft in this barn on this morning. It was Fagan who had hurtled him towards an uncomfortable moment where he would act as a witness to the old man's end, his final moment of life, in a ruthless assassination.

"I'll be there at 7:30 a.m. sharp," Fagan had stated. "You just be there with your camera charged up and your finger on that fuckin' shutter button, boy, and when it's over, get the hell out of there. Go home. Stay out of sight for forty-eight hours…and you'll be famous."

Then he hung up.

After the call, a thousand conflicting ideas buzzed through the young photographer's head. Scenarios for and against the assignment banged around and into each other, but when it all came down to it, one conclusion consistently jumped to the front of the line. Regardless of how ridiculous or reckless the whole thing seemed, how could he not do it? A twenty-eight-year-old reformed thief with a record, hustling for a living with his camera, gets a phone call from a national political figure to document his assassination. The fact was, he did long for that adrenaline rush that came with life on the edge. The whole affair was just too wild and appealing to not go through with it.

Another faint creak below snapped Brian out of his reverie. He might be addicted to adrenaline, but he wasn't a fool. He'd taken the precaution of mailing letters, explaining where he was going and why, to two of the only three people he trusted, and, if the night's event went awry, might care enough about him to help him out of the jam. His attorney, Harry Morgan, and his on-again-off-again girlfriend, Joanna

Johns, should have each received a letter by now. Brian was saving something special for the third person. If he survived the job. Frozen in place, camera trained and ready to go, Brian acknowledged to himself that he had no idea how it would all end.

Harry Morgan, his attorney, was a left-winger who loved a good conspiracy. He was the kind of guy who, after receiving his letter, would probably hope that something untoward would happen to Brian so he could yet again rattle the sacred cages of the federal government. Harry had kept Brian out of jail when accused of being the infamous "Cat Burglar of Highland Park" five years earlier. The city of Highland Park, an enclave of the richest people in Dallas, located in the middle of the sprawling Dallas metroplex, lies just outside the boundary line of the one of the most expensive schools in the nation, Southern Methodist University. Highland Park was a well-planned conglomerate of quaint, high-dollar specialty shops, multi-million dollar mansions with manicured lawns and multiple BMW's, Ferraris, and Mercedes parked in every driveway.

It also had one of the highest per capita ratios of police officers to citizens, with high-tech Tahoe patrol SUVs on every street corner. Brian's exploits had stirred quite a furor, when–allegedly–he'd helped himself to the upper crusts' belongings on a monthly basis. The hauls were considerable, but it was the predictable frequency of his trysts that drove law enforcement agencies bonkers.

The fence Brian had–allegedly–used to get rid of his ill-gained inventory, Harvey Sensabaugh, got caught in an unconnected sting operation and had ratted Brian out as the now infamous burglar who was regularly capitalizing on the rich folks. He did it in turn for a sweetheart deal with the prosecution for his freedom in return for Brian's incarceration. Of course, it also meant that he wouldn't have to pay for all the past merchandise Brian had turned over to him from previous jobs.

Lucky for Brian, Harry shot enough holes in Sensabaugh's deposition to drive a Panzer tank through. Never one to miss an opportunity in front of a camera, at one impromptu press conference just outside the courthouse, Harry was able to seize center stage.

"The word of a liar? A thief? A cheat? *A-a-nd* a broker of stolen goods, obviously trying to drag an innocent young man into the gutter with him! *Pa-leese!*" he roared. "These charges against my client, Mr. Braun, a well-known working man who's busy trying to make a living as a photographer taking pictures of your wife and kids, are totally bogus! No, there's absolutely no hard evidence against him, circumstantial or otherwise. You have only the word of an admitted fence trying to buy his way out of a prison!"

As shallow as it was, it worked. Mainly because, in the end, there was no proof. Lots of innuendo, but no proof, just as Harry had said. Despite all the negative publicity at the beginning of the whole affair, the indictment never made it out of the Grand Jury. The Crimes Against Persons Department never came up with any 'hard evidence' against Brian, in spite of Harvey's accusations. Brian had laid low, paid his taxes on time every year since, and stayed out of trouble while he hobnobbed with the rich and famous, putting their pictures on the front of local and national magazines. He got off scott-free, and so did Harvey. Harvey's immunity deal kept him out of prison, and Brian reaped the benefits of notoriety.

The Dallas/Ft. Worth news media did a good job of inadvertently turning Brian into a local hero among the middle-class. It was, of course, another brilliant stroke of genius hatched by Harry Morgan. With things kind of shaky worldwide and politics preaching doom and gloom, the average Joe didn't give a damn if Brian made a living breaking into over-priced, million dollar mansions and procuring a few precious baubbles belonging to those who were oppressing them. They liked it, as a matter of fact. And the rich didn't mind it, either. Being a victim of the Highland Park Cat Burglar catapulted the victimized family into even higher social status within the community. That didn't go over too well with the prosecution, and once Brian was tagged with hero status, everything started backfiring on the D. A., who stood by with his mouth slack-jawed and watched what he had on Brian slowly crumble before his eyes.

Joanna Johns was a reporter with the *Dallas Morning News* who, during this whole Highland Park fiasco did her best to defame Brian's already questionable character and connect him to every jewel heist in Dallas. She also wrote that Brian was not only the most notorious , but also the suavest burglar since Cary Grant in *To Catch a Thief.*

For his part, Brian resented being called a burglar. He considered himself an honorable, sophisticated Robin Hood who never harmed anyone. Everything he stole was insured. Even its best connotation, "burglar" sounded…demeaning. Cheap. Second class. So, Brian had called her and told her, in his best Cary Grant voice, how insulted he felt by the burglar tag, and could they have dinner somewhere and talk about it? They did. The rest is history.

But now, that all seemed very foolish. The past five years was little more than a flash of insignificance—a dream. Suddenly, life was exciting again. Very real. Very dangerous. And, though Brian hated to admit it, very refreshing.

Last night, sitting in his Jeep before heading off to Rusk to do the senator's bidding, Brian had held those letters in his hand. A moment later, they were poised half in and half out of the mailbox slot. He remembered feeling a calmness overtake him as he let them fall. When Brian heard the letters' soft landing at the bottom of the box, yet another feeling joined the calm already curdling in the pit of his stomach: commitment. By this act, Brian had sealed his fate with the senator's.

Chapter 4

William Duvall arrived at the Beulah Schoolhouse at 1:00 a.m. sharp and parked the black GMC Yukon SUV in the nearby woods. Grabbing a lightweight backpack from the rear compartment, he threw it over his left shoulder, closed the door so as not to engage the lock, and stood motionless. Still and quiet, the squad leader allowed his eyes to adjust to the black ink of night, and his ears to the sounds of the forest.

After five minutes, Duvall activated his radio, deciding it was time to contact the surveillance team on duty. He didn't worry about the transmissions being intercepted. There'd been no word from the team on duty of any unusual visitors today or this evening. And second, Edison had spared no expense when it came to equipment. Duvall had the same communication devices as FBI SWAT and Violent Crimes Task Force team members: A body harness unit with an earpiece custom-molded to his ear. The unit was hard-wired to a ruggedized radio transmitter/receiver that could be operated in encrypted mode. With a maximum range of a half-mile, the equipment was more than sufficient for the operation at hand.

"Sparrow One, this is Songbird One. Do you copy?" Duvall

whispered.

"Roger, Songbird One," came the reply.

"Everything okay in your neck of the woods?" Duvall asked.

"Quiet as a church on Saturday night...nothing at all since last contact. The target is tucked in for the night."

"Good. Move your team back to home base. I've got it from here. Songbird One, out," Duvall ordered authoritatively.

"You won't get any argument from me, Songbird. Sparrow One is gone."

Duvall had made a final reconnaissance of the area immediately after meeting with Edison. After checking everything out, he had driven miles out of the area, stopping at a Wal-Mart for a few snacks for the night, then taking in a late movie. The feature couldn't hold his attention, but it accomplished his need to be out of sight until it was time to return to Rusk. His mind was constantly reviewing and re-reviewing every step of the early morning operation, revisiting every possible contingency. He also had time to consider some of the implications of a hit on a United States Senator. Edison, he thought, just might be taking this all a step too far. He would need to talk with Edison about his own future at their scheduled meeting.

Duvall's earlier surveillance had paid off. There was a large oak tree located off the driveway leading up to the school. Its branches, almost the same circumference as the trunk, would provide an excellent perch from which to view the road in both directions and any traffic. It was good cover, comfortable, and provided him room to wiggle. Duvall climbed up about twenty feet to a comfortable crook in the tree, retrieved his night vision binoculars, water bottle, and energy bars from the back pack and then hung it from a branch stump on the trunk. By 1:32 a.m., he was settled in for the arrival of the team.

During the next two hours, three vehicles drove past. Two pickups, whose drivers obviously knew the road, zipped up the road, underneath him, and continued North. The third, a Jeep Cherokee, caught his attention. It was going unusually slow. He checked his watch. It was 3:30 a.m., about an hour before the team was due to check in.

As he watched, the Jeep continued to creep along the road now weaving from side to side. At first, he thought the driver drunk. He tried but couldn't make out the driver; the Jeep's windows were up and tinted. After passing Duvall and driving on a hundred yards or so, the driver hit the brakes and made an abrupt U-turn back in the direction of the school.

What the hell?

Duvall's reflexes kicked into gear. He straightened his back tight against the tree trunk and adjusted his position to get a better view of the now oncoming Jeep.

The driver maintained his slow pace and drove past Duvall and the school again. Duvall trained his binoculars on the taillights. They suddenly flashed and the driver turned left turn onto a barely discernible dirt road that led to an unoccupied mobile home Duvall had checked out earlier.

The man's so drunk, he missed his turn, Duvall assured himself, relaxing a bit as he watched the Jeep pull to a stop. As the driver's door opened, a dim interior light blinked on. A man in obscure dark clothing got out, walked unsteadily around to the front of the Jeep and raised the hood.

Mechanical trouble, too? So, why go to the darkened house?

The driver kicked at the front bumper and missed, then stumbled his way towards the trailer house, disappearing from view. A moment later, an interior light flashed on, then off.

Ah, it's your house! As drunk as he is, he'll be sleeping it off well into the day. Definitely not anyone to worry over.

An hour later, Duvall spotted truck headlights. This would be Eldawoody, right on time. As the truck neared his position, his earpiece came to life.

"Songbird One, this is Songbird Three. Do you copy?"

"Gotcha, Songbird Three," Duvall answered.

"I'm coming up on the intersection. All clear?"

Duvall hesitated, thinking about the owner of the Jeep quietly sleeping off his drunk.

"Songbird One? All clear?" Eldawoody repeated.

"You're clear, Songbird Three. You're first on site."

"Got it. Three, out."

Ten minutes later and right on schedule, Duvall spotted more headlights, and the next moment, his earpiece came to life again.

This would be Hat.

"Songbird One, this is Songbird Two. You copy?"

"Yeah, Two. This is Songbird One."

"I'm approaching the schoolhouse now. All clear?"

"You're good to go, Two. Only thing I've seen tonight is a drunk weaving his way back home and another Songbird."

The voice on the other end laughed. "Roger that. Out."

"Two out." Eldawoody added and the low hiss in Duvall's ear phone went silent.

"Over and out," Duvall said to a dead mic.

Shutterbug

Chapter 5

Brian heard Senator Fagan's truck before he saw it, lurching back and forth, sideways along the deep rutted road ahead of him. Ready, he brought the camera up to eye level, his finger poised just above the button that was about to make history. Approaching the barn, the older model, red and white pickup rambled along the track.

Still, no sound from below.

Brian zoomed in the lens on the figure behind the steering wheel. The senator had on a blue-jean jacket and a navy blue Dallas Cowboys cap with a white star on the front of it. Perfect target. Is that a grin on his face? He kept waiting to hear the barn door squeak again, anticipating the assassin's exit, but the would-be assassin remained as still and silent as Brian. The pickup stopped about fifty or sixty feet from the barn doors. A safe enough distance so that the automatic shutter sound couldn't be heard.

Then, the voice from below shattered the silence and Brian's nerves.

"Songbird Three. Two, here. Target is set and confirmed. When he lights the cigar, I'm a go."

Seconds screamed by in silence.

This is real. This is going to happen!

The words of his mentor when he first started in the photography business popped into Brian's head. *'Remember Brauny, don't be distracted by the moment. Take the picture. To hell with everything else.'* Taking heart, he kept the camera trained on the senator and the truck door.

"Roger that," said Songbird Two.

Fagan got out of the truck. Brian watched him slam the door shut, and then lean back against the front fender. He was relaxed, at ease. He didn't act like someone who knew he was about to get shot. He pulled out a cigar from the right front pocket of his jacket, rolled the tip of it around in his mouth and then pulled out a box of matches from the jacket's left front pocket.

Brian remained remarkably calm. *Not yet. Wait till the shooter leaves the barn. Wait until he won't hear the automatic shutter firing.*

Senator Fagan struck a match along the side of the matchbox, watched the flame flare, and then held it to the end of his cigar, sending large puffs of smoke signals skywards.

Brian sensed the front door below him opening, but without a sound this time; Songbird Two was on the move.

Keep the camera on Fagan.

The senator's head was tilted to the side; his eyes squinted against the drifting smoke from the cigar. Songbird Two came into view of Brian's lens. His walk was deliberate. No variance.

Now! With imperceptible movement of his finger, the automatic shutter whirred into action. Brian was catching every step the killer made. Every frame. Eleven per second. Songbird Two, a pistol in his

36

right hand, down to his side.

Brian noticed the barrel was unusually long. *A silencer?*

The senator looked up. Surprised. "What the..." but didn't have the chance to finish the sentence.

Aiming directly at the senator's head, Songbird Two, barely three feet away; his right arm lifted up to a perfect ninety-degree angle to his body, moved his trigger finger imperceptibly.

Click, click, click, click went the shutter.

A single spit-thud in between the last two clicks. One to the head. No scream, just a guttural cry from the senator. Fagan's limp body collapsed to his knees, crumbling to a halt prone on his right side.

Click, click, click, click...

Songbird Two took a single step forward, and lowered his pistol towards the chest of the fetal-shaped body on the ground. Two more spit-thuds, the senator's body jerked slightly with each. Touching his finger to his ear, the shooter said something Brian couldn't hear, turned, and walked calmly away.

Click, click, click, click...

Brian released his breath and his hold on the shutter.

Silence.

Shutterbug

Chapter 6

The instant Brian released his finger from the shutter button, his hands started to shake. He shifted slightly to his left to get out of the killer's visual field. It was the first clear view Brian had of the killer's face. Brian noted a brief look of confusion, maybe concern. Standing there by the barn, the killer touched a finger to his ear again and said something. Brian was too far to hear what he said. The assassin glanced towards the tree line, and scanned it with grim concentration.

Evidently, Songbird Three wasn't responding. Songbird Two didn't wait around, though. He removed the silencer from the end of the barrel, dropped it into his backpack, and then shoved the pistol into a shoulder holster beneath his jacket. Taking one last look towards the tree line, he turned, and with long, purposeful strides, disappeared behind the barn.

Brian listened for his return, but all he heard were a few twigs cracking as the assassin entered the woods. Brian's body abruptly deflated and relaxed. He closed his eyes and dropped his forehead onto his arm. There was no elation. The thought of a Pulitzer sickened him.

What have I done?

Senator Fagan had insisted that Brian leave immediately and lay low for a couple of days, and, that's just what he'd planned do. But, he decided, it would be prudent to stick around a little longer to make sure there was no one else left out there. *Where is Songbird Three? And what about a Songbird One?*

Brian wasn't even sure if he had the strength left in his legs to climb down the ladder, anyway. He felt the need to think. Hiding out like a fugitive for two days just didn't seem as good an idea as it had before the assassination. *Did I really just witness an assassination? Shouldn't I go to the authorities? The FBI...not the cops.*

Brian decided to go directly to their Dallas office. Lay it all out. Get some proper protection.

But wait. The whole thing's so outrageous, would anyone believe me? Wouldn't they try to pin this on me? I should've done more to protect myself. I should've recorded my conversation with Fagan.

The sound of an engine emerged from the distant tree line. He perked up as a black SUV burst into the open maneuvering towards the barn skillfully and at a high rate of speed. From habit, Brian pulled the camera back up to his right eye and refocused the lens on the approaching vehicle. The vehicle stopped directly behind the senator's pickup.

Brian tensed his shutter finger. Click, click, click, click...on and on the camera whirred.

What happened next eliminated all thoughts of going to the authorities, and made him decide to lay *really* low for the next couple of days.

Chapter 7

"Songbird One, this is Songbird Two. You copy?"

"Roger, Two. Go ahead," Duvall answered quietly.

"Houston, we have a problem."

"What kind of problem, Songbird Two?" Duvall asked.

"The target is terminated, but Songbird Three doesn't respond. Faulty equipment, a dead bird or one that's flown the coup, I don't know. We last communicated less than a minute before the hit. Then, nothing."

"Heard that, too. Understood, Songbird Two. Stick to your original exit strategy, and I'll clean up here. Repeat. Do not deviate from the original exit strategy. Songbird One out," Duval replied.

"It's your show, Songbird One. Two, out and gone."

Duvall had vacated his treetop surveillance cover at dawn, since he'd no longer be invisible in the morning light. This, too, had been carefully arranged from when he originally scouted the area. Now, he was settled into a new position on the ground, in a heavy overgrowth of thick vines that blended into the trees approximately twenty feet off the road. It provided good cover to watch the main road, FM 23, and the dirt road to Fagan's barn. He observed Hat's white Dodge pickup pull up to the highway from a tunnel of trees and make a left turn back towards Rusk. Duvall, on the other hand, had no plan to leave anytime soon.

Earlier, during his transition from tree to ground, he had taken a quick jog down the road to check out the supposedly disabled Jeep that'd been left by the unscheduled visitor. He circled it quickly, giving it a thorough once-over, committing the license plate number to memory. Then, checking to make sure no one was around, he knelt on one knee and placed a magnetic GPS tracking device behind the rear bumper.

We'll know wherever you go from now on, young fella.

Now it was another waiting game: waiting on Eldawoody, waiting on the owner of the Jeep, waiting to make certain there were no further deviations from the expected. For now, there was nothing Duvall could do about Eldawoody if the man didn't show up. He'd have to worry about that later.

It was almost 8:00 a.m., thirty minutes after the hit on the senator, and traffic was slowly picking up on the highway. No sirens, screeching tires, or a mass of government vehicles converging on the senator's house. Just another day in the country. Duvall knew he should already be on the road, but he wanted to wait a bit longer to see if the Jeep driver turned up. Too many things weren't adding up. Maybe no one's found the senator's body yet. That could explain the absence of law enforcement converging on the site. But with Eldawoody's disappearance *and* the convenience of a drunk sleeping off a night of drinking in an abandoned trailer house less than a quarter of a mile from the kill zone, alarms were humming in his head.

Another forty minutes went by. It was 8:45 a.m. and there was still no sign of Eldawoody, but Duvall spotted the Jeep owner stroll from the darkness still engulfing the mobile home and into the morning light. He was six feet tall, young, in his late twenties probably, with dark hair. He was wearing a baseball cap, the bill, like earlier, hiding the man's features. Nonetheless, he looked tired, haggard and nervous, constantly checking back over his shoulder at the woods to either side of him.

Duvall's sixth sense about the stranger paid off. He was awfully spry for someone who could barely walk five hours earlier. There was something in this man's body language that bothered Duvall. He'd been correct to assume this guy was and yet wasn't an amateur. He wasn't one of the authorities, but there was something about him that separated him from an everyday civilian. The young man turned left, and walked to his car. When he got there, he slammed down the hood, got in, drove back to the main highway, and headed off towards Rusk. When Duvall judged that the stranger was a safe distance away, he gathered his things, left his hideaway, and darted stealthily to the school house and behind to retrieve his Yukon. He flipped on the GPS receiver and waited. He'd give his prey plenty of room to get down the road before he started to tail him. His intention was to follow the stranger for a short distance to get a bearing on where the strange young man was headed, then return to Dallas.

The meeting with Edison would have to wait. Duvall had things to do first. He needed the office to run the plates on the Jeep, do a quick background check on the guy, then he would call Edison. Duvall was no longer looking forward to his meeting with Edison. Edison didn't like surprises.

Shutterbug

Chapter 8

Eldawoody was in a dream, emerging from a deep, dark tunnel. Episodes of the last twenty-four hours coming and going in flashes:

"Songbird Three. Two, here. Target is set and confirmed. When he lights the cigar, I'm a go," confirmed Hat."

"Roger, Two."

"All secure?" asked Hat a final time.

"Roger," repeated Eldawoody. *So, little snake, you've crawled your way into my yard, and that can only end in pain.* Eldawoody's heart had become a chipped-sharp stone, ripping through his chest with every waking breath, since Edison had handed off the key position—his position—to Hat. Eldawoody was supposed to be where Hatfield was now. *It was my hit!. Mine, you cursed...*

Eldawoody had prayed for Allah's guidance, and had worked and manipulated his way up through the ranks to get this coveted job. A dead senator on his resume would put him at the top of the heap in his field. His prayers assured him that he was the chosen shooter to take out the senator. *As I now desire to be the one to deliver the blow that will one day end you. And today would suit me fine!*

Immediately after yesterday's meeting, Eldawoody had had to

scrambled to signal his outside contact about the change of shooters, that he'd been betrayed by the infidel, Edison. Then, Edison had beeped him less than five minutes after the meeting, and he'd had to interrupt his message to his contact, ending up unclear how much of his message had gotten out. Edison's message had been equally cryptic. All he said was to make sure Hat followed through with the job.

And that's exactly what I intend to do, you bastard! From his perch in the tree line, Eldawoody trained the scope of his sniper rifle on the barn doors, waiting for Hat to exit and to make his move. *Shoot, so I can drop you dead right next to the senator...*

The barnyard door opened, but before he could see if it was Hat, he heard a snap and everything went black. *Snap. Snap. Somebody's fingers?* The dream ended.

The next thing he knew, his eyes were fluttering behind a blindfold. He didn't try to open them; instead, he mentally checked in with his body to make sure he wasn't hurt or damaged. He was sitting in a chair, hands cuffed, ankles bound to the chair's front legs. His chin was resting on his chest. He knew he'd lost time and couldn't quite get his bearings. His training told him his best option was to stay still and learn everything he could...

"You fucked up, Eldawoody," came a voice from the blackness to his right.

He refused to move.

"It's okay, Hasan," the voice continued. "I saw you flinch. You don't have to pretend. The drug's had time to wear off."

A new voice from his left said, "What do you think we should do with him, Larry?"

"What do we usually do with terrorist—scumbags like this who assassinate government officials?"

Eldawoody didn't recognize either voice.

How do they know? He raised his head slightly, his ears attuned to every sound in the room. His mouth was dry and his brain was screaming like he had a bad hangover. He nonetheless remained silent. *Wait. Just wait. All will be revealed."*

"You're totally screwed, Eldawoody. The jig's up."

Again he didn't answer. He tried to move his tongue. It felt thick and coated. His lips felt cracked, glued together by their dryness. He realized he couldn't respond even if he wanted to. Besides, he didn't know what to say even if he could. *Who are these guys...?*

The voice on his left, Larry, said, "I'm afraid your time has come to an end, my friend."

Eldawoody braced for the worst. Instead, footsteps from his right faded away across the room. A door opened, then closed. With the next sound, his balls drew up inside him. The room echoed crisply to the unmistakable sound of the slide mechanism of a 9 mm Glock, jacking a bullet into the chamber.

Shutterbug

Chapter 9

Driving along a series of two-lane black tops and obscure country lanes gradually coaxed Brian's blood pressure back to normal. He needed a plan, and with the extra time and the surreal contrast between the peacefulness of the countryside and the debacle back at the senator's ranch, he'd started thinking out his options. Returning to his studio was out of the question. After what Brian had just seen, he realized that laying low didn't mean sitting at home watching TV for two days. To be honest, other than the letters he had posted earlier to Harry and Joanna, he hadn't planned too much beyond the assassination, mainly because he didn't think it would really happen.

As Brian's head cleared from the shock of the past few hours, he found himself focusing more and more on what he needed to do, instead of obsessing on imaginary boogey men in the Jeep's rearview mirrors who might be following. And, as he did, a new plan eventually came to light. He knew he would need to stay out-of-sight for more than two days. Time was critical. It was his enemy, rather than ally. He needed to download his pictures, which, no doubt, would rattle the very core of the country.

There were things to do before he went underground. He had a few calls to make, and one more person to see before he disappeared. It was this third person whom he trusted and would need to rely on the most, more than Harry or Joanna.

Once Brian hit the city limits of Big D, his relaxed state of mind faded, his instincts went on high alert, and he headed for the one place he felt he'd feel safest, at least for the time being. Taking the Floyd Road entry into the sprawling campus of the University of Texas at Dallas in Richardson, he entered by way of a small side road rather than the main entrance. It was here, on this campus, his passion for photography had developed. While it had started out as a blow-off course, photography had ended up his only lasting future career.

The professor who had fueled his shutterbug flames was named Mickey Rockaway. Nowadays, they didn't get together as much as Brian liked, but they touched base with each other at least once or twice a month. It'd been a few years since Brian had last passed through the hallowed gates of UTD, but he had no doubt that the Campus Police would, as always, be out in force, if nothing else, handing out parking violations by the handfuls to cars without parking stickers. Brian drove slowly by the unattended side-entrance guardhouse, carefully watching his speed, turning eventually into a parking lot for visitors next to the McDermott Library. The advantage of parking here was that it was exactly where he needed to be. The drawback was that he'd be trapped like caged animal if he needed to make a quick exit. There was only a single narrow lane going back to the guardhouse. Brian parked, grabbed his camera and laptop off the passenger seat, pumped four quarters into the meter-money-eater, and headed for the library.

The main lobby was one big study hall, filled with students sitting in hard wooden chairs, hunched over or kicked back around over-sized, wooden tables. It had the typical higher education library atmosphere replete with subdued murmuring voices and an occasional, stifled outbreak of laughter.

He walked up to the information desk—the last line of security before entering into the cavernous interior with its never-ending rows of bookcases organized using a numbering system that even Einstein wouldn't be able to figure out. A twentyish-year-old female student was half hidden behind the semi-circular desk, stooped deep in concentration over a textbook thicker than a Dallas phonebook. With laptop case and camera bag hung over each shoulder, Brian looked like every other student on campus. He gave her his best student smile.

"Uh, excuse me."

She looked up and attempted a smile, though it appeared to hurt. "Can I help you?" She asked dryly.

Brian set his bags on top of the desk with a feigned sigh of exasperation. "Yeah. You think I could use your phone, there?" he said, pointing to a beige colored, multi-buttoned contraption on her desk.

She shook her head in the negative. "I don't think…"

Brian interrupted her with a shrug. "I know: school rules. But, hey, my cell battery's dead, and I need to call Professor Rockaway at the Arts and Technology Building to let him know I made it to the library. We have an appointment about my dissertation, and I wanted to make sure he's there before I walk all the way across campus. He's not always dependable about being where he's supposed to be. You know. Professors!" He gave her his best *give me a break* smile.

This time she returned a genuine smile, one that didn't appear to hurt at all. "Okay, sure," she said, picking up the receiver. "You know the number?"

"Two-thousand-one."

She dialed it, evidently waiting to hear a ring at the other end before handing the receiver off to him. Brian took the phone, knowing whatever he said would have to sound normal and proper, because she clearly planned to tune into every word. Two more rings and the professor picked up.

"Rockaway," he answered, like he didn't really want to talk to anyone.

"Professor Rockaway, this is Brian Braun, I'm calling about our appointment."

"You're shittin' me, right, Brauny?" Rockaway replied, instantly recognizing his friend's voice.

"Yes sir," Brian said sincerely, more for the benefit of his eavesdropper.

"You're in trouble again, right?"

"Yes sir," Brian said, giving the bookish girl another smile.

"I'll see you in a minute. I'm in the lab," He said and hung up.

"Thank you, Professor, I'm on my way," Brian said, speaking to the air as he handed the receiver back to the receptionist, appending, "I owe you one."

Chapter 10

Hatfield pulled into a Dairy Queen parking lot off I-45 in Corsicana and backed into a space opposite the building. He pushed the gearshift into park, let the car's engine idle, and scanned the parking lot before making a move to get out. Hatfield had to make sure that no one would see him here, not Hasan—whatever had happened to him—and especially not Duvall.

In the corner, he spotted his contact's car, and then saw him through the restaurant window, hunched over a table in the corner of the place. Hatfield killed the engine and went inside.

"Coffee, please," he said to the middle-aged woman at the counter.

"Anything else?" she asked.

"That's it, thanks," he said, smiling. He paid her, took the steaming cup, and headed to the back of the restaurant.

"How's it going?" Hatfield asked, stretching a hand over the table to shake.

"Good, and for you, Songbird?" the stranger answered. "How did it go? Okay? From what Jail Bird says, seems like it did."

Hatfield took a sip of coffee, set it down on the table, and sat back, spreading his arms over the back of the booth. "Almost perfect from my end…that I could see, anyway. I guess you got my message about the switch."

"Yeah, it would have gotten real messy if Edison hadn't changed his mind. You played him well."

"I was lucky. Nobody plays Edison. He's totally unpredictable. The whole operation would've collapsed if I hadn't got the go ahead from him. I'd have been forced to kill Eldawoody, then the shit would've hit the fan all the way around."

"But it didn't, that's the important thing." The man took a sip of his coffee. "By the way, what do you mean by 'almost'?"

"There's a problem," Hatfield said. "Eldawoody didn't answer a check-in call when he should have. No sign of him when I left, either. I don't like loose ends. You know."

The man's brow's knitted together, as he shook his head. "Me neither. Jail Bird didn't say anything about Eldawoody missing a check-in. That's a big loose end. You think he's gone lone wolf on us? We can't have a loose gun…"

"Don't know, but we've got to find out, and quick."

"Damn. I thought we had all possible contingencies covered. I'm on it, though."

Hatfield touched his cup to the man's. "I just need to tie this up. Everything else went well. The senator went down just like we planned."

The man sitting next to Hat took another sip from his cup, then set it down slowly on the table. "I know you're ready to finish and leave this assignment, Songbird. A year's a long time. Can't imagine doing what you do. Me, I'll take being the outside man any time."

They shared a quiet moment before Hat's contact spoke again. "Need anything?"

"Just to get this thing with Eldawoody cleared up," Hatfield replied.

His companion nodded. "John Lee wanted me to give you the word about seeing you. 'Very soon,' he said."

"Yeah, yeah, okay," Hatfield said, scooting to the end of the booth. "Tell him now's not the time. Edison and Duvall will be watching me like a hawk. I think something's up with Duvall, too. Something's not right with him. I can feel it, but can't seem to get a read on him. Not yet."

Hatfield stood, and the two shook hands. Winding down the conversation, Hatfield said, "I've got to get to Dallas for the fireworks that are about to start. Should be interesting. The next forty-eight hours are crucial, you know."

"Yeah," said the man, making a move to get out of the booth as well. "We've got things covered on our end, Songbird, and we'll make sure Eldawoody is out of the picture. You just watch your ass." The man stood and stretched. "Gotta take a leak. Damn coffee does it to me every time. See you later."

The middle-aged lady behind the counter smiled at Hatfield as he approached the front door to leave. "Come back to see us, now, hon. Ya' hear?"

"Will do," said Hatfield, pushing his way through the door.

Shutterbug

Chapter 11

Brian smiled thinking about his former professor. Mickey Rockaway was a trip. A late fifties,Vietnam vet, hippie throwback, he wore his gray hair in a ponytail that traveled midway down his back. In contrast, his long grey Fu Manchu mustache said he didn't take shit from anybody. But when you knew as much as he did about photography, computers, or anything with a digital chip in it, you didn't have to give a shit about administration or anyone else. And, he was a genius that the hierarchy at UTD respected, like him or not, and his close friends numbered among the elite families and founders of the university. He was bulldog loyal to his friends and would gladly go to hell and back for them. Brian was proud to call himself one of Rockaway's close friends.

Brian had been one of Rockaway's "projects" during his earlier years at the university, evidently recognizing something in Brian that no one else did. And, while it took Brian a while to see the light that Rockaway had seen earlier in him, even after Brian got busted, Rockaway steadfastly remained the one person Brian could confide in about anything and everything. He trusted the professor, and learned the hard way that lying to him never worked. For the moment, however, Brian would have to keep the professor at least partially in the dark, if for no other reason than for his own protection.

Brian strolled into Rockaway's combination lab/office, to find the professor in his natural position: kicked back in an old, worn, leather swivel chair, his legs stretched out, his scuffed cowboy boots crossed at the ankles on top of his 50's-style wooden desk, smoking a Marlboro. A crooked smile wandered across his lips as Brian approached.

"I thought you'd cleaned up your act."

"Nice to see you too, Rock," Brian said, dropping his bags on the floor and flopping into the single overstuffed chair Rockaway always kept opposite him. "I thought this was a non-smoking area," Brian kidded, pointing to what little was left of the glowing butt hanging from the corner of the professor's mouth.

"It is," he said, removing it and crushing it in an ashtray already overflowing with over-smoked butts. Without changing his position, he stretched his hand partway across the expanse of the desk; Brian had to get up in order to shake it.

"So, what's with the phone call? Your cell broken?"

"No."

"Shit. Then whatever it is, you're not going to tell me, are you? I can see it in your face."

He knows me like a book. "No, I'm not. Because it's better this way. At least, for now."

"I wish you wouldn't do this, Brauny. I don't want to see everything you've accomplished the last two years pissed away on another 'secret' scheme." He shook a new Marlboro from the pack on his desk and lighted it with a Zippo from his 'Nam days.

Brian shook his head. "It's not that kind of deal, Rock. I promise. I haven't broken the law. For now, let's just say I'm on a photo assignment. A big one. I'm here, but I'm not, if you know what I mean, and I need your help."

Rockaway gave a guttural, smoke-laden half-cough, half-laugh. "Yeah, it does. That's what scares me. So, what is it you want?"

Brian took a deep breath before speaking. "I shouldn't have come here, Rock. I might be putting you in the middle of something bad, something that could get messy, and by messy I mean dangerous. Shit. I'm just not sure…yet."

"Bullshit," Rockaway said, taking another deep drag, then exhaling a few well-practiced smoke rings at the ceiling. He flashed Brian his crooked grin again, this time with a glint of naughtiness in his faded blue eyes. "I'd 'uv been pissed if you hadn't. Whatever it is, I'm up for a little excitement. Tell me what you wanna do and what you need."

"I used the school phone because I probably shouldn't use my own cell for a few days. It'd be too easy for certain people to trace me…and the people I call." Brian pointed to the pack of cigarettes on his desk. "Can I have one of those?"

"No."

"Asshole."

"So now you come to me for help and call me an asshole?"

"Of course," Brian replied cheekily, though he stayed away from the pack. "I need for you to buy one of those pre-paid phones for me. I think you may have to fill out some paperwork or something on them. Maybe not, I don't know for sure because, up to now, I've never needed one. I need it clean. Just for now, Rock. I promise that nothing I've done or am doing is illegal."

"So you say. Yet you need *my* name on it instead of yours. You're asking me to get this 'clean' phone for you, yet you can't tell me what it's about because you don't want me involved in this." He grinned again, more of a twitch this time. "Okay, it makes a kind of sense. What else?"

Brian pointed at his camera bag. "I need to print some shots I made while you're out phone shopping." In actuality, Brian had no intention of being around when Rockaway returned with the phone.

"Umm," he said, prematurely stubbing out a half-smoked cigarette. "Am I going to have to pay for the phone, too, or are you gonna pony up for it?"

Brian stood and pulled a wad of bills from his front pocket. He'd raided his emergency stash "just in case" before leaving for Rusk. "How much do you need, you think?" Brian asked, peeling through the bills. "Twenty bucks?"

Rockaway cocked his head sideways, staring at the bills in Brian's hand. "You're prepared, I see." He got up from his chair, grabbed the money and held one of the bills up to a light as if checking to see if it was genuine. "You really think I know how much one of those damn things cost? Give me a hundred just to be safe," he growled, holding out his other hand.

"I can't tell if you're shittin' me or not," Brian said, reluctantly slapping a single hundred dollar bill into the professor's open palm. He didn't have time for verbal warfare.

Rockaway took it, and held it, too, up to the light.

"This'll do. When can I see the pictures?"

"Soon," Brian said, without hesitation. It wouldn't matter. He'd be long gone before Rockaway returned.

"Be back in an hour, then," Rockaway half-asked.

"Perfect."

"Asshole," Rockaway replied, walking to the door, adding a back-handed wave on his way out.

The professor strolled across campus at a leisurely pace, letting the crisp breeze blow against his face, stray wisps of long hair waving in the wind behind him. His friend had evidently fallen into something interesting, to say the least. Something involving intrigue. Obviously, Brauny needed to lay low and was taking precautions. That was encouraging. He shook his head. Leave it to Brian Braun to go legit from a life of crime and then fall back into something that Rockaway suspected must be even bigger and better than last time. He was convinced this ex-student of his had nine lives, but still…it didn't keep Rockaway from worrying. He was also not a little jealous. The kid looked alive again—he could see it in his eyes—and he was glad to be brought into the mix of things, even if in a minor way.

He spotted Brauny's jeep parked in the visitor's section, not far from his own car. UTD's president and the deans of each department had their own special parking places in front of the library, and even though he was neither, that didn't stop him from parking right alongside them. He was the only professor at the university allowed to do so. The old saying, 'It's not just what you know, but also who you know' was true for him, and he milked it for everything it was worth. As he angled in towards for his car, a large man with hurry and purpose in his step exited from the library front doors. Rockaway didn't break stride, but kept his eyes on him. Strangers on campus weren't an unusual occurrence, of course, but there was something about this guy that didn't fit: plaid shirt, scuffed army boots, the way he carried himself?

As one vet to another, Rockaway would have acknowledged, then brushed off the man's military bearing, and under any other circumstances, wouldn't have given the man a second look, but after his visit with Brauny, he did. He got to his car and fiddled with the key in the door lock long enough to watch the stranger head across campus towards the Arts and Technology Building. When the stranger was completely out of sight, Rockaway, on a hunch, trotted across the parking lot to Brauny's jeep. He checked underneath the front bumper first, then along the undercarriage frame on the driver's side, winding up at the rear bumper. He felt something. He got down on his knees and looked underneath around the gas tank and that's when his hunch paid off. A little black box approximately two inches square was attached inside the rear bumper. He recognized it immediately. It was a GPS tracking device.

Chapter 12

Brian didn't waste any time sorting through the printed pictures of the senator's assassination for the best shots; he grabbed those with the biggest potential overt shock and awe. He had to get out of Rockaway's lab before the man returned. The printer was still kicking out copies when the office phone rang. Rockaway had only been gone about fifteen minutes.

Pick it up or let it ring? Brian questioned. Surely Rockaway hadn't run into trouble acquiring the cell phone. Brian hesitated, then decided to answer the call.

"Professor Rockaway's office," he answered in his most studious voice.

"Does a guy built like a cement block, wearing a plaid shirt and jeans sound familiar?" It was Rockaway, an undertone of urgency in his voice.

Songbird Two? "Yes…maybe. Why?"

"Good enough," said Rockaway. "Get the fuck out now! He's headed your way! Stop whatever you're doing and shove it in my lower desk drawer. I keep it unlocked. When you close it, it'll automatically lock. Go out the exit stairway at the end of the hall and meet me at the back of the building. I'll be there in two."

Rockaway hung up the same time Brian did.

The printer continued spitting out photographs while Brian popped the camera's memory card out from the portal on his Apple MacPro laptop that was connected to the printer. Slipping the memory card in the watch pocket of his jeans, he closed the computer screen, shoved it in the case, hit CANCEL on the printer, grabbed all the photos, tossed the rejects into the bottom drawer of Rockaway's desk, and headed out the door like a man on the run. Brian took the steps two at a time down the doublewide staircase, praying he wouldn't miscalculate his footing. He burst through the exit doors to see Rockaway idling at the nearby curb in his 1969 Plymouth Road Runner. Rockaway jumped out of the driver's seat and motioned Brian over to his side of the car.

"Give me your keys and take my car," Rockaway said. "There was a tracking device on your Jeep. My cell's on the console. Use it for now and call me when you get low. Don't argue. There's no time to lose."

In spite of Rockaway's curt instructions, Brian started to argue. Rockaway grabbed both of Brians bags and tossed them on the passenger floorboard. Defeated before he could even speak, Brian obediently got behind the wheel. Rock slammed the door shut and was heading back towards the Technical Arts building before Brian could protest. Putting the hot rod in drive, he got the hell out of Dodge.

Having made his way across campus from the library, Duvall sat on a bench in the plaza, outside the entrance to the Arts and Technology Building. The plan, assuming Braun was in the professor's office, was to wait until the man left by the front doors to get into his car, then intercept him. He checked his watch; at least thirty minutes had passed since Braun would have entered the building. This was taking too long. Duvall needed to act, and get away before the campus police noticed him loitering.

The tracker he'd placed on the Jeep had led him to Braun, Professor Rockaway, and the Arts building. He had found Braun's Jeep parked in front of the library and took a shot at finding him in the building, or, at the very least, running into someone who might know where he could find Braun. With a modicum of friendly encouragement, a mousy-looking student librarian had provided him a wealth of information.

Duvall rose from the bench, ambled nonchalantly over to the front door of the Arts and Technology building, and, once ensconced, slipped into a stairwell. After taking the stairs two at a time up to the second floor, he located Rockaway's office. Duvall knocked.

"Come in," somebody growled from inside.

Duvall stepped inside and immediately recognized the grizzled, gray-haired hippie sitting behind the desk with his cowboy boots propped up on top. It was the same man he'd seen in the parking lot when he'd exited the library for this building. *How'd he get back here so fast?* Duval wondered.

Duvall remembered him not only because of the professor's unusual appearance, but also because of the equally unusual car he'd seen the man approach: a classic, metallic-blue Road Runner. Duvall stepped up to the desk, glanced around the lab as though curious, then stuck out his hand.

"Name's Dunagan. William Dunagan. Brian Braun was supposed

to meet me here about this time," he said.

The professor didn't reach for the proffered hand. In fact, he didn't move at all, or offer any friendly amenities. Duvall withdrew his hand and checked his watch.

"He had some pictures for me." Duvall continued as casually as he could while mustering an obviously contrived smile. "You must be Professor Rockaway."

"Really? He hadn't said anything to me about it. And, yes, I'm Rockaway. Brian's not here." Rockaway made a production of checking his own watch. "He's not very dependable, you know. We're supposed to meet over at the Fox and Hound on Campbell Road for a late lunch…" Looking up from his watch, he completed what he hoped would prove an effective diversion. "…in a few minutes," Rockaway returned the visitor's smile. "You're welcome to join us, if you like."

"M-m-m. That's disappointing. I'd just wanted to talk briefly with Brian. I don't have the time to chase him about." On Rockaway's bare left arm, Duvall noticed a Special Forces Airborne tattoo—a saber with three diagonal lightning bolts across the blade, and an accompanying silver MIA bracelet wrapped around his wrist. *Shouldn't make snap judgments, but….* Duvall pointed at Rockaway's arm. "Green Beret?"

Rockaway rotated his tattooed arm and glanced at it. "Yeah, 'Nam. And you?"

"Navy SEALS," answered Duvall, adding, "Desert Storm."

Rockaway nodded, grinned, but didn't say a word.

After an awkward minute of silence, Duvall offered, "He's not coming back, is he?"

"Nope," Rockaway answered. "And he never was here."

66

"He's in a shitload of trouble, you know," ventured Duvall.

Rockaway shrugged his shoulders. "Not my problem."

Duvall turned to leave. "Tell him I'll be seeing him."

As Duvall turned to leave, Rockaway called out, "Hey, Navy."

Duvall stopped abruptly and turned around.

"Hoo-rah," Rockaway crooned. "Never know. Different time, different place, we could've shared a beer together."

"Maybe so," Duvall mused. "Hoo-rah," he shouted as he shut the door behind him.

Rockaway lifted his shirttail and removed the .45 automatic from his waistband, set it on the desk, and dropped his feet to the ground. Grabbing the phone, he dialed his cell number. It rang twice before Brian picked it up.

"Dump the cell phone after this conversation. That block of cement came by to see me," said Rockaway, lighting a cigarette.

"Shit, Rock, I'm sorry."

Rockaway produced a key and opened the bottom drawer of his desk. He pulled out several photos. "Jesus, God, Brauny! What the hell have you gotten mixed up in?"

As Brian reluctantly began to explain, Rockaway interrupted. "Shut up and listen, Brauny. We don't have time for pleasantries. The man that came by wasn't the same one in the pictures you left behind. It looks like another block of cement offed your senator."

"I..." Brian began in reply, but didn't know what to say.

"You remember our old watering hole where we shot pool a couple of weeks ago? Where that asshole stiffed us on the bet?"

"Yeah," said Brian.

"Leave messages with Louise. And by the way..."

"Yeah?"

"You're one lucky son-of-a-bitch, you know that, right?" Rockaway stated. "These pictures are incredible! They've got Pulitzer written all over them."

"Yeah," said Brian. "I was told that would be the case once before. I just want to be alive to collect. Later."

"Later," echoed Rockaway, staring at the phone handset.

Chapter 13

Maxwell Edison was fuming. He paced back and forth in his office like a caged animal, occasionally glaring through the window at the waning afternoon horizon. He'd hung up from what should have been a routine face-to-face post-operational check-in with Duvall and had stormed out of the Dallas Country Club dining room without finishing his meal or signing the tab. *Fuck 'em.*

What was supposed to have been a quiet celebratory lunch over the death of his nemesis had ended in disaster. His brain swirled with questions. What had happened to Eldawoody? Who was the unexpected visitor Duvall had mentioned? Edison brooded momentarily on how the person had made it past their surveillance, before the questions resumed in earnest.

Had the intruder seen anything? How could the man have awakened so early, if, as Duvall had said, he had been drunk just hours before? Had Duvall finally identified him? Why did Duvall let him go instead of taking him down on the spot?

More troubling was that not a single news flash had come across the media reporting the senator's death. The hit had occurred eight hours ago. It should have been all over the news by now!

But most troubling of all, Edison now had doubts about Duvall. He'd never had reason to doubt the man, but Duvall's attitude during the last phone call was totally different from earlier when he'd called to report the "loose ends," forcing him to miss their lunch appointment.

Was Duvall the mole instead of Hatfield? On the phone, he had been what? Flippant? Disrespectful? No, more like aloof. And that alone was enough for Edison. Duvall's attitude was one more of the things he would need to address at their next meeting. A knock on the door snapped Edison to a halt.

"Yes?"

His secretary, Sandy, entered. "Mr. Duvall to see you, Mr. Edison. Is there anything I can get the two of you? Something to drink, perhaps?" she asked, stepping aside for the squad leader.

Edison's features relaxed slightly. "You know, Sandy, that wouldn't be a bad idea." He pointed at Duvall. "Bill? You up for a drink? With the day you've had, I'd think you'd be ready for one."

Duvall nodded. "Sounds good. Something to sip would be greatly appreciated at this point."

Edison nodded towards the open bar in his office. "Sandy, do you mind? We need to talk, Bill," he said, pointing at a round conference table in the opposite corner of the room. Once the two were there, he continued. "Tell me about your day."

"Busy, to say the least," said Duvall, sitting down beside his boss, relaxed.

Sandy placed two crystal shot glasses before each man. "Buzz me if you need anything, gentlemen."

The mock smile dropped from Edison's face the moment the door closed behind his secretary. He tossed the entire shot of bourbon at Duvall in one swift movement and slammed the glass down on the table. "Spill it. What the fuck is going on, Bill?"

Duvall, at first, looked aghast, his eyes reflexively narrowing, his body tensing. Then he relaxed and brushed of the drops of liquor that hadn't soaked in. Duvall looked up after the last drop was gone, and the two men faced-off, neither daring to blink first. Then Duvall smiled. "We've known each other a long time, Maxwell, and that's the first..."

Maxwell waved him off. "Fuck it. It's over. Just tell me what the hell's going on."

"Where to begin, Maxwell," he said casually as he took a sip from his shot glass. "Well, to start..."

Edison stood and started pacing back and forth behind his chair, interrupting Duvall. "First, why the hell isn't this on the news, Bill? Don't those vultures know there's been a fucking assassination? Do I need to call a damn press conference and do their job for them, for Chrissakes? Why doesn't anybody know about it?" A dark thought shadowed his mind, causing Edison to stop dead in his tracks. He turned around to face the squad leader. "There *was* an assassination wasn't there, Bill?"

"I heard the whole thing go down on the two-way, Maxwell. You can't fake that." Duvall flicked an imaginary drop of liquor from his jacket. I'll consider the circumstances, and the apparent strain you're under, in your even asking me that question, Maxwell."

"If it'd been anybody else but you, Bill, I'd have them fired, then immediately killed for emphasis."

Ignoring Edison's comment, Duvall stood, towering a full head over his employer. "Frankly, I don't know why it hasn't hit the news, Maxwell. That's not my department. Maybe the authorities are keeping it under wraps for some reason. Who the hell knows? They've got to release something on it sooner or later. A U. S. Senator can't just disappear for no reason. And don't worry, Maxwell. He's dead. Trust me on that."

"M-m-m. Of course, of course. It's just strange, that's all. Something like this should be all over the place by now. What about this fourth wheel? Who the hell is he? What was he doing there in the first place? Could he have anything to do with authorities not releasing the information?"

Duvall shrugged. "Here's the deal. There was some traffic on the two-lane in front of Fagan's place going on this morning, even at 3:00 o'clock in the morning. Nothing suspicious, really. It's farming and dairy country, for God's sake, everybody there gets up before the sun. Anyway, this guy weaves down the highway, and eventually drives down on a side-road across from where I'm observing everything. He pops the hood of his Jeep next to a mobile home, then wobbles his way in. The house lights flash on then off and don't come back on. Looked to me like a local drunk returning home from a bender with some kind of mechanical problem. Anyway, I radioed Eldawoody and Hat when they were in position. They acknowledged, but they apparently hadn't noticed anything amiss, 'cause the guy never came up in our conversation. I figure they never saw him holed up as he was in the dark mobile home. There're three other houses down that lane, too, you know. Shacks really."

Edison frowned. "But you must have been suspicious when he

reappeared just after the hit. Suspicious enough to at least follow him. Wasn't that why you missed our meeting?"

Duvall answered as if it was apparent. "Of course, Maxwell. You know me. I cover all the bases. I put a tracking device on his Jeep while he was sleeping, as a precaution. I waited at my location for almost an hour after Hat left the scene and the deed was done. I had good cover. I waited to see if any emergency or official type vehicles converged on the area, but they never did. Like I said, the only person that showed up was this Brian Braun character—that's his name. He looked distressed, but what the hell, he hadn't had time to sleep off the drunk, and he hadn't fixed the car . He ran to his car, slammed down the hood, and took off like a chicken on fire. That's when I decided to follow him. At first, I didn't think too much about the reckless way he was driving, assuming that he was trying to get somewhere fast before his Jeep stopped working altogether. Then I realized he was headed back to Dallas, and wondered if he was trying to be evasive. He obviously didn't want to be followed." Duvall had been sipping at his drink throughout the story, finishing both at the same time.

"And? Where'd he go?"

"Followed him to the UTD campus in Richardson. He stopped by the office of a professor there. Rockaway. Dr. Mickey Rockaway. An old hippie type. Long hair and shit. You know the type."

"One of those liberal shits. And?"

"I waited near his Jeep, but somehow missed him. Braun, that is. Then I went straight to the professor's office. Rockaway's a wily s-o-b. We chatted briefly. Actually, we sparred words for a few minutes. We didn't fool each other. He knew why I was there. Evidently, his boy told him something that spooked him. Braun must really trust him: It's the first place he went.

"Rockaway's a vet. Former Green Beret from the 'Nam days. Apparently, Rockaway spotted me in the parking lot as I was walking from the library. That's probably when he made me. He wouldn't have made me, I figure, unless Braun said something that alerted him. Or, maybe I just don't have that college look."

"I don't like it. Not one bit," said Edison.

"Yeah. Me neither. And Rockaway's no fool. I doubt it's the last we'll see of him."

"Hm-m-m," hummed Edison, as he strolled across the room to the bar and grabbed a bottle of Crown Royal. "Have a seat, Bill." Both men took their originals seats, and Edison refreshed each's glass. "Let's do this one thing at a time. The professor first. Who is he? A professor of what? And why was this Braun character there?"

"Photography," said Duvall. "I think you can figure it out from there. Former student, maybe."

"Shit. You think that little fucker, Braun, took pictures of the assassination?"

"Probably."

"And you think the professor is behind this?"

"It's possible."

"How could he know? Security on this was tight. Your team and me. That's all who knew."

Neither spoke while the implications settled about them.

"Do him first...the professor, that is," said Edison. "He'd be the brains and the loose thread that could unravel this whole operation. But first, find out what he knows, and if he's got any pictures. Maybe that's why Braun was visiting him. Get it all, then waste the motherfucker."

"Will do," said Duvall. "He'll most likely try to protect Braun and probably do a good job of it. I'll focus on getting the information and any photos, and contract out the killing to one of the boys. Hat can do it."

Edison held up a hand, shaking his head. "Not sure about him yet. I'll come back to Hat and Eldawoody in a minute. Okay, this Braun character. Who is he and what do you think about him?"

Duvall stuck a finger in his glass and slowly stirred the caramel liquid. "An interesting fellow. He's a thief. A thief turned photographer. And a good one. Good thief, I mean."

"Christ almighty!" exclaimed Edison. "What the hell's next? An old hippie professor and a fucking thief turned tourist with a Kodak. Does this get any worse?"

Duvall cracked a rare grin. "You'll have to admit, Maxwell, it's definitely interesting. At least they're not professional killers. Shouldn't be a problem taking them out and righting things. For now, I've just got the parameters of Braun's bio. I'll find out his hangouts and so forth. Shouldn't be too hard to locate him and talk face-to-face."

"It goes without being said that I want Braun dead, too."

Duvall nodded. "Of course, same as the professor. Okay, I'll do both of them. As for Braun, he dumped his Jeep, and is driving Rockaway's Road Runner. Shouldn't be too hard to spot. Stands out like a paisley Hummer. I'll have his place staked out by another team. They always go home for something. "

"Okay," said Edison. "Now, what about Eldawoody? You think

he's in on it? Maybe he contacted Rockaway and arranged for whatever it is he and Braun are up to. Maybe that's why you couldn't contact him after the assassination? Maybe Eldawoody's at the bottom of it all, and had something to do with the lack of public response?"

"Maybe," Duvall said, shrugging.

Edison shook his head. "I can't believe it. Eldawoody. After all these years. I mean...if he's turned, heaven forbid, we're both in a world of shit. You know that, don't you?"

"To be frank, Maxwell, I'm more concerned about Eldawoody than Braun. I can take Braun out without a problem. But Hasan—that would be a whole different story. If he wants to disappear, then he will, and there's nothing we can do about it. If he's waiting to bump off one of us, he can do that, too. If he..."

Edison waved him off. "I know. I know all that shit, Bill. My question is: What do we do about it?"

"At the moment, Braun's the key, not the professor or Eldawoody," said Duvall. "I don't know exactly what his part in all this is, but he's the key. Locate Braun, contain him, and my guess is, Eldawoody will show up. Then, we can find out his role in all this, and decide what to do. Rockaway is an afterthought."

"Okay, you work up a strategy on that," Edison said, "Now, how'd Hat do, and what do you think about him? Is he straight?"

"He made the hit, Maxwell, so he can't be FBI. Personally, I've never doubted him. That was your bag, not mine."

"I don't know. You said yourself there was no response team at the Senator's place after the kill." Edison stood up and tossed down the last inch of Crown from his glass. "You've got less than forty-eight hours to clean this mess up, Bill. Just do it."

Duvall left the remainder of his drink on the table. "No problem, I'm on it, Maxwell," he said, walking to the door and closing it softly behind him.

Edison returned to his desk to contemplate his next move. He needed to cover his ass all the way around on this one. Too much had gone wrong, and he wasn't putting the fate of his future in the hands of people he couldn't be one hundred percent sure of. Then, on impulse, he thought, *Fuck it,* and grabbed the cell phone from his belt. He scrolled down the directory of names on the screen to the one he wanted. The other end rang only once before someone picked up.

Edison didn't wait for a greeting. "Gib, Maxwell here. You available?"

"Depends."

"I need a team, off the record. It's your kind of job and it needs to be way under the radar."

"Where and how much?"

"Local, and double your usual fee. You'll need a team. I'm guessing six to eight. The job will be over in less than twenty-four hours. I want your best men. Plan on getting your feet wet."

"Okay," said Gib Rogers. "Anyone I'll recognize?"

"Yeah. It's one of my own. Your favorite rival, as a matter of fact."

"Duvall?"

"You got it."

"In that case, I'm definitely in. I've been wanting to fry his ass for some time. An hour? At The Shack?" asked Rogers.

"Order me some ribs," said Edison and hung up.

Shutterbug

Chapter 14

Brian parked Rockaway's Road Runner off Mockingbird Lane, grabbed his backpack with the pictures in it off the seat, and sneaked into his favorite bar and restaurant, The Shack, through the back door. The sweet aroma of barbecue hit his smell sensors immediately. Brian waved half-heartedly to eighty-year-old cook and co-owner known to everyone locally as "Sam," and his latest new dishwasher from south of the border. Sam never talked. He just grunted and cooked. Anti-social tendencies, Brian surmised, but who cared as long as he kept putting out the best home cooking in Dallas County.

For restaurant-goers, the lighting was unusually dim, but, for the the myriad of regular barflies, it was perfect. The Shack mainly served neighborhood and business locals. It was a great place to eat, drink, play pool, and listen to the Bob Robertson Society Blues Band on Friday and Saturday nights. Clientele and patrons all knew each other by first names. The fact that Sam served ribs so tender the meat fell off the bone before you could lift it to your mouth made up for the bad lighting, forty-year-old décor, and ancient standup Pac Man and Galaga videogames located in the corner of the pool room.

Brian stopped at the end of the bar and slipped onto a barstool sporting worn, deflated black vinyl seats from the 60's. Louise, the bartender and co-owner, didn't see him come in; she had her hands full pouring beers near the other end of the bar.

"Hey, gorgeous, what's it take to get some service around here?" Brian teased loudly.

Without turning around, Louise quipped back, "A lot more than you got, Honey," while she scooped up four iced beer mugs by the handles with one hand and aimed them at four regulars posted on their favorite stools at the opposite end of the bar. The men turned, and, recognizing Brian, waved, then immediately attacked their drinks.

Coming his way, Louise smiled, showing off a set of ivories that glowed in the dimness of the bar. "Where you been, Honey? Ain't seen you in a couple of weeks. I was afraid you'd dropped me off your favorite's list!" She moved towards him as gracefully as a synchronized swimmer, and threw her arms around his neck, burying his face in the cleavage between her more than ample breasts. Brian relaxed and enjoyed her attention until his supply of oxygen grew short. Sensing his need for breath, she let him up, grinning ear to ear. "You been gone too long, Honey."

Brian had sorely missed Louise, every five-foot-five, two hundred pounds of soul in her black body. "I know, I know," he said nodding agreement. "Things have become pretty wild lately, Louise."

She frowned and planted a thick, meaty hand on each hip. "You look rough, Honey. You gittin' enough sleep?"

"Yes, Mother, I am," Brian said. "How 'bout a beer?"

"Sure. First one's on me," she said winking.

"One's all I need. Say, Rockaway call in today?"

"Sure did. Said to get your skinny ass off the barstool and call his office. Said he'd be checkin' in regularly for messages. What you two rascals up to? Ya'll got somethin' sly goin' on? Huh, Honey?" She winked again. She did that a lot.

Using Rockaway's cell phone, Brian called the professor's office number and left his name. Five minutes later, Rockaway called back.

"I told you to dump that phone!" he growled.

"Hello to you, too. And don't worry; I'm okay," Brian said with attitude.

"Be there in ten minutes," he said.

"We'll have company," Brian answered. "I called Harry and Joanna on your cellphone while I was on my way."

"Thought you were keeping all this under your hat, Brauny. Now you're bringing in a lawyer and a newspaper lady? You wouldn't make a very good secret agent, kid."

"That block of cement that showed up at the campus spooked me. I've got more pictures, and they're gonna to blow you away. I thought some folks other than just you and me needed to know about things. Just in case."

"Gotcha. See you in a few." Rockaway hung up.

"Louise," Brian called out, pointing to an isolated booth in the far corner of the restaurant area. "I'll be over there. There'll be four in all."

Louise nodded and winked, letting him know she'd take care of it.

Minutes later, Harry Morgan and Joanna Johns walked in, and Louise pointed them to the corner where Brian waited.

Drinks? she mouthed silently, lifting a cupped hand to her face.

Harry nodded in silence, holding up two fingers. She nodded and winked.

Brian stood as they approached, giving Joanna a hug and kiss on the cheek, and Harry a warm handshake. Harry sat opposite Joanna and Brian in the booth; he wasn't smiling. "What's so important I had to cut my run short, Brian? It isn't a working day, you know."

"Since when have you had a working day? And when did you start jogging?" Brian asked sarcastically, noting the expensive designer-brand jogging suit the attorney was wearing.

"Since his secretary ordered him to, I'm guessing," laughed Joanna nodding her chin at the bulge showing just above the attorney's waist. She squeezed Brian's thigh gingerly under the table. She knew him well.

"You look like shit and smell like a barn, Brian. Have you taken to breaking into barns instead of mansions, now?"

Louise came to the table and set down two frosted mugs of beer. "We eatin' or just drinking today?"

The three of them in unison sang out, "Rib plates."

"An extra Bud and plate of ribs for Rockaway, too," Brian added. "He should be here in a minute or so."

Louise did her usual wink and left.

"Okay," said Joanna once Louise was half-way back to the bar "Let's hear it." After a moment of dead silence, she added, "You're in trouble, aren't you?" with a bite of annoyance.

"He didn't break the law," Rockaway said, striding up to the table.

Brian pointed at Rockaway. "My savior is here."

Turning to look Joanna directly in the eyes, he said, "I promised you five years ago that I'd never break the law again, and I meant it.

Let's just say I'm in a bit of a situation," appending, "but I didn't break the law."

Rock slid in beside Harry and slapped him on the back. "How's it hangin', Lefty?"

"Screw you, you old hippie. All that hash you snorted in 'Nam has clearly fried your brain." Harry faked an exaggerated glance at Rockaway's ponytail while he lifted his eyebrows. "The barbers all die in Richardson, Professor?"

"Smoked, Harry, not snorted," corrected Rockaway with a grin.

"Just like a couple of children," Brian mumbled just loud enough to be heard. Brian opened his backpack and pulled out a stack of 8x10 glossy inkjet photos from a plain brown envelope. "I don't have any time to waste. That's why I called together our happy, dysfunctional group." Brian stared the faces around him, and continued, "I've got a story to tell, and just so you don't think I'm crazy, I've brought pictures to prove it. First, the story…"

Brian stumbled through an account of the last day, beginning with his initial contact with Senator Fagan about *Faces of Texas*, then moving to the phone call from the politician about photographing his assassination, the letters he had mailed to each of them, the events at the barn, Songbird Two's appearance, and finally everything that happened at UTD.

Harry and Joanna listened in stunned silence. Rockaway filled in the details of what had taken place in his office. "I sincerely doubt that William Dunagan is his real name," he ended.

Brian leafed through the stack of pictures, moving a few to the bottom of the pile. "Look for yourselves," he said, pushing them towards Joanna and Harry.

After a few minutes, Harry looked up at Rockaway. "Have you seen these?" he asked.

"Just a few Brian left behind," he answered. "The one with the man pointing a gun in Fagan's face was most telling." He removed a couple of pictures from the inside pocket of his jacket and tossed them onto the table. "They were more than enough for me to know Brian's story was true, and that he was, indeed, in serious trouble."

Brian retrieved the pictures and slid them into the middle of the stack. The photos were now in sequential order, beginning with the first shots of Senator Fagan's pickup as it drove towards the barn to the final shot of Songbird Two walking away from the dead body of Senator Fagan. Harry leafed through them, one at a time, then passed them on to Joanna. Joanna looked through them and passed them on to Rockaway. When all three had finished, all eyes focused on Brian.

Harry leaned back from the table and took a breath. "Why haven't we heard anything about this in the media? All of this happened," he checked his watch, "about eight hours ago!" All eyes, including Brian's, now turned to Joanna.

"I really don't know! This is the first I've heard about it. There's been absolutely nothing on the wires! My God, how could this be?"

"Can't blame the liberal press on this one, Harry," Rockaway smirked.

Brian resorted the photos. "I think I can answer that, at least partially," Brian said, glancing at Rockaway. "You see, I haven't finished the story. I think someone's trying to cover it up, and that's related to the person who's trying to get me."

Harry gave a short uncomfortable laugh. "You mean there's more? Something more damning than a pictorial essay documenting a senator's assassination? This I've got to see."

"What is it, Brian?" Joanna asked, curiosity etching her face.

Brian laid the first of the several photos he'd selected out into the center of the table. Simultaneously, their eyes zeroed in on them. "After the shooting, I remained in the loft of the barn. I wanted to wait as long as I could to make sure the shooter and Songbird Three, whoever he was, and anyone else who might be hanging around, had left. I sure as hell didn't want anyone seeing *me* leave the barn. This picture was taken shortly after I saw the shooter, code-named Songbird Two, leave the scene." The picture showed a black SUV in the background, approaching the senator's truck and his dead body from the tree line. All eyes returned to Brian after they'd examined it.

"How long afterwards, Brauny?" Rockaway asked.

"Not long. Maybe fifteen minutes or so," Brian answered, as he laid out another picture. "This one shows four men in suits getting out of the SUV." Each person at the table took turns examining the shot. Brian waited for them to finish, then placed a third picture on top of the other two. "But this is the money shot."

To everyone's surprise, Joanna scooped up the pile and dropped them quickly onto her lap. "Louise," she whispered.

Louise approached the table with a tray full of steaming plates and Rockaway's beer, and set them down one at a time. "Here you go, sweeties, enjoy." She straightened up and looked at each of them intently, dropping her usual smile. "Somebody just die or somethin'? You folks look whiter than usual."

Rockaway laughed nervously. "Nah, we're okay, Louise, just talking business," he answered, pulling his plate closer, "but you're right, we're taking things way too serious with these ribs staring us in the face like this. Time to eat!"

Louise wiped her hands on her waist-apron. "I'll leave you to your business then." She said, winking and leaving.

After Louise was out of sight, Joanna returned the pictures to the table, carefully avoiding the steaming plates, standing alone and ignored.

"Check out the senator," Brian challenged. Everyone looked closely, and he watched as three mouths hung in disbelief. "Now this," Brian said, laying a fourth picture on top of the pile. He waited for their reaction. It only took seconds. A collective gasp came from the table.

"It's a hoax!" Joanna exclaimed.

Rockaway chuckled. "No wonder they want your ass so bad, Brauny."

"Another fucking government conspiracy! I knew it," spat Harry.

The last picture showed Senator Jimmy Fagan standing on his own two feet, shaking hands with the driver from the SUV.

Chapter 15

Hatfield picked his way through the downtown afternoon traffic on Main Street on his way back to Elite headquarters. His plan was to meet with Edison for the debriefing, swing by the garage to turn in the company truck and equipment, grab a bite to eat, and then wait for orders from Duvall. He kept his radio tuned to the local news station, but, oddly, as of yet, nothing had come across the airwaves about Fagan.

Eldawoody's disappearance worried him; it had to be driving Edison to the brink. *The shit's hit the fan, hasn't it Max old buddy?* he thought to himself.

Hatfield's phone vibrated. He checked the caller. It was Duvall.

"I was wondering when you'd call. How'd it go with the boss man? I'm on my way there."

"Not too good," Duvall chuckled. "I wouldn't go there now if I were you. He's in the process of having a coronary. Nothing on the news, and Eldawoody's spooky vanishing act has got him more shook up than he's willing to admit. Did you see or hear anything that should've caused alarm bells, Hat?"

"Nope. You know I would've told you if I had. I was in the barn the whole time prior to the job, Bill. Eldawoody and me, we chatted back and forth right up to the time. After he confirmed the final all clear, that was it. Whatever happened to him had to have happened after I walked out of the barn. We're talking seconds, here. Know what I mean?"

"Yeah. Whatever it was…he was disappointed when Maxwell jerked his chain, but, hell, he's a professional. He wouldn't just pick up his toys and leave because he got his feelings hurt. Given everything, it seems to me there may be something to Maxwell's paranoia about a mole in the organization after all. This will likely come back to bite us in the ass if we don't somehow clean up this mess."

"A mole? What are you talking about? You never said anything about a mole."

"Boss said was on a 'need to know' basis, Hat. The only reason I'm telling you now is because of Hasan. Maxwell thought it was you. That's why he gave you the job instead of Hasan. He figured that if you were FBI, you couldn't make the hit. He figured you'd squirm out of it somehow if you were a fed." Duvall hesitated. "The heat's on our vanished friend now. Right now, it's all up to you and me, friend."

Hatfield let what he'd just been told soak in. Finally, he volunteered, "Things are really fucked up. It sounds to me like a storm is about to hit, and I don't want to be standing in front of it. Listen, Bill. We need to talk."

"I think together we can handle damage control, but you still haven't heard the worst of it. We've got some fish the boss wants us to fry," answered Duvall. "What's your twenty?"

Hatfield hesitated before answering. "I'm on I-30 about fifteen minutes out from the office. What fish?"

"There was visitor at the scene, Hat. No idea how he got wind of things, if he was hired, or what. Don't know enough yet. I'm guessing he took some pictures. At least, that would figure, him being a photographer and all. Maxwell wants us to track him and a photography professor friend of his down and neutralize them."

"What? You're shittin' me! A photographer?" Hat's dismay was genuine. "That means the assassination could be on film! I could be on film!" This wasn't good. "Where was he? I didn't see or notice anything at all out of place. After Hasan gave the final all clear, it only took a matter of seconds before it was over. I was back in my truck driving away in less than five minutes. There couldn't have been anybody in the barn. I was there. I would know."

"I'm not pointing a finger at you, Hat. If you go down, all of us do. He was probably in the woods. The appearance of the photographer and Hasan's disappearance seem like more than coincidence," Duvall stated.

"You got a lead on the photographer?"

"Braun, Brian Braun. He's from Dallas, but let's not do this over the phone. Why don't we…uh, wait a minute, Hat."

There was silence on the other end of the line. Hatfield waited almost a full minute before Duvall returned.

"Listen Hat. There's something I've got to take care of. Keep your phone handy. I'll get back to you about the cleanup work. Later."

The line disconnected before Hatfield could respond. *Now what's that all about?* "Shit." Hatfield mumbled, and started punching in a number on his cell phone.

The moment Duvall ended his call with Hatfield, he slipped

around the corner of the Bank of America Plaza Building. During the conversation, Duvall had spotted Maxwell Edison exiting from the front entrance of the office building, rushing up to the valet parking attendant, and didn't want to be spotted.

And where the hell would you be going in such a hurry?

Duvall slunk deeper into the shadows to watch. Edison seemed edgy, impatient. The ringleader checked his watch several times over the next few seconds. His anxiety was understandable, maybe, given the enfolding fiasco, but Duvall also read something else in his boss's body language.

Chapter 16

"Who do you think's behind this farce, Brian?" Harry asked, gathering his wits enough to begin an attack on his plate of ribs.

"I'm more interested in who's putting GPS trackers on my Jeep and a hitman on me," Brian shrugged. "I'm guessing FBI, maybe."

He looked at Rockaway for confirmation. "What do you think?"

Rockaway shook his head. "I don't think the FBI is out to kill you, Brauny. If it is, capture and interrogate, yes, kill, no. There's something more sinister going on. This doesn't seem CIA or any other of the fifty acronyms out there. It has to be some rogue group. But why? What's really going on? I don't get it. Fagan has a well-known tendency to piss-off a lot of people, but I can't think of anything he's been up to lately, that'd rate a hoax like this."

"That sorry wing-nut has also been known to create every opportunity possible to appear before a camera," added Harry, wiping a dribble of sauce from his chin and grabbing another rib. "Hey, aren't you guys gonna eat? You know, come to think of it…ol' Fagan hasn't been in the news in a while. That alone should be newsworthy."

"Does Elite Security ring a bell for anyone?" Brian interjected.

Joanna finished a sip of beer, then raising her hand. "Yes! There's a Senate Hearing about them next week. And guess who's chairing it?"

"That's right. I ran across something about it on the internet," Brian said. "I was looking for something on Fagan after he called me, but what I read didn't look like a big deal. An article also appeared in the *Times*, but was tucked away on a back page and written more like an afterthought, not some big hoopla."

"What's the hearing about?" Rockaway asked.

"I don't know for sure," said Joanna, "but I heard through the journalist grapevine it was something about alleged kickbacks, dirty dealing, the usual. I think I also heard it had something to do with Iraq. Elite Security is the biggest international security company in the world. Its home office is right here in Dallas. They do contract protection of political figures; they're the dominant private security force in Iraq."

"Yeah, and Zeta Corp is their main competition. Zeta Corp has its ass is on the line right now for the 'accidental' deaths of some civilians. Elite marched in and took things over right out from under them," added Harry. "Sounds like our Texas Senator from Rusk has Elite Security in his gun sights, so to speak, but why?"

Brian pushed back his plate. He needed food to keep going, but hearing what he'd heard, he had no appetite anymore. "You think Elite would put a hit out on Fagan for that? What could a Senate committee do that would warrant taking out the Chairperson? I mean, what could Fagan's committee do to Elite Security? Levy them a big fine? Slap their business wrists and cause them to temporarily lose some business? Corruption's nothing new, and certainly not enough an excuse to kill a United States Senator, for Pete's sake. There'd have to be something more. Something that would drive them to do the unspeakable, if that's even what this is all about."

Rockaway shook his head slowly. "I think we're missing the whole point here, boys and girls. Just think a minute: Boy Wonder here," he nodded at Brian, "took pictures of a man shooting a senator. Then there're pictures of that same dead senator's miraculous resurrection. Of him shaking hands with a bunch of suits. So, here's the real question: Who was the shooter working for? Elite? And why bring in a third party like our Boy Wonder here," he said, pointing again at Brian, "to blow the whistle on the whole she-bang? It doesn't make sense."

"It's a conspiracy, I'm telling you," stated Harry, flat out. "There's no doubt about it. I can smell it."

Rockaway rolled his eyes. "No shit, Sherlock. I'll concede that to you. It's because it doesn't make sense that there must be something bigger behind it all." Rockaway pointed towards the backpack. "What about those photos? That's a lot of dynamite you've got there, Brauny. You gonna give them to Joanna? Bust this thing wide open? It's probably the only way to protect yourself against whoever's after you. I don't know that there's anywhere left to run. If it is Elite that's after you, they've got the same or maybe even better resources than the feds. Probably better, if you think about it. No internal laws to hinder their enthusiasm to skin you alive.

"Right now, you're the target regardless of who's behind it. And that's the way they would want it. Fagan's obviously not the target. He's protected by the suits. He most probably never was in danger. Otherwise, he never would've called you to take those pictures. Those

8x10's can send a lot of people to the hoosegow and make heroes of the leftovers."

Harry pushed back his plate full of bones he'd picked clean, and took a healthy swig of his drink. "You could turn yourself in to the feds, unless they're the ones that wanted Fagan dead. Then you'd be shit out of luck. I wouldn't put anything past the feds."

Joanna stuck a couple of fingers in her beer and flicked them at Harry's face. "You're such an asshole."

Harry licked his wetted lips and wiped his face. "Only stating the facts, my dear."

Before she could respond, Louise again appeared as if from nowhere, catching everyone by surprise. "Ex-cuse me? I see three full plates and only one satisfied customer. Am I missing something here?" she asked, wagging a finger at them. "I ain't never seen food left on a plate in my restaurant."

"This one's yours," Brian whispered to Rockaway across the table, looking for a quick retreat.

"It'll be gone before you come back in ten minutes to refill our drinks, Louise," Rockaway said, holding up his half empty bottle of Budweiser. "Promise."

"You guys, okay?" she asked. The look on her face showed she understood they were in serious conversation.

"We are," Brian said. "Could you make sure we're not disturbed for just a little bit longer, please? We need a little more time to figure out a few things, Louise. Okay?"

"Consider it done. If'n you all need anything, just call me. And I mean anything, you hear?"

Brian grinned, appreciating her light-hearted presence ever more. "I hear you."

While at Rockaway's office, Brian had printed four copies of the picture showing Fagan's fatal shot and another of him being helped by the suits from the SUV. He handed a copy of each to everyone at the table. "We need to split up. If they find out about this meeting, we could all be dead."

Harry knocked back the rest of his drink. "And I'd like to thank you for that."

"Harry. Joanna," Brian continued, scoffing at Harry's remark and handing them each a manilla envelope. "I'm entrusting you two with copies of the whole sequence of pictures. Keep them safe."

Harry nodded. "I'll put them in my safety deposit box at the bank."

"It's a holiday. They're closed today, idiot," quipped Joanna.

"That's what I said. I'll lock them in the safe at my law office. What then, Brian?"

"Well, if anything happens to me, I'm sure you'll think of something," Brian answered.

"But what can we do in the meantime?" Joanna asked. "Leave you all alone among the wolves? I don't think so. I'm going to stick to you like glue.

"Rock?" Brian asked, looking for support.

Rockaway shook his head. "Looks like you've now got two handicaps. As for me, somebody's got to protect the bad guys from Joanna. I'm up for that," he replied obliquely.

"I'm not at all sure what to do in the long run," Brian commented, ignoring Rockaway's flippant remark.

At that, Joanna turned to Brian again. "So, that's your plan for now? Isolate from us and make yourself a better target? Look, I could splash these photos across the front page and put a stop to this whole thing right now. The notoriety alone would provide us instant protection. Nobody could touch us," Joanna stated firmly. "Think, Brian. This isn't a game. If we don't, everybody's life will be at stake, not just your own."

Brian paused, then nodded. "I know, but first I'm going to have to start eating my ribs before Louise comes back. Right now, I'm more scared of her than all of the boogeymen that might be out there."

"And then?" She continued doggedly.

Brian smiled, "Then, I'm going to call Senator Fagan, of course."

Chapter 17

Cell phone in hand, Hatfield drummed the steering wheel with the fingers of this other hand while he waited for the traffic light at Main and Griffin to change to green. His phone didn't even finish the first ring before it was answered.

"Hell-o?" The man from the Dairy Queen said.

"FUBAR," said Hatfield. "I need to talk to The Man. ASAP."

"Can I help?"

"This is above both our pay grades."

"Want me to patch you through now or set up a time and place?"

A silver, late-model Mercedes idled in front of Hatfield at the light. All he could see of the driver was platinum white hair extending out on either side of the driver's headrest and a pair of female eyes checking him out in the Mercedes' rear view mirror. He took his eyes from the woman driver and glanced idly to his right across the street at the front entrance of the Bank of America Plaza Building, and did a double take. There was Duvall, standing just beyond the corner of the building. He was dressed in civvies and blended almost imperceptively with the downtown crowd. Almost. *I thought you were out and about?* thought Hat.

But it wasn't Duvall's clothes that held his attention. It was what he was doing. The man was clearly slinking as best he could in the shadows. *Who are you following, Bill?*

Then, he saw Maxwell Edison standing at the valet stand.

"Uh, you still there?" The voice on the other end of Hat's cell phone questioned.

"Yeah, listen, I'll have to get back to you. I'm okay, but something's just popped up I need to check it out. Just let The Man know I need to talk, and I'll get back."

As Hatfield disconnected, a horn blared behind him. He immediately looked ahead and saw the Mercedes pulling away.

Hatfield punched the gas and made a sharp left turn, barely clearing the onslaught of oncoming cars and pedestrians. He had to find a position of cover, where he could watch Duvall and see what was about to unfold. He spotted an open curb space on his right in the shadow of a tree, and pulled in, wrenched the truck into park, and twisted around in his seat to watch Duvall and Edison.

After getting his car and tipping the attendant, Edison drove to the end of the block and made a quick right going the opposite way on the same street that Hat was on, and accelerated; at the same time, Duvall ran into a nearby parking lot assumedly for his own ride. Hatfield slid down low in his seat. There was only one exit/entry into that particular lot and it was on the same street as he and Edison were on. Hatfield turned on his left blinker, forced his way into traffic, and started to circle the block, hoping to spot Duvall without being spotted himself.

A moment later, Hatfield recognized Duvall's big Yukon turning right from the parking lot and onto North Lamar in the same direction as Edison. After letting several cars pass, he immediately maneuvered to follow Duvall. The old pickup Hatfield was driving wasn't the ideal vehicle for tailing another. Size, age, and color would make it stand out among the sleek, later-model cars on the road. Luckily, the sheer size of Duvall's vehicle made it an easy target to follow even at a distance.

Occasionally, Hatfield could catch a brief glimpse of Edison's black Ford 500 up far ahead, but his main focus remained on Duvall. Recognizing the route, Duvall and Edison were undoubtedly heading for Interstate 35. As their cars were hugging the right lane, Hatfield assumed they were headed north. He was right.

As expected, the interstate, was heavily congested, and Hatfield figured he would stay unnoticed as long as he hung far enough back. Far ahead, Hatfield noticed Edison's Ford with its right blinker on, indicating he was planning to get off the interstate, probably at the next exit, Mockingbird Lane. Hatfield smiled to himself. This told him two things: First, Edison hadn't spotted Duvall or him. Second, Hatfield knew exactly where Edison was headed: his favorite bar and barbecue place, The Shack.

Exiting well behind Duvall, Hatfield cut left across the Mockingbird Lane traffic and whipped into the parking lot across the street from The Shack. From his vantage, he watched Edison park his Ford directly in front of the restaurant's entrance and Duvall double back after passing and making u-turn. As Edison entered the restaurant, the squad leader turned into The Shack's parking lot and double parked just out of sight in a narrow driveway beside the building.

Pulling up his last dialed number on his phone, Hatfield hit the call button.

"Yeah?" said the man from the Dairy Queen.

"I'm ready, patch me through."

"Hold the line," the voice responded.

Hatfield had to wait for only a few seconds before a new voice came into his ear. "I understand things are heating up. You okay?"

Hatfield watched Duvall emerge from the shadows and casually stroll the sidewalk. "Yes, but I've got to make this quick, John Lee. There was a photographer at the barn. I think I was caught on film killing Fagan."

"What? Are you..."

"Something's up, so just listen." Hatfield continued to monitor Duvall's casual stroll down the sidewalk, watching him occasionally stop before a shop window as if looking at the window-merchandise, then moving ahead. "Duvall's added the photographer and another person onto my hit list. Also, my hunch about the mole search was right on the button. Edison thought it was me, which is why he switched hit men at the last moment. But now, Duvall and Edison are focusing on Eldawoody since he disappeared. Edison's about to shit his pants. But there's more. There's dissension among the ranks. Duvall's tailing Edison on the sly. I've followed them both to The Shack on Mockingbird. Something's about to happen, so I've got to move. Don't send in the Marines just yet. I'll be in touch."

"Wait! Don't hang up!" shouted John Lee at the dead line.

Chapter 18

Harry nursed a Salty Dog while the rest of the group wolfed down their rib dinners. No one wanted another reprimand from Louise. Thankfully, the eating process silenced everyone, offering Brian a welcome respite. Wild and varied scenarios raced through the minds of each and every person at the table, and each as they ate, was engulfed in their own deep thoughts about what to do next and how to do it.

Brian gave Joanna a quick glance. From the look on her face, Brian assumed she was fantasizing about her own Pulitzer. Though momentarily disappointed, he couldn't blame her. After all, that was what had gotten him into the mess he was in. He shifted his gaze to Harry. He knew what was going through his head. This would be his opportunity to throw his hat into the political ring, maybe make a run for the Senate, railing against corruption and injustice. He would finally have to get his chance to bring down Big Brother. Brian moved his focus to Rockaway and grinned. Rockaway caught his young friend staring at him, returned the grin, and nodded. He'd be the one Brian knew he could count on when things got down to the nitty-gritty. And he knew they would. Soon. He could feel the nitty-gritty breathing down his back right now.

Brian and Rockaway gnawed at the last vestiges of meat from their final ribs, then pushed their plates away from the edge of the table at the same time. Rockaway silently fired up a cigarette. Surprisingly, no one objected.

"Hey," said Rockaway, taking a deep drag, "where's my Runner, Brauny?"

"I parked it around back. Came in through the rear entrance. Is my Jeep still at school?"

"Nah, I drove it here."

"Here?" Brian hadn't expected that. He had thought that Rockaway would surely tuck it away somewhere out of sight. "But they know about it, Rock. It'll make you, maybe all of us if we're caught together, a target. What did you do with the tracker you found on it?"

Rockaway grinned. "I stuck it on the rear bumper of Professor Sorenson's car. He lives in Sherman. If they follow that Swede anywhere, they'll end up almost in Oklahoma." He took another drag. "He's a prick anyway. He steals my parking spot at least once a week to piss me off."

Brian didn't like the idea of bringing yet another innocent person into the mix. Rockaway must've read his mind.

"He'll be fine, Brauny. Don't worry. And if they spot your Jeep, I can lead them on a wild goose chase. Away from you."

"I'm not sure I like that idea either, Rock. You don't need to be putting yourself in the front of this."

Rockaway waved Brian off. "Shit, Brauny, I haven't had this much fun since 'Nam."

Brian shook his head in disbelief. He didn't like it. It was time to go on the offensive. "Harry, let me see your cell," he said, holding out his hand.

"Excuse me? What's wrong with yours?"

Brian waved his hand again. "Come on, as my attorney, you're supposed to protect me. Right?"

"Ye-ah," Harry said, but it came out more like a question. "And your point is?"

Brian sighed. Everything was a sparring match with Harry. "Look, it's a given that, even though they may be withholding it from the press, the authorities are probably all over Fagan's place by now and will have started tracing whoever calls. For now, we don't know if they're aware I was even there snapping pictures or if this is something the senator did alone."

"I'm guessing they know," added Joanna.

"Maybe," said Rockaway.

"Exactly," Brian said. "We don't know."

Brian turned his eyes back to Harry and stretched out his arm again. "You and I aren't going to be running in the same circles anytime soon, so if they're going to trace or follow somebody, it would be better you than me. Besides, you're a lawyer. You'd have reason to call a senator involved in an upcoming hearing. So-o, Harry, as my attorney, you should be..."

"But, what if..."

Brian held up a hand to stifle him. "Think of the political clout you'll have after this is over, Harry. You're at the forefront of exposing the biggest coverup since Watergate."

Harry nodded in concession. "Okay, okay. You've twisted my arm

Shutterbug

sufficiently," he said, grinning. "You want me to call the senator for you?"

"That was easy," Rockaway mumbled.

Brian thought for a minute. All eyes were on him. "Yes. You talk first. If everything sounds kosher, hand me the phone, but if someone else picks up, or you hear clicking on the line, or if the senator tries to stonewall, do your outraged lawyer thing. Let 'em know we're on the run from the bad guys. Demand protection for your client."

"That should be easy enough," he said. "After I piss them off, then what do you want me to say?"

"Just get the senator on the phone, and I'll take it from there."

"And then?" Harry asked.

Brian shrugged. "I'm not sure. We'll have to see." That was the truth. Brian was counting on his ability to think on his feet, to react and feed off what Fagan had to say.

Harry pulled out his cell phone. "Number?"

Brian had memorized Fagan's number, and recited it to Harry. Harry punched in the numbers then looked up at Brian, his thumb poised on the TALK button. "Ready for this, Bucko?"

Brian nodded.

Harry made a big deal about pressing the button then put the phone to his ear. "One ringy-dingy," he sang.

"Cut the playing, Counselor," Rockaway said with an edge. "There's nothin' at all funny about this!"

Harry frowned at Rockaway, and then his eyebrows abruptly rose in surprise. "Uh, yes. This is Harry L. Morgan, the attorney on record for Mr. Brian Braun of Dallas. Could I speak with Senator Fagan, please?"

"Really? And may I ask your capacity in regard to the senator?"

"Really? And your name is?"

Harry nodded his head at the receiver with a mischievous look.

"Oh, real-ly," Harry crooned. "Well I'm sure you're a fine political aide, but I need to speak directly with the senator. It's about the upcoming hearings…" Suddenly, Harry's tone turned low, guttural and threatening. "That shit ain't gonna fly with me, mister. So listen up. What? Oh really? Okay, but before you hang up and put yourself at risk, give your 'boss' a message for me: Can you say the word 'photographs'?" Harry winked at Brian. "Tell the senator that unless he calls this number in the next, oh let's say, minute or so…I've advised Mr. Braun to show the photos to the *Dallas Morning News*. We're about a block from there now."

A pause.

"You have my number, right? Good. Oh, and tell the senator Mr. Braun has *all* of the pictures. The befores and afters. He'll know what I'm referring to, as he well should, since he's the one that hired my client. Mr. Braun is a very thorough and professional photographer, you know." Harry checked his watch. "The second hand is ticking on my watch."

Another pause.

"What's that? You want to know what pictures I'm talking about? Ask your boss, the senator," he replied calmly, then snapped the cell phone shut and set it on the table, a Cheshire Cat grin spreading from ear to ear across his face. He spread his arms out wide. "So, how'd I do?" he asked, looking from one concerned face to another.

Rockaway snubbed out his second after-meal cigarette on the floor. "How the hell are we supposed to know? We don't know what the other asshole said."

Harry pointedly ignored Rockaway. "It means they don't know, Brian! I could hear the tension in the aide's voice. They don't have a clue! I guarantee it!"

"Unbelievable," said Joanna. "What in the world is Fagan up to? Why the big assassination ruse?"

"And why hire Brauny here to photograph it?" Rockaway added.

"Politics," chimed in Harry. "I know…'conspiracy nut, Harry'…but, think about it: Fagan's no fool. Whatever he's got up his sleeve will mean *mucho grande* political points in the end. That you can count on."

It was then that Brian remembered something the senator had mentioned on the phone when he had pressed him on the same question. "I asked the senator the same thing once. I told him that it looked like he was getting the short end of the stick. I get to take pictures that'll rock the world and he gets dead. He said, 'Don't you worry about me, son. I always come out on top.' It didn't register with me then, but I should've seen that he was already laying down a smoke screen. I guess I was too caught up in the moment."

Rockaway took another sip of his beer. "Don't fault yourself there, Brauny. I don't think anybody would've been thinking clearly in the same circumstances. So…what now?"

Brian shrugged. "According to Harry's ultimatum, they've got about thirty seconds left to call back. If the senator doesn't call back, then we head to the *Morning News* and bust this thing wide open."

No sooner had the words left Brian's mouth than Harry's phone began bouncing around on the table. "It's probably for you," Harry said drolly, pushing it towards Brian.

Brian picked it up, flipped it open and spotted the senator's home number in the caller identification window. "Nice talking to you again, Senator," he said, as pleasantly as he could. Brian pressed the speaker button and set it back on the table for all to hear.

The usual, familiar, down-home gaiety was absent from Senator Fagan's voice. "Where are you, Brian?"

"Here. You know, livin' the dream, Senator Fagan. Tryin' to stay alive long enough to cash in on that Pulitzer you promised me. Avoiding an assassin the size of a small bus. And you? You seem to have had a miraculous recovery after being fatally shot. Three times. We all know that Texas has the best health care system in the world, but this is nothing short of resurrection."

"Listen, boy. You've no idea what you've done by calling me. Weren't my instructions explicit enough? Despite what you might think, neither of us was in any real danger before. Now we're both screwed."

That got under Brian's skin. "Well geez, *Senator*, I'm really sorry about the inconvenience I'm causing you. But I assume you're surrounded by federal and state agents, while I'm out here all alone, not knowing who to trust anymore. So fuck you and your problems, Senator. I'm taking this story to the papers. It's the only way I can assure my safety and those around me. Matter of fact, I'm walking that way now." Harry waved to get Brian's attention and pointed to himself. "With my attorney, I might add. We'll be in the lobby in less than two minutes."

Rockaway gave Brian a thumbs up. Joanna's eyes widened with interest and curiosity. Harry smirked and mouthed an "'atta boy."

"Now, wait a minute, Brian," said Senator Fagan with an audible trace of panic. "You can't do that! Not yet, anyway." There was a pause. "Listen Brian, we need to meet. Face to face. Come out here to the ranch. Like you said, there's enough agents out here to start a whole new division. I can protect you. Come on, Son. Don't go to the papers just yet."

Rockaway frowned and shook his head in the negative. Brian glanced at Joanna and Harry, who nodded in agreement.

"You don't understand my situation here, Senator. Someone has turned their bulldogs loose on me, and I don't know who they are or who the 'someone' is. Hell, I'm not even sure I can trust you. Not knowing who the 'enemy' is, I doubt I'd even make it to your ranch alive."

Brian paused for effect.

"I've got to do what I can to protect *me,* senator. That's all I'm concerned about at the moment. Not you. Not whatever it is you're hatching. You've proved you can resurrect from the dead, but I haven't mastered that trick."

The other end of the line remained silent. Brian had to strongly resist the temptation to continue speaking.

The senator finally broke silence. His tone changed from panic to deadly. "First, Brian, I don't believe a fucking word you're saying about being minutes away from the *The News*. You're on a speaker, and I don't hear a damn thing in the background. Not a bus, not a car horn, not a soul. So shove that little lie up your ass, boy."

Brian shrugged in silent compliance.

"However, I don't doubt that you believe you're in danger, as am I. Turns out we're going to be in bed together a little while longer whether either of us likes it or not. Are you with me so far, Brian?"

"I'm listening," Brian said. "But I've been in one spot too long already. I'm about to move, so make it quick."

"All right. I'm holdin' aces and spades you don't even know about. If I even get a glimmer that you're trying to fuck me, I'll do something worse than get you killed. I'll send your sweet ass to jail and make sure they throw away the key. You see, I've got proof of the identity of the real Highland Park Cat Burglar. Remember that whole fiasco of yours never came to trial, so your lawyer won't be able to plead double jeopardy. I might even be in good humor enough to exchange the goods I have on you and that Sensabaugh character for the pictures of my 'murder'. Think about it, son."

Silence screamed across the phone line. *What the hell?* "So are you done talking?" Brian asked calmly refusing to give Fagan the satisfaction of hearing any panic on his part.

"Oh, I've just started, son," spat Senator Fagan. "And another thing, who the hell do you think would believe that *I'm* the one that sent you out to take pictures, even if you did publish them? Why, it looks to me that you might be in cahoots with the ones that tried to kill me. Who do you think the public would believe? A senator or a thief? I've got the goods on you, young man, and I'll make damn sure you spend the rest of your natural life in jail if you try to fuck me over on this."

Another pause.

"Now do I have your attention?"

"In that case, Senator Fagan, you're not going to be in my photography book." Brian snapped the phone shut, and then handed it back to Harry. "I think I'm beginning to like the senator less and less."

"Well, that seals it," said Harry, taking his phone. "I'm running against that son-of-a-bitch for his office next election." Harry looked over his shoulder. "Where's Louise? I could use another drink."

Chapter 19

Having observed Edison entering The Shack, Duvall returned to his car and drove it into the parking lot behind the restaurant. It was a narrow affair with just enough room for one long row of cars and was divided from the public alley by a six-foot brick retaining wall. The moment he entered, he hit the brakes. There, parked closest to the rear entrance of the restaurant-bar was a 1969 metallic blue Plymouth Road Runner. *Rockaway's?* Duvall thought. *What are the chances of running into two such cars the same day?*

Duvall didn't believe in coincidences. That morning, when he was tracking down Braun, he had spotted this very car in the library parking lot. Rockaway had been fiddling with his car keys right next to it while checking him out, yet somehow the professor was in his office waiting for him when he got there to confront Braun. While he'd played Twenty Questions with Rockaway, Braun must have been making his getaway in the professor's car, probably about the same time Duvall was climbing up the steps to the second floor of the Fine Arts Building. Questions about Braun, Edison, Hatfield, and Eldawoody swam within his tired mind.

Duvall had thought Edison was going to The Shack to eat. Perhaps he was also meeting someone at the same time. *Braun?* In this less than desirable neighborhood of hookers, muggers, and thieves, he couldn't window shop, and hanging around the parking lot for any length of time would likely catch the usual roving parking lot security officers' notice, wherever he was at the moment. He needed to come up with an alternate plan that would keep him close enough to observe what Edison was doing, and not be blatantly conspicuous.

Duvall maneuvered his Yukon behind the Road Runner and put it into park, blocking any possible escape for Braun, if indeed Braun was here as he strongly suspected, and walked around to the front of the building.

As he slipped past the door, his peripheral vision caught a quick glimpse of another classic. It was a red, '68 Mercedes 500 SEL making a left turn from the opposite direction off Mockingbird Lane.

What the hell? Duvall's features and thoughts both grew simultaneously dark. An old hate from the past stirred in his gut. Keeping his eyes glued on the garish car, he stepped back into the dark recessed entrance of a beauty shop for African-American clientele located adjacent to The Shack. It gave him perfect cover, and a good view of the Mercedes. Duvall knew of only one person who drove one of those. *Is he here to meet Edison, too?*

Duvall followed the coupe as it pulled up behind Edison's sedan. The driver unfolded from the low slung seat; a black Stetson hat popped out first above the roof confirming his suspicion. It was the infamous contract assassin Gib Rogers. Duvall had unfinished business with the killer. "Gib," he said, gritting his teeth. *Perhaps its time to kill old and new demons at the same time? Still, Braun, Gib and Edison, together, here, at the same time? What the hell's going on? Maxwell must be planning some personnel changes.* "Time to make your peace with God, boys," Duvall mumbled.

Duvall continued to hide in the shadows, contemplating plans and contingency plans one after another. Then it hit him, and he knew exactly what he needed to do next.

Shutterbug

Chapter 20

Maxwell Edison found a parking spot near the front door of The Shack, which was unusual this late in the afternoon. He strode in, briefcase in hand, stopped just inside the door for a second to let his eyes adjust to the dim room, then made his way to the bar. The barstool groaned beneath him as his two hundred plus pounds settled onto the seat. He noticed a few customers he vaguely recognized at the end of bar and nodded at them. They were regulars, very regular from what he remembered, but he had no desire to know who they were, or for them to know who he was. *Deadbeats. I wonder if they ever get their asses off those stools to do anything besides take a leak and go home to sleep.*

Edison tapped the bar nervously with his fingers, and, as if on cue, his favorite bartender in the world showed up next to him from the annexed dining room.

"Hel-lo, Lu-eez. Long time, no see," he greeted with a smile.

"Why, Mr. Maxwell! Where you been so long?" Louise exclaimed, giving him a hug.

"You alone, Mr. Maxwell or is somebody joining you today?" Louise casually asked.

"I'll need a table for two and...a bottle of Corona."

As Louise worked her way behind the bar, and a second later placed an opened Corona on the bar in front of Edison, Gib Rogers appeared from behind and sat down beside him. Rogers touched his fingers to the rim of his cowboy hat and threw a smile at Louise.

Louise pointed Edison and Rogers to an unoccupied booth at the opposite end of the annex, and followed them there. After the two men had found their seats, she asked, "What'll it be, boys? Somethin' to drink first?"

Maxwell held up his Corona. "One more of these for me, Louise. Then, cut me off, and hand me a rib plate."

"How 'bout you, Mr. Gib?"

"Just tea, Louise, and same thing to eat."

"Gotcha," she said and left.

Both men were silent until Louise was out of earshot. Rogers spoke first. "So much for small talk. What's the deal?"

Edison looked down at the lime curl in the bottom of his bottle, making it twirl in circles on its end by moving the bottom of the bottle in a circular motion with his hands. He kept his eyes on the lime while he spoke.

"There are short and long term considerations here."

"Let's do the short term one's first, then."

Edison took a drink, then rested his back against the wall. "I've a very delicate operation that may have gone completely haywire this morning. A simple job, really. You'd think three trained assassins could bump off one old man."

"And?"

Edison finally shifted his gaze to Rogers. "And shit, that's what. You know Eldawoody?"

"Of course. We worked that operation together in the Sudan. Remember? Good man. Ruthless."

"Well, he disappeared. He was the spotter for this morning's operation. Gave the all clear, and, poof! Vanished before the job was even finished." Edison's stretched his arms out like a magician performing a disappearance act. "Voila! Gone. Not a fucking word. Not a sound. Nothing."

Rogers frowned. "You mentioned Duvall earlier. He involved you think?"

Edison shrugged. "Don't know. He's supposedly chasing down two leads right now. Get this…there was a photographer on the scene who may have taken pictures of the hit. I haven't been around to debrief the shooter yet. Michael Hatfield. Know him?"

"No. What about the target?"

"That's not your concern right now. But I'm beginning to think that Duvall's on the take somewhere. He may have planned this whole fucking thing. The photographer. Eldawoody. Blackmail maybe. I'm not sure of anything right now, except for one thing: I've got a number of people to eliminate, and I mean eliminate. Now. Within the next forty-eight hours."

Rogers looked to his left and saw Louise returning. Neither said a word as she arrived at the table and set down the drinks. She looked back and forth between the two men.

"Do I smell bad or sumthin'?"

Edison smiled, then patted her arm. "Louise, you're the finest

117

woman I know. It's just one of those days. You know."

"Seems to be a lot of that going around today," she said without humor. "Food'll be here in a minute. Want me to shout out that I'm comin' so ya'll can quit talkin' 'fore I get here?"

"You know how to whistle, don't you?" Rogers joked.

Louise waved him off and laughed. "Ya'll full of somethin' 'round here! That's for sure."

"Great girl," said Edison after she'd left. "Wish my life was as simple as hers."

"Right," said Rogers, "and that'd last about two minutes. So tell me what you want so I can get to work."

Edison reached down and pulled his briefcase from under the table, popped it open, and pulled out two large folders, tossing them across the table. "My people pulled this together for me before I came to meet you. I'll have the rest by the time you finish your first rib. This is the basic info. Two guys to start with," he said pointing to the folders.

Rogers opened the top folder and pulled out a laminated copy of a newspaper article about Brian Braun and his cat burglar exploits. There was another half-inch of paper complete with photos, an up-to-date biography, business and home addresses and phone numbers, and known associates.

Edison pointed. "That's the photographer. I want him dead, and I want any fucking pictures he took."

"Okay," said Rogers. Placing the first folder aside, he opened the second, briefly scanning each page. It was a dossier on Mickey Rockaway. "Three tours in 'Nam and former Green Beret. I hate those fuckin' green weenies. Photography professor at the University of

Texas at Dallas. Fucking hippie who never grew up. I seen the type before. This one'll be fun." Rogers, finished scanning the dossier, tossed it back on the table. "Okay. For the short term, one hundred K each."

Edison didn't blink. "Nothing, if one or both is still walking around tomorrow."

Rogers nodded in agreement. "Understood. And the long term deal? That's what I'm really interested in. I'm tired of freelancing."

"I want you to take out the entire team. Duvall and Hatfield first. They'll be the easiest to locate. I can even help you there. Eldawoody will probably take some work, but he's doable, I'm sure. I don't want any loose ends from this morning. I don't want any trail that connects them to me or the company. If this goes down wrong..."

Edison paused to size up Rogers before his big finish. "Your reward will be a fat salary and permanent employment."

Rogers shook his head, objecting. "How fat? I'd want at least..."

Edison stopped him in mid-sentence. "Not here. You take care of the short term, and you can name your price on the long term."

This time, Rogers nodded in the affirmative.

Shutterbug

Chapter 21

Louise stepped up to Brian's table and examined their plates. "Now that's what I'm talking about," she said. "Clean as a whistle! How 'bout dessert?"

Everyone groaned. "No way," replied Joanna. "I just blew a week's worth of dieting on that meal."

Louise laughed. "Honey, I'd kill if I thought I'd get me a skinny little butt like yours to pack 'round!"

"Just the check, Louise. We gotta split in a few minutes," said Rockaway.

"They's a couple of tables I need to open up," Louise stated, with intent, off-handedly.

"We appreciate your patience, Louise. You're the best." Brian offered for the group.

She winked at Brian. "I'll be right back, Honey," she said, and sauntered away, swishing her large hips.

Brian dug into his pocket for some money.

"Put your money away, Brauny. You'll need it," said Rockaway. "So? Now that you've had some time to think, what's 'the plan'?"

Brian knew they weren't going to like it, but it was the only way he could think of to be safe. For them, anyway. "Your silence and my stuffing my face with food have brought me new resolve."

"I'm against it already," interjected Rockaway. "I can already guess your plan."

"Then, shut up and listen so I can tell everyone else."

Rockaway shot Brian a friendly finger. "Asshole."

Ignoring his old friend, Brian continued. "We simply each go our own way."

"Now wait..." started Joanna.

"Hear me out," Brian said, holding up a hand to stop the expected blowback. "Joanna, you need to go to the paper and camp out. That's the best and safest place for you. I need you there if something breaks, and I can't do my job if I'm worrying about you.

"There, you'll be constantly surrounded by co-workers. I think you should even give your editor a scaled down version of what's up. This thing is going to break soon, real soon, one way or another. This way, you'll be right on top of everything, and the scoop will be yours."

Despite Brian's overwhelming logic, Joanna managed an objection. "Listen, if you think..."

Brian cut her off. "You know it's the right thing to do, so just stop with the objections." He pulled the camera's memory card from his pocket and slid it across the table to her. "Take this. If anything happens to me, at least I'll know this is in safe hands. You know what to do with it."

"Brian, I..."

"Just take it."

"Now, Harry, as for you..."

A wry look on his face, Harry repeated Rockaway's hand gesture. "I'm not going home, and my office is closed. Besides, I made the fucking call to the senator, remember? That alone most likely placed me on everyone's hit list, so any suggestion you have on where I should hide needs to be a damn good one, *kemo sabe*. Do you know of such a place?"

He's right, Brian thought. *I've placed Harry directly in harm's way.* "Yeah," he acknowledged, and nodded at Rockaway. "With him."

In the background, they could hear Louise talking to some dinner guests as she escorted them into the annex to a corner opposite them. Brian glanced up at the noise, and saw her seating two men. The shorter overweight one with his back to Brian had a distinct military bearing about him. The taller looked like a commercial refrigerator dressed all in black like the bad guy in a cowboy movie. Despite the dim lighting, his eyes were hidden behind a pair of shiny, bug-eye aviator sunglasses.

"Unless you have a better idea," Brian said, bringing his thoughts back into focus, "where you can stay surrounded by lots of friends for the next twenty-four hours or so, Rockaway's your best bet."

Harry smiled a weak smile, but a smile nonetheless. "I'm an attorney, Brian. All of my friends are sitting at this table." Then, he threw his right arm over Rockaway's shoulders and pulled him close. "Looks like it's you an' me, buddy!" Evidently his second Salty Dog was kicking in.

"Shit," said Rockaway, throwing off Harry's arm. "What exactly do you have planned for me and Perry Mason?"

"My office is sounding better every minute," said Joanna, fingering the memory card.

"You'd know that better than me, Rock," Brian punctuated.

"Okay, I'll think of something and let you know. Where're *you* goin'…that's the question?" Rockaway asked. "In my opinion, you'd be better off with Joanna. Where else better than a newspaper?"

"I've got a plan for my own protection," Brian riffed. "Something even you'll be proud of, Rock."

Rockaway spotted Louise returning from the new customers' table, pulled out a wad of bills and held them up in the air to get her attention. "Over here, Louise. I'm buying today."

She laughed. "Why, Mr. Rockaway!" she exclaimed, crinkling her eyes and winking at him. "Since when did you become the big spender? My baby, Brian here, usually picks up the tab."

"Sh-h-h, Louise. Don't be so loud," Rockaway retorted, annoyed at her mentioning Brian by name.

"My, my, I don't know what ya'll been up to today, but ya'll are mighty touchy! Seems like everybody's on edge."

Rockaway handed her enough bills to cover the meal plus a more than generous tip. "This should make up for our rudeness."

She looked at the bills, then Rockaway, wide-eyed. "That surly will cover it all."

As Brian stood, he looked again towards the back corner of the room. The rhinestone cowboy in the last booth was looking their way, but casually conversing with his company. Brian shrugged it off.

"I need a moment before we leave," said Harry, nudging Rockaway to move. "I've got to go to the men's room." Rockaway moved out of his way and let Harry slip by. Harry headed for the restrooms, located off a narrow hallway not far from them. "I'll be right back," he reassured everyone.

Rockaway shrugged and turned to Brian. "Okay, so where are you hiding out till this blows over, Mr. Braun?"

"I've got some friends I plan to stay with. Collectively, we can muster almost as much fire power as the 101st Airborne Division," Brian said, being purposefully vague.

"Come with me," Joanna pleaded. "You don't need to be hiding out like a common thief, especially in your own neighborhood. That's the first place they'd look."

"I'm not a 'common' thief," interjected Brian.

"Whoever *they* are," added Rock. "We don't even know for sure who's after Brian. You know, Brian, Joanna might be right."

"I've got this covered, I tell you. I know what I'm doing and why I'm doing it," Brian said, not wanting to justify his actions. "I'm not an amateur, either, you know."

"What neighbors are you talking about? Those young thugs you sometimes hang out with? You're kidding, right?" asked Joanna, her concern evident.

"Don't make judgments you know nothing about, Joanna." The remark came out harsher than Brian intended, but he didn't care.

Joanna pursed her lips tightly together and said, "Like you did when you took on this photo shoot, I suppose. Fine, then! Do it your way."

An uncomfortable chill settled around the table.

"You two can quibble later. Right now, we need to get moving," said Rockaway, standing next to Brian. In the distance, the rhinestone cowboy rose, walked towards the conspirators, brushing by Rockaway and Brian, moving smoothly towards the restrooms, giving no notice to the three as he passed. Rockaway, Brian and Joanna, for their part, paid him no mind.

"Look," Brian said to Joanna, "I'll get in touch with you as soon as I'm settled in. For the time being, if you don't know where I am, then you can't tell anybody."

"Let's go," said Rock, "we've been here too long. I'm gonna go roust out Harry. He's taking all day."

Brian heard the restroom door in the hallway behind them open. His first thought was *Good, Rockaway won't have to chase down Harry*, but then Brian saw Rockaway's body tense and his eyes narrow to small slits. Brian immediately turned around. Harry had come through the door with a face as pale as the moon, the rhinestone cowboy close behind. The man in black, a full head taller than Harry, was obviously controlling the lawyer.

"Shit," Rockaway whispered to Brian, "we've got to get you out of here. Now! We've been had."

Brian saw Joanna slip the memory card off the table and into her lap, and reached over to pry it from her clinched fist. She resisted at first, but then relented. A wave of guilt flushed over Brian for giving it to her in the first place. What had started out as a defensive game had suddenly turned into a deadly confrontation. Their lives likely hung on what each did during the next few seconds.

Rhinestone gently nudged Harry to the table, making sure everyone saw the gun pressed against his spine. "You know, I really love the food here, and I especially like that loose-mouthed Louise," Rhinestone said in a calm, cold growl. "I really don't want to hurt her or

126

any of her beloved patrons. Know what I mean?" Then, he looked directly at Brian. "Right, Mr. Braun?" The man with the gun turned slowly towards Rockaway and grinned. "Right, Mr. Rock-a-way? If there's even a twitch that makes me uncomfortable, I'll not hesitate to waste your attorney."

"Go ahead," returned Rockaway. "The world's got too many smart-ass attorneys like it is."

Shutterbug

Chapter 22

Edison had been in The Shack for almost thirty minutes. Hatfield watched Duvall, hunched over, knife in hand, maneuver his way between the parked cars in front of the restaurant, and quickly puncture the right rear tire of the Mercedes. Duvall moved to Edison's ride and did the same, then disappeared behind the rear of the building.

Hatfield frowned. Something big was about to happen, and to know what was about to go down, he'd need to get closer to the action.

Duvall, having finished his work on the tires, retreated into his Yukon. He wasn't sure if Rogers, Edison, and Braun would come out together or separately. He'd have to be ready to evaluate and re-evaluate the situation on the shortest notice, and be flexible in his actions.

Gib Rogers. The Congo. Duvall had tried to sequester away the two thoughts in the back of his brain for the past three years. Since his recovery, Edison had kept him busy with jobs that required his mind and body to be in constant motion. The physical wounds had healed nicely, but the emotional scars were still fresh, and the nightmares remained.

It was April 2006. The Democratic Republic of the Congo was in the throes of its second and what threatened to be its bloodiest civil war. Rebels outside the town of Kafe were callously murdering Bangladeshi *Mission de l'Organisation de Nations Unies en République Démocratique du Congo*, or MONUC, Peacekeeping soldiers, in the end, taking seven hostages. Elite Security was secretly contracted to make sure the end-results were better for the hostages than their captors. The two men assigned to the job, Rogers and Duvall, had been paired together on several previous operations under the Elite Security umbrella and had worked brilliantly as a team, even though they didn't much like each other.

The operation started off smooth, but after the uneventful hostage rescue, returning the peacekeepers to the MONUC lines while rebel troops attempted to cut off their escape route turned out to be another story all together. The peacekeepers were in bad physical condition, having been tortured and severely brutalized by their militia captors. Hacking through the thick Congo jungle, and the frequent necessary stops for the injured allowed the rebels to surge ahead of the rag-tag group and set up an ambush, one that resulted in the death of all seven peacekeepers, leaving Duvall badly wounded and left for dead by Rogers, who had run into the jungle to save his own life.

It took two days of crawling on his belly through the jungle and almost bleeding to death, before Duvall reached the safe haven of the United Nations' lines. Only Duvall's survival training and the constant thought of gutting Rogers like a pig had kept him from succumbing to the temptation to just give up and die.

Fate had, in the end, smiled upon Duvall, and the time had finally come for Rogers to answer for deserting his combat-buddy. And Duvall planned to make it a slow death. Duvall slipped into the rear seat of the

Yukon and recovered a canvas bag from under the front seat that contained a compact Steyr Tactical Machine Pistol and four extra clips of ammunition. It was time to take out Rogers. And find out the bottom line about Edison and Braun as well.

While Duvall hid in the rear of the strip center parking area in front of The Shack, Hatfield took advantage of his absence and drove across Mockingbird Lane to cruise through the parking lot of the neighboring Taylor Publishing Company. Hatfield was lucky enough to locate a parking spot close enough to an exit driveway to allow for a quick retreat should it prove necessary, yet far enough away from the street to remain unseen. On foot, weaving through the many cars, the massive employee parking lot provided good cover to make his way back to The Shack, all the while watching carefully for Duvall. He stopped behind a jacked-up Chevy 4x4 pickup with mud tires as tall as his waist and a front hood as high as his chest. *Only in Texas.* It would provide the perfect cover. He was about thirty yards from the strip center corner and could easily stand behind the right front fender and get a perfect view of the entrance to The Shack.

While he waited, Hatfield tried to make sense of the day's events. Here he was, hiding in a parking lot, waiting for something to happen. His gut told him nothing good would come of the situation. A photographer, in possession of incriminating pictures of him shooting a United States Senator at point blank range was probably right now sitting at the editor-in-chief's desk of the *Dallas Morning News,* about to bust the story of the century wide open. Still, he had to know what was going on in The Shack before he could appropriately initiate damage control. Duvall's sudden appearance snapped Hatfield from his reverie. Things just kept getting worse.

Hatfield eased back from the front fender so he wouldn't be spotted and watched as Duvall lopped along the side of the restaurant-bar. He was carrying a long canvas bag. *A gun bag*, Hatfield surmised. Hatfield watched Duvall squat down, unzip the bag, and open it. Duvall didn't have to take anything out for Hatfield to know its contents. *Firepower.* Duvall stayed in a squat position at the corner of the building, apparently waiting for the same thing as Hatfield: someone to appear from inside.

Edison? Is he going to ambush Edison? I thought they were long-time buddies? Hatfield knew their history went back as far as the 80's, from when they served together in the CIA. Hatfield pulled his favorite Heckler and Koch P30 automatic from his waistband holster and attached a silencer to it. He'd wait, too, just like Duvall. Wait to see who he should shoot first, then next.

Chapter 23

While Louise stood behind the bar filling orders, Brian's group, increased by two, marched slowly towards the front exit. It was obvious that Louise was confused about their processional exit. She stepped around the bar to greet them. "Mr. Edison! Ain't you and Mr. Rogers going to wait on your food? It's almost ready."

"We're just going to step out for a minute, Louise. We'll be right back," Edison said in a rush.

Maxwell Edison? Brian motioned to Louise. As she exited from behind the bar to join him, Rhinestone moved closer beside him. "Careful, picture boy," he whispered.

When Louise stood in front of him, Brian reached up hugged her around the shoulders with one arm, grasping her hand with the other, making sure his two new 'friends' could hear him clearly. "The food was delicious, as usual, Lou-ee-za," he teased. "We'll all be back in a minute."

Louise squeezed Brian's hand back.

"Tomorrow," she said, with a still-questioning look. He could feel her eyes on his back as the party resumed marching forward.

The early dinner crowd hadn't hit the restaurant yet. Louise's only customers were the same bar flies that were there earlier, with the exception of a couple of fellows shooting pool in the adjacent game room.

Rockaway and Harry were forced to lead the way, Joanna and Brian following, the two new 'friends' bringing up the rear. While the last two had pocketed their hardware, the four hostages were keenly aware of their existence. Seeing Rhinestone's automatic pressed up against Harry's spine earlier at the table had proven sufficient incentive to get them to leave.

Brian broke the silence. "So, what do you...?"

"Shut up and don't say another word," said the Rhinestone Cowboy, patting him on the shoulder like they were best friends. "You'll find out everything you need to know in just a few minutes."

Brian shrugged the cowboy's hand away from his shoulder and resisted the temptation to respond. He had to wait for the right moment to act, and, right now, provoking the guy further wouldn't do anything except get him, Harry, Rockaway, and Joanna prematurely killed.

Short and Stocky moved around them to the front of the group. "Here's what we're going to do," he said in a low voice, bringing his captive audience to a halt in front of the doorway. "There's a black Ford 500 parked outside this door." He nodded at Brian. "Braun, you and your girlfriend are going to get in the back and ride with the two of us," he said, pointing at Rhinestone and back to himself. "We have some things to discuss."

"As Mr. Braun's attorney, I must insist..."

Short and Stocky jabbed him in the ribcage with an elbow. "Shut up, asshole." He nodded again at Cowboy, standing behind the group.

134

"Once we all get out the door, you usher Big Mouth here and the professor around back. I'll meet you after I get these two lovebirds loaded. I don't have the room or time to fuck around with these two." Shorty turned to Harry, grinning this time. "Tell me, counselor, does the term 'collateral damage' mean anything to you?"

"It does to me," interrupted Rockaway, before Harry had a chance to respond. "And I'm sure we'll have the chance before too long to see it in action."

Brian knew Rock was trying to draw Shorty's attention away from Harry before one of two dropped Harry right at the door. Brian didn't think it mattered to either of the two goons if they shot somebody here or in the alley.

He also knew Rock would make some kind of move, probably as soon as they got outside, and readied himself to react on his and Joanna's behalf.

"Fuck you, professor," said Short and Stocky, "that Green Beret shit goes nowhere with me. I used to chop up you mother-fuckers every morning and serve you for breakfast. Now move."

Rhinestone moved cautiously forward to hold the door. Outside, the Ford beeped twice as Short and Stocky unlocked it with a remote. As the bright outside light hit their eyes and they all squinted from the glare, Brian, taking up the rear, saw Rockaway slowly raise his left hand to his brow as if to block the sun, and ease his right hand into the small of his back, then glide between Harry and Joanna.

Brian got ready. He sensed that Rock was about to make his move, and he'd have to make it before either one of the group's new friends had a chance to draw and level their guns again. Rhinestone closed the door behind Brian. Short and Stocky moved to the Ford's back door on the driver's side, motioning Joanna and Brian to follow. Cowboy stuck an arm out to separate Rockaway and Harry from Joanna and Brian. It was at that moment that all hell broke loose.

Rapid fire from an automatic weapon peppered the Ford 500 with a violent spray of bullets. The windshield and side windows exploded in unison to the staccato sound of extreme firepower. Then, rows of holes appeared along the hood and passenger side of the car. This wasn't Hollywood with slow motion, special effects; everything happened simultaneously as if in one quick motion.

Brian spotted Rhinestone Cowboy bolting in the opposite direction from which the shots were coming, leaving Rockaway and Harry in the kill zone on the sidewalk, bullets whizzing around them and thunking on the car.

Brian jerked Joanna backwards by the collar of her jacket, twirled her around, and slammed her face into the recessed corner of the doorway. He shielded her body with his, but the space was so small, he knew he was partially exposed to the sidewalk. Joanna didn't scream. He wondered how she could be so calm, then decided that was something to be pondered later, not now. Though his back half was exposed to potential ricochets, he had a perfect view of the action including the shooter, standing sideways on the sidewalk at the end of the building to his right: a big guy wearing a plaid jacket, pointing his automatic weapon with careful aim, designed to spray lead in a narrow area and create chaos.

Short and Stocky had been opening the back door of the sedan for his captives when the shooting started. He immediately dropped down, scrunched against the left rear tire, knees to chin, gun out and ready to return fire. He was a cool customer.

The moment the shooting started, Rockaway gave Harry a violent shove out of the line of fire with one hand, while reaching for the .45 in the waistband of his jeans with the other. Trying desperately to keep his balance, arms waving in circles, Harry landed face down two cars down from Edison. Catching his breath, he had enough consciousness and state of mind to pull himself forward and well away from the line of fire. Rockaway, instead of running away from the hail of bullets, rolled forward in a controlled shoulder roll, landing safely behind the cover of the left front tire. Brian was stunned by his mentor's agility.

As bullets continued thump-thump-thumping about him, Rockaway whirled to his left, his gun chest high in a two-handed grip. He had a point blank bead on Short and Stocky's forehead before the man even knew he was there.

Rhinestone ran humped over between the same two cars where Harry had kissed the asphalt, but ignored the lawyer, instead, making a run for the cover of a parked cars in the next row over.

That's when the firing shifted.

There was a brief pause, and the shooter changed his focus from the Ford, to the red Mercedes coupe behind it. This seemed to get the attention of Rhinestone Cowboy, who stood, shook a fist in the air and screamed, "No-o-o! Son-of-a-bitch!" the car clearly of more value to him than his life.

Hatfield, in the meantime, gawked at the whole magnificent scene unfolding before him, sad that he couldn't allow it to continue. If he did, people were going to get killed, and he damn sure didn't want the blood of innocents on his hands. He leaned across the hood of the pickup, steadying his automatic with both hands, and put two shots into the corner of the building inches above Duvall's head.

Shards of stucco plaster sprayed in every direction, some flinging down and stinging Duvall in the face. Crouching lower, Duvall twisted around, and, temporarily holding his fire, fanned his Steyr back and forth across the parking lot behind him, searching for the shooter. Frightened and frustrated, he grabbed his bag and retreated quickly to the back of the building.

The shooting stopped as suddenly as it began, and the resulting silence was deafening. Brian's ears were ringing in a constant, high, whining tone. Joanna, mashed against the door, stiff and silent. No screaming, no hysteria. Rhinestone emerged from behind the pickup where he'd taken cover while his Mercedes was shot to hell, stooped over and trotted away hugging the back end of the cars, giving a final glance at the destroyed Mercedes coupe, and then disappeared around the opposite corner of the building.

Rockaway had frozen, his .45 still aimed at Short and Stocky's head. "Drop the weapon," Rockaway ordered in a low growl. "It's over."

"Fuck you," said Shorty, swinging his weapon towards Rockaway.

A final explosion shattered the dusky evening. Sirens began wailing and screaming in the distance, as blood and brains splattered against the tire and along the parking lot, and Short and Stocky slumped to his side.

"Eat that for breakfast, motherfucker," mumbled Rockaway.

Chapter 24

The sirens screaming in the distance couldn't drown out the sound of that one last shot that shattered the momentary silence surrounding the parking lot. Hatfield jerked his weapon towards The Shack and waited. The shot sounded heavy. *Probably a .45,* he thought, watching and waiting. Time, however, was short. Gawkers were already beginning to poke their heads outside of windows to see what all the commotion was about, and the place would be crawling with cops in a matter of minutes. Hatfield made his decision, and moved quickly but with caution. Somebody out there had a gun, and he didn't want to walk into whoever it was.

The old hippie with the ponytail was the first to appear. Hatfield observed him tucking a pistol into his rear waistband as the man moved forward to help the jogging suit guy to his feet.

If that's my shooter, where's Edison?

The younger man, who protected the female, stepped out from the entrance shadows, motioning her to stay. Hatfield could see the tension and mistrust in everyone's face. Ponytail's arm returned to his waistband, but he didn't draw his gun.

At that point, Hatfield slipped his weapon in his own waistband

and resisted the impulse to bring the P30 back into firing position. Instead, he held both arms over his head as in surrender. He was going with his gut on this one. "Don't shoot! Take your hand away from your back. I'm on your side!" Hatfield shouted, and began approaching. Ponytail kept his hand fixed to the small of his back, and didn't move.

Good. Just take it easy, old man.

Someone attempted to open the restaurant door, but the young man shoved it closed with the palm of his hand and yelled for whoever it was to stay inside.

Hatfield made his way to the group without getting shot. *Okay, good, but the next part's crucial.*

Everyone kept their distance as Hat approached, as if waiting for him to make the slightest untoward move. The young man in front of the door, stepped back in front of the girl. Hatfield stopped and glanced to his left. The body of Maxwell Edison was sprawled on the pavement. Blood oozed from a fleshy pucker in the center of his forehead. Slowly, the four formed a circle around the dead man. The sirens were closing in and Hatfield realized it as up to him to get them out of there. The young man was staring at Hat with a look of distant revelation on his face.

"Listen," Hatfield said, keeping his hands shoulder high, "we've only a few seconds, here. I don't fully know what's just happened, but I can tell you this…if you want to live…", he pointed at the street, referencing the wailing sirens, "outside of a prison…you need to come with me."

Hatfield pointed at Edison's body. "That's going to be hard for you to explain, my friend," he said looking at Ponytail. "You just shot the

140

owner and CEO of Elite Security, the largest private international protection agency in the world."

"Not anymore," Ponytail answered.

"You're Songbird Two," said the young man flatly.

This time, it was Hatfield's turn to show his surprise. "How do...? Are you Braun? Brian Braun?"

"I saw you at the Senator's ranch this morning. You shot him... dead. Yet somehow it didn't take..."

"Now you *have* to come with me. All four of you. As I said, we've only seconds before we're knee-deep in cops. We can still make it if we leave together *now*."

"And just who the fuck are you, that we should trust you," said Rockaway.

"My name is Michael Hatfield...I'm with the Federal Bureau of Investigation."

Shutterbug

DAY 2

Sunday, September 6, 2009

Shutterbug

Chapter 25

"SECURITY FIRM CEO MURDERED," read the headline in the morning newspaper of the article written by Joanna Johns.

The reporter's name triggered a memory as Fagan skimmed the article. The more he read, the more her name nagged at the back of his brain; he couldn't get it out of his head. Then a terrible thought came to mind.

"Oh-h-h," he moaned. "Fuck, no! Please tell me I'm not right on this!" Fagan jumped to his feet, a panic-driven bolt of energy catapulted him from the dining room into his private home-office in the next room. His hands scrambled across stacks of folders that lay haphazardly on top of his desk, until he found Brian Braun's folder . He leafed through the information he'd gathered on him weeks before, until he found the newspaper articles about the Highland Park robberies. There she was, a small headshot inset next to her name in the several of the articles.

Fagan picked up the telephone receiver on the desk and dialed the three-digit number to the guesthouse. After two rings, he heard the other line pickup. He didn't wait for a reply. "Get your asses over here. The shit's hit the fan, and I'm standing right in front of it. Get your asses over here now!"

Minutes later, four grim men with Zeta Corporation stood in a line facing Senator Fagan on the other side of his modest conference table. The looks on their faces conveyed their displeasure about having been interrupted from their own projects and preparations.

"The shit has hit the fan, boys," the senator repeated.

"You already said that, Senator," said Mark Freeman, the leader of the security team. "I knew that yesterday, when I listened on the speakerphone to that photographer who you hired. A dumb-ass move on your part…no matter how you attempt to justify your motives."

Fagan's eyes narrowed. He sat in his chair and leaned back, pretending to relax, flashing his best politician's smile, knowing this was not the time to antagonize Freeman. He held up his hands in mock surrender. "You're right, of course, Mark. I know that, now. But that's spilled milk—we can't moon around about what's happened. We have to stay focused on what we *can* do now and in the future."

Fagan slid the five-year-old article on Brian Braun toward the center of the table so the team leader could see it, pointing at Joanna Johns's byline picture at the top of the article. "That little cunt right there," he snarled, jabbing a finger at the paper, "wrote this article, too!" He pushed the morning paper with the front page article about the shootout on Mockingbird Lane in front of Freeman. "She was there when Edison got blown away."

Freeman picked up the paper and quickly scanned its contents. "There's nothing at all in here about you, Senator. Could just be a coincidence. She's one of the paper's top reporters. And The Shack is a popular eating place in Dallas. Nothing particularly unusual about that."

"The senator thinks they're connected," added Luis Diaz, another member of the team.

"Damn straight I do!" Fagan tapped his forefinger on top of Joanna's picture. "I did my research before I talked to Braun. I know for a fact that he's been givin' that girl the big slip daddy for the past five years. They've been hooked up ever since she started reporting on him about the Highland Park heists. Just think about it for a minute: Braun's got pictures of a United States senator getting assassinated. The little prick stays longer than he was supposed to, and then takes some additional fuckin' pictures of that dead senator getting up and shaking hands with *you* four," he said, pointing from one to another of the squad members.

Freeman shifted uncomfortably in his stance. "You don't know that for a fact."

Senator Fagan grinned. *That's it, squirm.* "Hell, boy, I don't have to know it! That's the kinda deal where a maybe is as good as a done deal. You read me?" Fagan leaned forward, resting his fists on the table. "He's got the pictures—you can trust me on that." Then he leaned back in his seat, again. "So, let's say, for interest's sake, he hooks up with little miss reporter and says, 'Hey baby doll! I've got something you gotta see!' It's his fuckin' insurance policy against me. He can blow this whole scheme sky high! Zeta Corp continues to slide down the slippery slope it made for itself and goes plum out of business. People start going to jail, including you, boys," he emphasized stabbing a finger at each of the security men.

Fagan checked their faces as he pointed to make sure they understood him before continuing: "With Edison dead, it'll make it that much easier to shove Elite out of existence. Edison's little brother and obvious successor, is a pussy. But I'm not really that worried about him. While he's trying to wrap his head about all this, Zeta will be resurrecting from the flames like a phoenix, bigger and stronger than ever."

"Just say it, Senator," said Diaz, "we don't have a lot of time. But, you're the one who's got to say it. Not us."

Fagan nodded. "Shit, boy. The words don't scare me: Kill Braun. Kill the girl. Kill anyone who's connected to them. I want them taken care of like you did that fuckin' raghead who was hiding in the woods with a gun."

Diaz frowned and stared at Freeman. "What's he talking about Mark?"

"I took care of two birds with one stone. Don't worry about it. It doesn't concern you."

Fagan stiffened and waved an arm in front of Freeman's face. "Hey! *I'm* talking here. I don't give a shit about that asshole. I want the fucking pictures! If the pictures go public...we're all ruined. And I won't be able to protect myself, let alone any of you boys or your the head dick at Zeta Corp. If we do them...then everybody's healthy, Zeta's back on top due to my senatorial generosity, I end up with enough money to kiss the government good-bye at the end of my term, and everyone's happy." The senator stood and turned to Freeman. "You're the head dick of this outfit. Come up with a plan we can chew at over at lunch. But whatever it is, we move on it today."

Chapter 26

Joanna Johns checked her watch while waiting for the city editor, James Durrett, to return to his office. She'd been cooling her heels for almost ten minutes and was getting antsy. When she tried to slip out of the office unnoticed for a meeting with Michael Hatfield, Durrett's secretary caught her at the last minute and made it clear he wanted to see her before she left.

During the early part of last evening after the firefight at The Shack, when Special Agent Hatfield had Brian, Rockaway, Harry, and her sequestered in a safe house, it took a lot of convincing to get Hatfield to let her go back to the *Dallas Morning News* offices to file her story about the Mockingbird Lane shooting.

"Sorry, this is well above above my pay grade," Hatfield said, and handing her his phone. Joanna had to argue, cajole, and beg for close to an hour with John Lee Pedamore, Special-Agent-in-Charge of the Dallas FBI Office, before she got his permission to send the story on to her editor. Pedamore reviewed every detail before giving the go-ahead. She was surprised at his candor and willingness to listen to her views on what should and should not be revealed, if, he constantly reminded her, he decided to let her send anything in at all. Although her victories were small and few, the promise of exclusivity for not only this blockbuster, but also all future stories, helped seal the deal for both of them. Her time with Hatfield and conversation with Pedamore gave her a whole new outlook on the FBI.

Now, it was her editor she needed to fend off. Joanna checked her watch again; it was a minute later than the last time she'd looked, and she switched to mentally preparing for the upcoming joust with her boss.

James Durrett had been in the news game for over thirty years and had been a hard-nosed investigative reporter with a Pulitzer Prize of his own under his belt. He could recognize, better than anyone she knew, when a reporter was sandbagging a story. After she'd warned Pedamore that Durrett would see right through any smoke and mirrors, he had also laid on her exactly what she could and could not reveal beyond the printed story. Joanna had promised and planned to stick to their deal.

"Sorry about that, Joanna," Durrett announced, entering the office from behind her and closing the door. He walked briskly around his desk and plopped into his chair. "You've been busy. Have you gotten any sleep this morning? You look like you've been here all night."

"No, but I'll catch some sleep after I get out of here. What's up?" She asked innocently.

"Well, I just had a few questions and comments about your story. We haven't had a chance to really talk about it." He leaned back in his chair and gave her a small grin. "Tell me about it."

Nonchalant. That's the ticket. "You read it, right?" She asked.

Durrett's grin dropped away and he nodded deliberately. "You know I did, Joanna, so let's not play games. The article would read good enough to the everyday reader; however, you and I both know there're holes in your story big enough to drive a Mack truck through. Would you like a 'for instance'?"

Joanna gripped the arms of her chair. *Here it comes*. "Of course, James. You know I'm always open for input."

"'Open for input' my ass, Joanna. You're intentionally dodging me here." Durrett stared her and held her eyes, then the grin gradually returned. "Okay, we'll do it your way for the moment. Just answer a few questions."

"Okay. If I can."

"You mentioned witnesses, but you make no effort to identify them. You mention a shooter, but make no effort to establish a motive. Was this a random shooting into a crowd that had just finished scraping the bones on Louise's ribs, or was Maxwell Edison actually the target? There were fifty or more spent shells from an automatic weapon scattered around the sniper's ambush position, yet a single shell, probably from a .45 automatic pistol, was found behind the car where Edison was killed. I presume, therefore, he wasn't killed by the sniper, though that's what the story implies. How's that for a start?"

Joanna remained deadpan, showing no shock or embarrassment. "As usual, James, your information is impeccable. How'd you come up with all that?"

Durrett ignored the question. "Are you aware that Maxwell Edison was due to go to Washington to attend some Senate Hearings next week?"

"Really, how'd you find that out?"

"There's a new invention called the Internet. You should try it sometime. Listen, I may be sitting behind a desk these days, but I still know my way around city hall, and I know a good a story when I see it. And so do you. By the way, speaking of Senate Hearings, were you aware that Senator Fagan called here wanting to talk to you?" He checked his watch. "He called at around…oh, five o'clock this morning! Now why do you think that is, Joanna?"

"He's mad because I didn't mention his name?"

Durrett spread his arms and rolled his eyes in frustration. "Normally, that'd be funny…and true. But not now. What're you up to, Joanna? There's a lot more to this story than what you've written. This isn't like you. And why are you sandbagging me here?"

Joanna glanced away from Durrett and stared out the window behind him. "I can't tell you, James. I've been sworn to secrecy." Her eyes shifted back to the editor. She felt bad about what she was doing, but she had no choice.

"Are you kidding me? You're pulling the first amendment card on *me*? I'm your boss, for Christ sakes!" Durrett paused, took a deep breath, and squinted his eyes at her. "Who were you with at The Shack, Joanna, and how did you just happen to be there right in the middle of it all?" He paused to wait for her answer, then his jaw dropped just enough to show that a realization had came to him. "You were there with that Braun character, weren't you? Are you trying to protect him in some way? Tell me you're not still seeing that thief."

Joanna needed some leverage, so she reached down and grabbed her leather tote bag from the floor and set it in her lap. "You remember Woodward and Bernstein, right?"

The city editor pushed back from his desk in exasperation. "Of course I remember Woodward and Bernstein. I also know you weren't even born then."

She continued, "They brought down the President of the United States, his staff, the United States Attorney General, and..."

Durrett cut her off. "I don't need a history lesson from you, Joanna. I was working as a reporter for the *Washington Post* when that all came down. I know both of those men personally." His next words dripped with sarcasm. "What's your point? Are you about to bring down the President?"

Joanna gave her boss a slight grin and opened the tote bag in her lap. "Close."

Shutterbug

Chapter 27

In his office, Agent Pedamore used his few remaining moments of solitude to gather his thoughts and prepare for his session with the Fab Four, as Hatfield had dubbed Morgan, Braun, Johns and Rockaway. Pedamore was aware that the four were operating as a cohesive group and would, together, be formidable opponents. That's why he decided to place them in separate safe-houses after initial interviews. However, even separate, they could be a challenge.

Last night, Pedamore had the intelligence unit dig up as much background info on the Fab Four as possible, before he pulled them individually into his office. There was no lack of information on Morgan, Braun, or Johns. Rockaway was another matter. Pedamore had to admit, they were a colorful group.

Braun was the obvious leader. There was nothing outstanding in his background or past associations that Pedamore could find that might have led the young photographer into a life of crime. Nonetheless, somewhere along the line, Braun had developed unmatched skills as a master thief. Why had an All American kid turned to crime, and how had he gotten so good? There was no doubt about his guilt in the Highland Park exploits. None whatsoever. To everyone's apparent surprise, he dodged that bullet entirely because of a lack of tangible evidence. He had also had an excellent attorney.

According to some agency informants, the word on the street was that the burglaries he had been arrested for were mere child's play compared to some million-dollar, high-tech heists for which Braun was likely to have been responsible. If Brian had so much stashed away, he certainly wasn't living off it. He'd been clean for the past five years, at least on the surface, and had managed to stay well under the radar of the law.

Braun also did an excellent job of picking his attorney. Harry Morgan may have a liability to come off as a court jester from time to time, but that was also one of his assets. It was a clever front. Play the fool; disarm the competition. Research confirmed to Pedamore that Morgan had never lost a case. Never. And twenty-five percent of his cases were *pro bono*. Politically, the man leaned heavily left and loved to chase conspiracy windmills, but he always stayed carefully in the fringe, making sure when operating from the outside that his name was never linked to any organizations. With Morgan by his side, Braun could, in the future, prove an even bigger problem than he was now.

Mickey Rockaway was, by far, the most interesting of the group. He appeared an open book—but that really said very little. He served three tours in Vietnam. After several unsuccessful attempts to pull the professor's military records and hitting the proverbial "need-to-know" stonewall, Pedamore called in a few favors from some military brass he was acquainted with. He was rewarded with a two-word return phone call: *Black ops*. No hello, no name, no goodbye, just a burned favor followed by the dial tone.

Upon return to the states from his last tour, Rockaway landed in Durango, Colorado, a one-horse town in the early 70's that served as a refuge for burned-out Vietnam veterans who spent their time smoking dope and living in nature. Today, most of these nature-lovers drove Cadillac Escalades, and owned most of the businesses as well as the land around Durango, having finally recovered, and discovered the advantages of capitalism.

Rockaway, however, had taken an entirely different route. He went back to Austin, Texas, his hometown, and attended the University of Texas on the G.I. Bill. He excelled in photojournalism and worked freelance, traveling around the world taking pictures of the carnage of war and civil unrest, selling his photos to the likes of *Post, Time Magazine* and major newspapers across the U.S. and Europe. During the 80's, he covered every hotspot that popped up, from the rebel uprising that overthrew the ruling government in El Salvador to the Tiananmen Square Revolt in China in 1989.

Perhaps photographing, and through it, re-experiencing death for almost two decades had motivated him into taking a teaching position at the University of Texas at Dallas in 1990. Since then, there was little of interest on him except numerous academic honors. He appeared to have settled into a more normal academic lifestyle. Until now, that is.

Joanna Johns was the only straight arrow among the bunch. An Abilene, Texas girl who worked at her father's local newspaper while attending high school, and eventually gained a scholarship to SMU School of Journalism. She got a job with the *Dallas Morning News* straight out of college, starting at the bottom of the totem pole writing obituaries, gradually working her way up the ranks with hard work and determination. He couldn't find anything negative about her. Johns' series on Braun, as the Highland Park Cat Burglar, was the lucky break that moved her from the Dallas social and entertainment scene to full-fledged invesitgative reporting. She'd been at the right place, at the right time, and had the necessary reporting experience to take her to the next level.

The chemistry between her and the thief hadn't hurt, either, making her series even more intensely engaging. Over the next five years, she learned how to hold her own with the big boys. He suspected she was a career-first kind of girl. The tears routine she tried to pull on him over the phone hadn't swayed him, though for a few moments, it *almost* had. *She'll be a definite challenge to handle,* he thought, *keeping this matter under wraps.*

Pedamore checked his watch. Hatfield would be checking in with him to report that The Fab Four were all lined up and ready for debriefing any minute now. In anticipation for what would undoubtedly be an interesting morning, Pedamore loosened his tie and rolled up his sleeves.

Chapter 28

When Agent Hatfield refused to answer their questions, the Fab Four collectively decided to quit answering his. Hence, while Joanna was preparing to accompany the agents with her from the *Dallas Morning News* back to Dallas FBI Office, Hatfield ended up driving Brian, Rock and Harry in awkward silence from their safe house to the same to meet with Pedamore. Brian sat in the passenger seat, Rock and Harry occupied the back seat of the FBI's Ford Expedition. The black SUV pulled up to the security booth at the entrance to headquarters; Hatfield showed his ID to the guard, then gave him the names of the men in the car with him. "I need your driver licenses," Hatfield said, holding out his hand. All three gave them up, and he passed them on to the man in the booth. "Here you go, Luther. Good to see you again."

"You too, Agent Hatfield. Been a while." The guard said while checking them against his roster. Still not satisfied, Luther leaned out the window towards the vehicle. "Could you roll down the windows for me, Agent Hatfield?" Luther then matched their faces to each's license. He stopped abruptly at Harry. The attorney's nose was broken and both his eyes blackened. A wide strip of white tape stretched across the bridge of his nose.

Harry recognized the guards hesitation. "Plastic surgery," he stated flatly pointing at the center of his face.

"He's good, Luther. Potential eyewitness," Hatfield explained.

Luther grinned and nodded his acknowledgement.

The black and yellow steel barrier recessed into the ground, and the mechanical arm blocking the entryway rose to allow them access into the parking lot.

The security guard handed the licenses back to Hatfield. "Have a good morning, Special Agent Hatfield."

"You too, Luther," Hatfield returned.

After parking, the three visitors followed the agent into the Dallas FBI foyer. To their right was a large bulletproof glass that divided the lobby from an open office space occupied by four women. Hatfield and visitors had to slide their ID's through a slot to the other side of the glass, where an attractive woman in her mid-30's took them and noted names, driver license numbers, time of arrival, and then passed them back. "Good to see you again, Agent Hatfield," she said smiling.

Hat returned the smile. "Good to see you too, Maddie. How's Henry?"

"A nine-to-fiver, now" she said, smiling big. "No more field work. I get to see him every night in time for dinner. Love it."

"Good for you, Maddie." Hatfield pointed at the double elevators. "This way," he said to the three accompanying him.

As the elevator rose, each man stood silently, back against a wall. Harry finally broke the silence. "So, Agent Hatfield, is anybody going to tell us what the hell's going on now that we've arrived at the Land of Oz? Every time we try to find out what's going on, you defer to 'headquarters'."

All eyes turned to Hatfield.

He shrugged. "Hope so."

"Could the feds at least consider something besides basic cable at the safe house? I get a little cranky when I don't get my nightly fix of HGTV," Harry stated. He reached up and gently touched the tender bridge of his nose. "By the way, your man did a good job on my nose. I didn't expect such good medical care from the federal government. Who was he?"

"Don't know," answered Hatfield.

The elevator stopped and the doors opened.

"Fifth floor, gentlemen. To your right." Hatfield led them down the hallway and stopped at a door on the left with no markings. After swiping his ID card through a slot and then punching in a code, the door clicked, and Hatfield opened it, motioning everyone inside.

Inside, the three men, Brian, Rock, and Harry, stood side by side, scoping out the office, increasingly curious about who it was they were going to see.

"Nice place," whispered Rockaway, finally breaking his silence.

The room was a large waiting room, tastefully decorated with modern paintings, fresh flowers in large vases placed around the room, two couches-and-numerous chairs arranged about a large coffee table stacked with neat rows of magazines. The sitting area was strategically located before a large plate-glass window that showed a scene of groomed gardens, a picnic area with an outdoor fireplace, tables and chairs, all of which was circled by a thick forest of trees that blocked the view of the surrounding freeways. To their left was an attractive woman, professionally dressed, sitting behind a large, semi-circular secretarial desk.

"I'm thinking head honcho's place," Harry whispered to Rockaway."

"You think, Harry?" Rockaway responded.

"Michael," the secretary exclaimed seeing Hatfield. "I heard you were back! He's expecting you," she said, nodding in the direction of the closed door behind her.

"Got you working a Sunday, huh?"

"And holiday," she added with a pout.

"Well, it's good to be back, Yvonne," Hatfield said, smiling at Yvonne and directing his visitors sit. "Wait for me. I'll be right back," he said skirting the desk and waiting patiently at the door till buzzed in.

"All this warm and fuzzy homecoming bullshit for Special Agent Hatfield is starting to get on my nerves. He sure gets around," Harry commented under his breath, as he checked out the room a second time. "They can't hold us for anything, you know. We haven't broken the law. I know the law. We're victims. Eyewitnesses, not criminals."

Rockaway and Brian sat down on the couch and Harry took a leather chair next to them.

Rockaway shook his head and leaned forward so Harry could hear him. "Harry," he whispered, "I killed a man. You think they're just gonna let me walk out the door?" He looked over his shoulder nervously at the secretary, but she was busy typing, paying her guests no apparent attention.

"Don't worry," Harry whispered back. "You have the best attorney money can buy standing right beside you."

Rockaway gave Harry a sly grin. "I thought Racehorse Haynes retired."

Harry smirked. "That's a low blow. I could go face to face with him and win any day of the week," he said, carefully touching his nose.

Shutterbug

Chapter 29

The secretary stood. "Can I get you something to drink? Coffee? A soft drink? Some bottled water?"

"No ma'am," all three answered in unison. Rockaway tapped Brian on the leg. "So you've changed your mind and decided to say something?"

"I'm unsure about what's happening, so I'm keeping my trap shut until I know more," answered Brian.

Hatfield had been away less than ten minutes, when the door behind the secretary re-opened. A tall man in dark slacks, white starched shirt with the sleeves rolled up, and necktie pulled loose stepped out to greet them. He looked more like a workingman than a senior agent. He strode directly up to Brian. "Mr. Braun?" he said, sticking out his hand.

Brian nodded and shook the hand.

"My name is John Lee Pedamore. I'm the Special-Agent-in-Charge of this division. Welcome." Pedamore followed the same formal introduction of himself to Rockaway and Harry, addressing each man by name followed by a firm handshake.

Brian warmed to John Lee Pedamore immediately, infinitely more so than he had Agent Hatfield. Hatfield presented himself as a silent brooder of few words the entire night they were sequestered in the safe house. Trust was something Brian wasn't handing out free cards for, even to the likable head FBI agent. He wanted to test the waters and see how things played out.

The three men filed into Pedamore's office. It was another large room with the same window placement and same view as in the outer office though from a slightly different angle. The décor was split: One wall was covered with photos, plaques, and trophies all associated with an obviously successful career in the Bureau. The opposite wall was covered with autographed memorabilia from the four big professional sports franchises in Dallas. Evidently, Pedamore was a big sports fan, and knew or glad-handed anybody connected to the organizations, from Eddie LeBaron and Dandy Don Meredith to Charlie Hough and Nolan Ryan to George Bush from Bush's days as the owner of the Texas Rangers baseball team.

"You're a sports fan," Brian noted, stating the obvious aloud.

"You think?" Harry mumbled.

Pedamore nodded and smiled. "Grew up in Pittsburg, which means I was born a Steelers and Penguins fan, but when in Rome..." he said, shrugging innocently, then strolled easily to a massive desk adorned with pictures of his family and pressed a button on the intercom speaker.

"Yvonne?"

Her voice came across crisp and clear. "Yes, sir?"

"Could you bring us five waters?"

"Right away, sir."

In the far corner of his office, a comfortable looking couch and three chairs circled a low table. Pedamore waved an arm towards the sitting area. "Gentlemen, take the chairs, please. Agent Hatfield and I will use the couch. We have a lot to talk about."

Brian started, "Uh, Agent Pedamore…"

"Call me 'John Lee' if you don't mind. I prefer to drop the formalities. I have a feeling we're all going to be communicating with each other frequently in the upcoming weeks."

The secretary entered the room with a tray full of bottled water, set it on the table, and left without a word.

Brian waited until the door closed behind her. "Okay," Brian said, "John Lee. Agent Hatfield, I'm sure, has told you that we're currently at an impasse in regard to communications. He knows who we are and some of what we know, but he's not reciprocated in kind. So, neither are we…that is, until we know what this is all about."

"Sounds fair. You show me yours and I'll show you mine, right?"

"Right," injected Harry. "But you show us yours first."

Brian noted the change in Harry's demeanor and tone. He was definitely in lawyer mode now. The wisecracking whiner routine was gone. Even Rockaway glanced at him with surprise and respect.

"For the record," Harry stated, "I'm legal counsel for Mr. Braun, Mr. Rockaway, and Ms Johns, though she's not present. I'll be advising them on what questions I deem appropriate to answer and what facts to divulge in these proceedings." Harry gave him his famous grin. "Your turn."

"Understood, Mr. Morgan," answered Pedamore. "Hopefully your legal services won't be necessary. But I'm happy to begin there, since circumstances that occurred on Mockingbird Lane could have some blowback later on. Let's hope not." Pedamore made a thoughtful pause. "This meeting is for information gathering only, gentlemen. I'm not here to arrest anyone. At least, not from this group." He smiled broadly. His initial assessment was correct: He had his work cut out for him. "Gentlemen, what I'm about to tell you is most likely going to be much more revealing than anything any of you right now may be reticent to offer. Some, you might find…let's just say…shocking. I must insist that everything said in this room remain here. Is that understood by everyone?"

Each nodded silently in agreement.

"Very well," said Harry. "I assume that includes you, Mr. Pedamore, and Agent Hatfield?"

Pedamore nodded in agreement. "With the exception of any orders necessary to bring this operation to a successful close, of course. From my point of view, I'm not aware of or interested in any less than legal activities on the part of the three of you. Let me again clarify myself: This is an information gathering meeting."

Rockaway shifted in his chair and crossed his legs. "Uh, Agent Pedamore…"

"John Lee, please."

Rockaway continued, "John Lee, are you completely aware of everything that occurred at The Shack?"

"Pretty much," said Pedamore. "There are some holes I'd like filled in; however, I'd prefer starting from the beginning before we get to that."

Pedamore looked from man to man. Brian was obviously feeling uncomfortable.

Harry jumped in. "Excuse me for interrupting, John Lee, but could I have what you just said in writing before we dig into all this? The part about no charges being against anyone in this room including any that might result from what might sound like incriminating statements?"

Pedamore grinned. *Now, I'm getting somewhere.* "I was waiting to hear something like that from you, Counselor. I can't give it to you in writing, but I can offer you my word, Harry, and my word is my bond. I'm old school. You'll have to trust me. As I said, I'm not interested in arresting any of you. As far as I'm concerned, you're all victims. Collateral damage, in Senator Fagan's view, I'm sure."

Harry turned to Rock and Brian in turn. "Do you trust him?"

Brian looked at Rock.

Rockaway got up from his chair and sauntered around Pedamore's digs, silently checking out the sports memorabilia and pictures. "Who's your favorite pitcher? Of all time?" he asked Pedamore, not taking his eyes from the wall of fame.

"Charlie Hough," Pedamore said without hesitation. "Best knuckle-ball of all time."

"Singing group?"

"Joe Cocker. Brought the house down at Woodstock."

"You drink?"

"When I can."

Rockaway turned to face the agent. "Do you keep your word?"

"Yes," answered Pedamore emphatically.

"Then, let's get this rodeo started," Rock said with a sigh, returning to his chair.

"You were saying, Agent Pedamore?" Harry continued.

Pedamore began as though nothing had just transpired. "First, I'd like to hear from each of you, so Hatfield and I can get everything in sequence." Pedamore flashed a look at his watch. "By the way, Miss Johns will be joining us soon. She's being brought here now by several of my agents.

"After I hear your four stories, Special Agent Hatfield and I will plug in the holes from our end. Is that agreeable, gentlemen?"

Pedamore turned to Harry. "I know you wanted me to go first, Mr. Morgan, but in order for me to lay all my cards on the table, I really need to hear Brian's version, then yours, then Rock's and finally Joanna's. I assure you I'll commit to my part. Agreed?"

Once again all of them, including Harry, nodded in silent agreement.

Pedamore turned to Brian. "Now…Brian, since all this started with you, why don't you begin?"

Chapter 30

Watching the sun peek over tree tops on the eastern horizon, Duvall savored the steaming cup of coffee on the deck of his 2,500 square-foot log cabin. This was his favorite time of the morning: a time to reflect, think, and plan before the stresses of everyday life completely encompassed him. Duvall was on an isolated, five hundred acre spread west of Dallas between Fort Worth and Abilene. He loved the place. It was his secret home away from home, his refuge paradise unknown to anyone but him. His condo in Dallas was a careful ruse, but not this place. The land, house, barns, assorted outbuildings down to the thoroughbred horses were paid in full. The spread was set up through a dummy corporation that couldn't be traced back to him in a hundred years—his former days in the CIA had taught him many things, one of which was how to become a non-entity amongst the human race. Reflecting on the events of the day before, Duvall knew it was time to retire from the crazy business. Just a couple more few loose ends to tie-up and he'd be free.

It was definitely time to sever all ties to Elite Security. That was simple enough: Don't show up for work. No one, including the corporate office personnel and Maxwell Edison's younger brother,

Rigby, knew anything about him. Duvall assumed Rigby would take over the reins of the company, but without any clue about the Elite Squad, its members, or the black-ops they conducted over the years under his brother's direction. Unlike Maxwell, Rigby was a weak, pathetic drunk who survived at Elite Security only through his older brother's generosity. Left alone, Rigby would likely end up bankrupting the firm before the end of the year. More likely, he'd take the first buy-out offer that came to his table, which would be an even better outcome for Duvall.

The second matter he had to contend with was yesterday's attack at The Shack. He'd learned about Maxwell Edison's death from a text he received from Hatfield on the company cell phone. Duvall didn't answer it, of course; instead, he read the message and immediately destroyed the phone. He wanted nothing left that could tie him to Elite. He was sure Hatfield wanted to meet and talk about their next move, especially now that Maxwell was dead. Even if Hatfield didn't want to disappear, such a meeting would never happen. He liked Hatfield, but he didn't trust him or anyone else at this moment. A peripheral movement broke his train of thought. In the distant pasture, a two-month-old palomino colt pranced around his grazing mother, vying for her attention. Duvall savored the sight. Three days maximum, and he'd be done with this and all other business entirely.

Characteristically, Duvall didn't feel a snippet of remorse, regret, or sadness at his employer's death, even though they'd worked together for over twenty years. And, he didn't give a shit how Edison had died. As a matter of fact, it was damn convenient the way it worked out. He could disappear from the scene and into obscurity right now if he chose, now that Maxwell was out of the picture.

However, there were a couple of nagging details he didn't want left hanging around his neck, and, after his next little bit of business, he'd never set foot in Big D again, anyway. Once he returned back to his heavenly ranch, he wouldn't leave it again. And if anyone came to his place uninvited...well then, they'd be toast.

Duvall noisily slurped the last vestiges of his coffee, and stared into the bottom of the empty cup. The sounds of nature intensified in his ears, and the smells of the ranch consumed him, washed over him, clearing his head. In three days, he'd be a free man, obligated only to his horses and the land. And if he hadn't finished his business by then, he'd walk away and leave the old debts unsettled and forgotten. They weren't worth sacrificing his future for.

The plan came together like the rhythmic ringing of church bells. Duvall decided to focus on the woman reporter. Re-reading her article in the morning paper, confirmed his decision. He admired how skillfully she held back just the right amount of information to the public, while presenting just enough to hook the reader. Obviously, she was writing within imposed FBI limitations, but still...she was one smart lady. Miss Joanna Johns would make the perfect conduit. Since she was clearly working with the FBI on this, he just needed get close enough to her, and she would lead him to the answers to some of the more elusive questions regarding the ever-increasing strangeness of this situation.

If this news reporter turned out to be the one who could unravel things for him, then he would send her a package that would expose all the dirty dealings Elite had perpetrated over the past ten years. He

173

would include everything he knew: how Edison framed Zeta with threats of exposing Zeta's abuse of civilians and prisoners, abuses and, in some instances, outright murder, that would cause them to lose their lucrative contract with the Defense Department; details on the assassination squads; everything he knew about Senator Fagan and his under-the-table dealings with Zeta; and all the dirt he could scrape up on Gib Rogers. That last part was personal. His "brother" who had left him to die in Africa. Every murder, every swindle, every government official bribe here and around the world, everything. Along with names. Names that would shake the halls of Congress, the British Parliament, the Kremlin. It would all be in the packet for Johns, if she turned out to be the right one. There wouldn't be a rock in the world that any of those implicated would be able to hide under. No more secrets.

Soon, he would reluctantly leave the sanctity of his West Texas ranch for one more trip to Dallas to fulfill the plan. As he went about prepping his gear, packing the car, and getting underway, Duvall's mind continued working on contingencies, tangents and opportunities.

Duvall's plan hinged on the assumption the feds would have whisked the four civilians away from yesterday's shooting melee, presumably to one or more safe houses. Of course, he had no idea of which they had used. The FBI, if anything, was predictable when it came to matters such as witness protection. The hang up was their release. If the feds kept them holed up, it'd create problems. None he couldn't overcome, but it would be infinitely better if they deemed safe and released early on. If anyone, they would probably release the newspaper reporter first, and he needed to talk with her. He climbed into his car and set his plan in action.

It being Labor Day Weekend, traffic was light on Interstates 20 and 30 and remained so all the way into Dallas. In truth, heavy traffic normally plagued the byways in town at this time of morning, would have been even more ideal for Duvall's purpose: It would have provided excellent cover and camouflage. Dallas FBI headquarters, off the beaten path from the Northwest Highway and normally obscured, by traffic and construction workers, stood boldly out. He'd have to find a spot to blend in with the local scenery, and still be able to observe the comings and goings from the building's parking lot, which he didn't expect to be heavy because of the holidays. Feebies took holidays like everybody else.

Duvall exited I-35 and looped west onto Northwest Highway, which at this point only supported two traffic lanes. Everything outside the two lanes was dug up. Bulldozers and trucks lay dormant, and pickaxes, shovels and piles of dirt were abandoned all about. He spotted a strip center just off the highway in similar disarray. *Bingo,* Duvall thought, pulling his silver 1987 Ford Taurus to a stop next to a worn down mini-mart. A smattering of rough-looking homeless men bringing to their lips short nondescript bottlenecks protruding from brown paper sacks staggered around the parking lots in front of several tired-looking stores. Duvall went inside, bought a tall can of Schlitz, with the mandatory brown sack in which to hide it, took a seat on the trunk of his car, and waited. He looked like all the other bums waiting for something, anything, to happen, and he had a perfect view of the road leading into and from FBI headquarters.

It took one and a half hours, but there was no doubt in Duvall's mind who was inside the black SUV that turned into the FBI entrance.

Shutterbug

He took a small sip of warm beer. *I just need to wait a little bit more.*

Chapter 31

Brian saw Pedamore's eyes avert to his bag. "In there? You've got the pictures with you? Have you shown them to anyone?"

Brian nodded once.

"Just Harry, Rock, and Joanna. That's why I wanted to meet them at The Shack. If anything happened to me, I wanted someone else to know what was going on. I was covering my ass using people I trust."

"Has Agent Hatfield seen them?"

Brian looked at Hatfield, but made no move to confirm or deny. For a fleeting second, Brian thought he detected a flicker of anger pass across Hatfield's face. It made sense to Brian. *I bet you don't want to believe these exist, do you, Agent Hatfield?* "No," Brian finally answered aloud.

"I see. May I see them, please?"

Brian lifted his bag off the floor, unzipped it, removed the large manila envelope and tossed it on the coffee table. "That's my Pulitzer there, John Lee."

Pedamore removed the pictures from the envelope and thumbed through them."Are these in sequential order?"

"Yeah."

"And this is all of them?" Pedamore asked, without looking up.

Brian didn't answer immediately. Pedamore gave Brian a questioning look.

"No," Brian answered. "There're more."

"More copies, or more pictures?"

"Both," Brian answered simply and clearly.

Pedamore's poker face expression remained unchanged and inscrutable. Pedamore held out one picture to Hatfield. "Damn good likeness of you, Michael," he said smiling.

Hatfield glanced at the photo of him pointing a pistol at Senator Fagan's head. He didn't return the smile.

Pedamore returned his attention to Brian. "These are digital, I assume? They're good. You're a very good photographer."

"Thanks."

"These *are* digital, right?" Pedamore asked again.

"Right," Brian confirmed.

Pedamore shuffled through the pictures a final time, then replaced them in the envelope, and handed the envelope back to Brian. Brian was surprised. He'd figured the Pedamore keep them as evidence.

"Do you have the memory card with you?"

Brian placed the pictures on the coffee table. "You can keep those. I've plenty more. And no, I don't have it with me."

Pedamore smiled again. "Okay. Then, let's move on to the shootout." He turned towards Harry. "This time, I'd like to begin with you, Harry."

"Saving the best for last?" goaded Rockaway.

"Always do."

The intercom on Pedamore's desk buzzed, and he got up to answer it. "Yes?"

"You asked me to buzz you when Miss Johns arrived. She's here now," the secretary on the other end reminded.

"Send her in, please."

Joanna entered, bottled water in hand.

Pedamore grabbed an extra chair, slid it next to Brian and walked to her. "Miss Johns. Special Agent John Lee Pedamore. A pleasure to meet you, in person," he said, offering her his hand. He pointed to the empty chair with his other. "You're just in time."

"Hello all," she replied, shaking Pedamore's hand, her inquiring eyes scanning the room."And thank you," she said to Pedamore over her shoulder as she sat next to Brian and gave his knee an assuring pat.

Pedamore returned to his place on the couch. "I read your article in this morning's paper. Excellent job. I'm glad to see you stuck to our deal. I knew I could trust you."

Joanna grinned. "And I expect you to keep your end of our deal as well."

"Of course, of course," Pedamore assured. "Brian just finished filling us in about his unusual day yesterday, and Harry was about to do the same from his perspective." He turned to the lawyer. "Now as I understand it, you had no idea about what was going on until you met with Brian at The Shack. Correct?"

"That's correct," stated Harry, like a compliant courtroom witness.

"So, from there, please fill us in."

Harry's demeanor remained professional, in spite of the comical twin blackened eyes and the white tape across the bridge of his nose.

Shutterbug

"Brian basically told us everything he just told you. As you can imagine, I was more than a bit dumb-founded, but when he showed us the pictures...well, after that I—we—took him deadly serious. We tried to help him explore the connection between Senator Fagan and Maxwell Edison, which, at the time, was very thin. You must remember that the hearing thing hadn't gotten much print. We came to no real conclusions. The visit by the man searching for Brian at Rockaway's office at UTD earlier definitely seemed ominous. Our—my—number one goal was to make sure Brian was safe. And that we were safe, too, of course, since we were now in the folds of this conspiracy alongside him."

Rockaway rolled his eyes. "Damn, Harry, don't start with that conspiracy bullshit again."

"Conspiracy? Are you aware of a conspiracy concerning all this, Harry?" Pedamore interrupted.

Again Brian noticed a flicker of emotion pass across Hatfield's face. It ended in the slightest hint of a grin.

Harry seemed shocked. "What would you call all this? This might be standard operating procedure for you, 'John Lee', but I don't come across this kind of circumstance every day."

It was Pedamore's turn to smile. "I see your point. Continue," he said, scribbling on his pad that appeared on his lap.

"Well, the last part is kind of embarrassing," Harry said, shifting awkwardly in his chair. "We still had no definite plan, and were trying to agree on our next move as a group. I'd had a couple of beers and a few Salty Dogs during the meal, and needed to go to the john. While I was in there, before I started my business, I might add, this guy came in

180

dressed like a bad version of Johnny Cash. He stuck a gun in my back, and ordered me to stay quiet and follow instructions. I almost pissed myself." When no one responded, he added, "But I didn't, of course."

Pedamore inched forward on the couch. "Did he give a name? Identify himself in any way?"

Harry shook his head. "No. Or, if he did, I didn't hear it. I don't mind telling you, I was mighty scared."

The mention of names sparked Brian's memory banks, and he vaguely recalled a shouted name just before all the shooting started. Turning to Joanna, he asked, "Remember when we were at the front door and Louise called out, asking where we were going? She called Edison and the other guy by name. Remember?"

Joanna's brows furrowed together in thought. Then, she snapped her fingers. "Yes, it was...Rogers!"

"Rogers?" Pedamore questioned. "You're sure it was Rogers? Did she use a first name?"

"No, just Rogers."

"Okay, that's helpful." Pedamore wrote down the name. "Ring a bell with you, Mike?"

Hatfield just shook his head in the negative. "It might've been his Mercedes that got blasted. We're checking."

"Okay. Harry, what happened next?"

"We went outside and all hell broke loose. I remember hearing shots, and somebody shoving me." He pointed at his face, "it left me with this little number."

"You didn't see the shooter?" Pedamore asked.

"No," answered Harry, "but I can describe the parking lot

pavement pretty well for you."

Pedamore relaxed back on the sofa. "I'm sure you can. You're all very lucky that none of you were killed." He turned to Rockaway. "Can you add anything to what's just been said, Mickey?"

Rockaway frowned. "Jesus, John Lee, only my mother calls me Mickey. I prefer Rock or Rockaway." His indignation was lost on the agent. "Yeah, well, for my part…"

Harry reached over and placed a hand on Rockaway's forearm to stop him. "I'd like to jump in here a minute, if I might, Agent, uh, John Lee. Before Mr. Rockaway continues, I want to remind you of our agreement about incriminating statements and that everything said in this room will not be held against us."

"I gave you my word on that, Harry." Pedamore responded. "And to give you further assurance," he added "I'm quite aware that Mr. Rockaway had a gun. He willingly gave it to Agent Hatfield at the scene, and told him that he'd shot Maxwell Edison in self-defense. The fact that a nine millimeter was also found beside Edison's body bears that out. Considering the circumstances, it appears to me to have been a justified shooting. But that's just me, of course."

"Good," said Rockaway, "then there's no reason for me to waffle. After I pushed Harry out of the way, I landed on my butt behind the front wheel of Edison's car. Edison was so close, I could almost touch him. I couldn't'uv run, even if I wanted to."

"Just one question," said Pedamore. "Why were you carrying a gun to begin with?"

Rockaway shrugged his shoulders. "You'd think it'd be obvious to a lawman." He turned to Hatfield. "Do you carry a gun when you're off duty, Agent Hatfield?"

"Never leave home without it, Mr. Rockaway. You ex-law enforcement?"

"No," answered Rock, "but I'm ex-Green Beret. I've got a license to carry a concealed weapon, and I sometimes do. It seemed particularly appropriate after that Dunagan fellow visited me looking for Brauny-boy."

"Dunagan? That's the name the man used when he came to your office on campus?"

"Yeah."

"So, to return to what we were talking about, the group had made no definite plans of yet?" Pedamore asked. Acknowledging Joanna with a nod he quickly added, "Except for Miss Johns, who was planning to consult with her newspaper editor. With photos. Correct?"

"Correct," answered Joanna.

Pedamore scribbled a few more notes, then turned to address the reporter. "What about you, Joanna? What can you add?"

She gave a short, nervous laugh. "I'm probably your worst witness, Mr. Pedamore. I've nothing to add to anything said at the restaurant. All that seems to have been said and gone over. Once we were outside, after the first shot, Brian...he yanked me back away from the line of fire...then...pressed me into the corner of the front door, shielding me with his body." Joanna's eyes wetted.

Brian, noticing, reached over, took her hand in his, and squeezed her hand gently. She returned his squeeze with enough pressure to turn his fingers red. She hesitated a moment, sniffled, took a deep breath and continued. It was the first time Brian had seen the hard-nosed reporter's façade break.

"I…I'm sorry," she said, recomposing herself. "Since all this occurred, I haven't slowed down enough to stop and think about what all happened. Even when the shooting was going on, I was busy thinking about how to write the article. Dying never entered my mind, until now." She took a sip from the water bottle in her free hand.

Pedamore nodded, tossed his legal pad on the coffee table, and stood. "I think this is as good a place as any to stop. We could all use a break."

"A break," said Harry, "then you'll fill in *your* blanks. Right?"

"Right. And, Brian, anticipating this might be a long process, I ordered lunch. Yvonne will take you to the food. We've a nice buffet arranged. I'll join you shortly." Pedamore called his secretary on the intercom into the room.

As the four filed out of the office behind her, Rock pulled Brian closer. "Listen: I'm done here, I don't buy that 'John Lee' crap, and I don't like where this all seems to be going, Brauny. I'm gonna eat their food and make a break."

For a moment, Brian looked surprised. It seemed increasingly unlikely to him that Pedamore would, indeed, live up to their bargain and actually 'fill in the blanks.' In fact, it felt to Brian as if he and the group were being manipulated. He smiled and answered, "I'm with you. Our lawyer can fill us in later."

Chapter 32

After the secretary led the Fab Four from the office, Pedamore flopped onto the couch and stretched his legs across the coffee table. Hatfield took a chair opposite him.

"So, what do you think, John Lee?"

"There's no doubt we've got to contain this situation. And them. I'm definitely going to place of them in a separate safe houses where we can keep them under wraps until we finish our part in what we've started. I'll take care of it from here. In the meanwhile, you've got your own things to do."

"Where do you want me?"

"Let's tie up some of the loose ends. The Attorney General is ready to drop the hammer on Elite and Senator Fagan as soon as we give the word. With Edison's death, the defense has begun to crumble. Cut off the head and the beast will die."

"Our boys have determined that Rigby, Edison's alcoholic brother, doesn't know a thing. Maxwell kept him totally in the dark. I doubt he even knows there's a hearing next week."

Pedamore nodded in agreement. "Do you have any leads on Duvall? Anything at all?"

"No. I texted him about a meeting, but if it was me, I wouldn't have answered either. Rockaway mentioned a Dunagan who came to his office. Duvall's used that alias before. He was probably following up after spotting Braun at Fagan's. What's the deal on Eldawoody? Any word from Dairy Queen or Jail Bird?"

The corners of Pedamore's mouth dipped. "Eldawoody's dead. Zeta took care of him. That one bothers me. I really wanted him in my house, not theirs."

Hatfield didn't react.

"Any idea of who this Rogers character is?" Pedamore asked, moving things back on track.

"No, but there's got to be some connection between Rogers and Duvall. Maybe that's who he was really shooting at instead of Edison?"

"Maybe…nothing for sure, yet. I'll run it down from this end and get back to you." Pedamore grabbed his notes and scanned them. "Braun mentioned that the waitress at The Shack, called out the name 'Roger's and it was a last name." He tossed the pad back on the table. "You know…if this Louise character knows the man's last name…she just might know his first. You want to follow-up on that? I know it's not usual protocol for someone in undercover operations," Pedamore scratched his chin, "but...uh, I have the feeling you've got some...concerns...of your own that need further investigation before you're ready to share them. If visiting with her would help…"

Hatfield nodded. "No problem, I want to go back and re-examine the scene, anyway. See if there was anything I might have missed last night. Any more from Fagan's camp, yet?"

"Just what I mentioned about Eldawoody," answered Pedamore,

"but there are two things for sure I want from you by tomorrow at the latest, if you're going to run with us on this."

"Shoot. What do you need?"

"I want the memory card with Braun's pictures of you, Fagan, and the team he's surrounded himself with. It was obvious Braun wasn't going to give 'em up. That's his ace-in the-hole. He's covering his ass... can't blame him for that...but I can't let him keep them, either."

"And second?"

"I want the letters that Braun mailed to Morgan and Johns. I don't want to leave any loose ends there, either. They are essential to containment, on this end. We've got too much time and manpower invested in this effort, and I don't want to see it fall apart because of a few renegade civilians." Pedamore stood. "For crying out loud, Mike, we've got a top-notch newspaper reporter, a left-wing, conspiracy nut attorney, a gun-toting ex-Green Beret, and a master thief, slash, photographer to keep from blowing the biggest political scandal investigation since Watergate."

Hatfield shrugged. "Doesn't sound too complicated, does it? I mean, after all, we *are* the FBI, you know."

Pedamore ignored Hatfield's attempt at lightening the moment. "I just don't like it. No more collateral damage, Hat. This has to be a clean operation. Understand?"

"Understood, John Lee, and I don't want to see a full year of undercover work go to shit, either."

"We're closer to that happening than you think," said Pedamore. "I feel it in my bones."

Shutterbug

Chapter 33

I can bring down international hit squads and corrupt CEO's, but I can't seem to get a five-minute interview with a barmaid at a barbecue joint.

Hatfield hunched over the bar with a tall, frosty, refilled mug of sweet tea in front of him. So far, Louise had done an excellent job busying herself, looking overworked and unable to attend to his request for a brief conversation. The suit and badge probably had something to do with it. His undercover assignment, for all intent and purposes, was done, and he wasn't sure if he wanted to ever go back undercover again. Normally, the Bureau would never have allowed him into the field to question a civilian about an ongoing case—too much danger of blowing his cover—but, evidently, Pedamore had picked up on the hints Hatfield'd been dropping wanting to followup on this particular case, and about coming out in general. No more deep cover, after this case, Hatfield promised himself in Pedamore's absence. With the notoriety of the principals involved in this case, his cover would ultimately be blown at some point, anyway. In this, what he envisioned as his last undercover case, he wanted to be at the forefront of closing things down, not in the background. Several rules had already been bent around these last few days and this was just one more to add to the list.

Hat continued waiting patiently; he knew Louise wasn't going anywhere, and neither would he. It gave him some time to reflect and figure out his next move with the matron of The Shack.

She'd be a hostile witness, for sure—he could see that already—and there was her innate reluctance to cooperate with any law enforcement officials. He had therefore decided give her some rein. Eventually, her loyalty to a customer would win out, and she'd talk. Then, he had only to gain her confidence, and he felt certain she'd tell him everything she knew.

Louise, as he anticipated, eventually edged closer, busying herself stacking some newly washed and dried beer mugs beneath the bar. Finally, she looked in his direction.

"You ain't leaving are ya," she stated as a matter of fact.

"No ma'am. Not till we talk."

She wiped her hands on a dish towel and tossed it to the side. "Let's do it, then," she said. "I got things to do 'round here."

"I appreciate your time, Miss…"

"Louise is fine; ain't no formalities 'round here. What you wanna know?"

Hatfield retrieved a pen and a small notebook from his inside jacket pocket. "I've got to write everything down nowadays, Louise," he said, making an excuse to take notes.

"That's fine," she said, "I ain't sayin' nuthin' incriminating, anyway. Shoot, Mr. Agent, time's wastin'."

"Louise, I know you've told all this, probably numerous times already to the Dallas Police, but I need a statement from you for the FBI, too. We're actually the ones in charge of the case. So, if you'll just be patient with me for bit, we'll get this done and you can get back to work. Okay?" Hatfield gave her an innocent grin, hoping to chip away some of the ice clinging to his adversary across the bar.

Louise propped her hands on her ample hips. "So you gonna ask a question or write a book?"

Hatfield gave her a short laugh. "Okay, do you know Misters Braun, Morgan, Rockaway and Miss Johns very well, or just as customers?"

She shrugged one shoulder. "As customers, 'course. We don't run in the same circles," she winked, "after work, if you know what I mean. I feed 'em. We joke around. They tip good. But, I do count them friends. They've been comin' here for many years, now. I'd do anything they asked, and they'd do the same for me. How's that? That what you want to hear?"

Hatfield scribbled some notes, then looked up from his tablet. "I just want to hear the truth. Nothing more, nothing less. Did they ask you to do anything for them, Louise? Did any of them give you something to hold? Anything like that?"

This time, it was Louise's turn to laugh. "Just a nice tip...no military secrets or nuthin'."

"Can you show me where Mr. Braun's group was sitting and where Mr. Edison and his companion were sitting when all this took place yesterday?"

Louise sighed with boredom. "Yeah, sure, come on this way," she said with annoyance, motioning him to follow her. She walked him to the annexed room, stopped before entering, and then pointed to her right in the direction of the restrooms. "Mr. Braun and his bunch were sittin' in that last booth against the far wall." Then, she pointed straight ahead to the booth in front of her. Misters Edison and Rogers, they were sittin' in that one. Opposite end."

"Mr. Rogers? You don't happen to know Mr. Rogers' first name, by any chance?"

"It's Gib. Ain't that a funny name? I know, 'cause I usually call him Mr. Gib," Louise said with a chuckle.

Hatfield scribbled in his notebook. "Do you remember who was sitting where? In the booths?"

Louise glared at him. "You're kiddin' right?" She gave a big sigh that raised her large breasts to new heights. Then, she surveyed the room as though thinking out. "Okay, best as I remember, Mr. Edison, he was facin' the restrooms an' Mr. Rogers—Mr. Gib—he was facin' the other wall," she said pointing again. Then, Louise turned on her heels with a bit of exaggeration, focusing on the other booths at the opposite end of the room. "I think Mr. Braun and Miss Johns was facin' towards Mr. Edison's booth." She hesitated a second and then nodded. "Mr. Rockaway and Morgan, they faced the restrooms. That's it," she said nodding, "that's the way they sat." Staring intently at Hatfield, she said with liquid sarcasm, "Now that you know that, you solved the case yet, Mr. Agent?"

"A few more question, please, ma'am. Just the facts."

Louise laughed suddenly. "I used to love that show," she said, her tone softening a bit, which was about all she would allow herself to muster for the federal man. "I think I'm startin' to like you, Mr. FBI. So, what's next?"

Hatfield returned the grin. *Making progress.* "Could you walk me through what happened next? When they went outside? Try to remember everything, like you did with where they were seated, Louise. What might seem unimportant to you might be important to me. Okay?" Hatfield said, trying to melt away any remaining barriers.

She pointed at the bar area. "I was back there waitin' on customers." She raised an eyebrow, "Like I should be now—anyways, I was waitin' on some customers, and everyone started marchin' out together in a bunch. I remember I was surprised 'cause I hadn't taken Mr. Edison's food to him yet. I think I asked him 'bout it, and he said he'd 'be right back'."

"How exactly were they 'bunched'? Who was where, do you remember?"

Louise scratched her chin as she contemplated. "I think Mr. Morgan and Miss Johns was up front with Mr. Rogers, and Mr. Edison, Mr. Braun, and Mr. Rockaway were at the back. That's when I asked Mr. Edison where he's goin' and didn't he want his food."

"Did he say anything else besides saying he'd be back?"

"Nope. None of 'em was very chatty. They were all serious and stuff."

"Did Mr. Braun say anything to you?"

Louise hesitated, shifting from one foot to the other, as if she was trying to remember. "Hm-m-m. Nope, don't think so. Well, maybe something like, thanks for the food, or something like that."

Hat sensed the woman was holding back something. Something she didn't want to let go of, regardless of how much he probed and

193

cajoled so he moved on."Then, what happened, Louise?"

She shrugged her shoulder again. "They went outside, an' all hell broke loose. I never even went outside when it was all over. Stayed in here the whole time until closin' time at midnight."

Hatfield asked, perplexed. "Weren't you even curious? Didn't you want to know what happened to your friends?"

Louise shook her head. "No way I'm goin' out there. Sent Sam," she said, motioning her head back to the kitchen area. "He just stood 'round and listened to what everybody was saying." She chuckled, "I think the cops tried to ask him some questions, but they figured out real quick that ol' Sam don't say much and wasn't goin' begin to just for them."

"Do you think…" Hatfield started.

Louise waved him off immediately. "No use wastin' your time, Mr. FBI." She looked over her shoulder towards the kitchen. "He's choppin' ribs. Got a cleaver in his hands. If it was me, I'd stay away from him."

Hatfield closed his notepad and stuffed it in his jacket pocket, hoping the gesture would give Louise a sense that everything from this point on would be off the record. He nodded in friendly agreement. "That sounds like good advice. Is there anything else you can think of, Louise? You've done a wonderful job recounting things so far."

Without hesitation, she said, "Not off-hand."

Motioning towards the bar, Hatfield said, "Can we sit down together for just a minute more? I know you need to get back to work, but this'll just take a minute. I promise."

She nodded, quietly led the way to the bar stools, and sat down first. Hatfield followed suit. He gently laid his hand on her forearm, which she had rested on the bar, then he removed it. He was going for the sincerity approach. "Louise, I know that these were more than just good customers to you. That's why I'm going to reveal some things I normally shouldn't in a case like this."

Louise frowned, but moved closer. "What you tryin' to say, mister?"

Hatfield matched her movement. "What happened yesterday wasn't an accident. It wasn't a 'being in the wrong place at the wrong time kind of thing' for *any* of those people. Someone—a killer—was waiting outside for the two groups to leave. They were specifically targeted, Louise. Now, Mr. Braun's group, I believe, are innocent of any wrong doing, but what we're afraid of is that the killer might not know that. Are you with me so far?"

Louise bit her lower lip. Her concern was obvious and sincere. "Y-you mean somebody could still be gunnin' for those young kids? That's awful, Mr...what is your name, Mr. Agent? I can't remember what you..."

"Hatfield. Agent Hatfield. My friends call me Hat," Hatfield said almost in a whisper.

"Mr. 'Hat'," she said. "I like that name."

"So, if there's anything at all, Louise..." He stopped and let the sentence hang in mid-air.

She shook her head slowly, as though wishing she could think of something to tell him. "I just can't, Hat. But if I do, can I call you?"

Hatfield reached in a side pocket and pulled out a business card. "That number on the bottom right is a 24/7 number, Louise. All you have to do is call." Hat knew the interrogation was over; he'd gleaned all he was getting from her. So, without further hesitation, he got up from the stool and offered his hand to Louise. "It's been a pleasure to meet you, Louise. I'd like to come back and try some of those ribs you're so famous for."

Louise gave his hand a firm squeeze and released it, depositing Hatfield's business card in an apron pocket with the other. "They's the very best in town, Hat. An' if I remember something I'll call as soon as it hits me," Louise said with a grin. *Cracker.*

Chapter 34

After their catered lunch at the Dallas FBI Offices, the Fab Four followed the secretary back to Pedamore's office; after their chattiness over lunch, their change in demeanor back to what felt to Pedamore like an enforced silence was obvious. Each returned to their previous seats. "Agent Hatfield had to leave," Pedamore informed the group. "How was your lunch?"

"Very good," answered Brian for the group.

"Good. I have just a few more questions and then I'll bring you all up to speed from my end. Is that okay?"

Harry nodded his affirmation. "As long as you do it, and it's something we don't already know."

"I assure you," said Pedamore, "you won't be disappointed. Now, Brian, I want to ask you about something that I know you want to avoid, but I'd be remiss in my position and duties if I didn't."

"You can ask anything you want, Mr. Pedamore...I just can't promise you'll get the answer you want."

"Fair enough. Okay, pictures like those you took, as you well know, would rock the nation to the core if, or when...they are published," Pedamore glanced at Joanna. "Through Miss Johns, I assume."

"That's a good assumption," said Brian, "but I'm not telling you where the memory card is or turning it over to you. I think you can understand why."

Pedamore gave him a knowing grin. "I know a pre-emptive attack when I see one. Okay. I probably already know your motives, but re-enlighten me anyway."

Brian relaxed slightly. "Sure, it's quite simple: Those pictures will save the lives and careers of the four of us sitting in this nice office of yours. Whether they get published or not, at the moment, is irrelevant to me. It's what they prevent from happening, if you get my drift. I've no idea what's going to happen to Fagan, if anything. I'm not completely clear about your motives in keeping us prisoners like this, or, as you call it, 'safe'. But what I've already surmised is that we're all targets for somebody, and right now it's hard to tell the good somebodies from the bad ones. See my point?"

Pedamore frowned thoughtfully, hesitated, then spoke. "I do, though I think calling yourselves prisoners is a bit over the top. I prefer 'special guests'," he said, smiling. "And as for the pictures and memory card, I'm hoping before we're done here, you'll see the wisdom in turning them over to me." Pedamore paused again, then added, "For safe keeping."

Switching gears, Pedamore started again, "I think it's time for me to open up to you, and then maybe you'll see the importance of a straightforward dialogue between us in this matter. I'm certain that with a fuller, uh, appreciation, let's say, of the situation, maybe you'll come to my way of thinking."

"You can try," said Harry, "but don't get your hopes up. It's not like the government's never lied to us before, is it?"

Pedamore nodded supportively. This was part of Harry's act and he refused to nibble. "Okay, let's get to it." Special Agent John Lee Pedamore took a deep breath, hoping he was making the right decision in sharing confidential information with this crew. "We, that is, the FBI and the United States Attorney General's Office, have been involved in an extensive investigation into Elite Security—principally, Maxwell Edison, a few others, and Senator Fagan—for quite some time now. As you've probably figured out on your own by now, Agent Hatfield has been operating undercover as an employee of Elite Security for the past year or so. I don't have to tell you that working his way into a trusted position in that short of time was, to say the least, a chancy piece of good luck on our part. Because of the intricacies of the case and the involvement of different government entities, and the amount of manpower, money, and most of all, the extent of endangerment of lives...I'm not in a position to divulge everything about what's taken place or who's involved."

"We understand that, Special Agent Pedamore," Brian said solicitously. "As you said, it doesn't take a rocket scientist to figure this much out."

"Right," injected Joanna, "I did a little more digging on my own this morning, and now that I'm seeing the details from the inside, as opposed to an uninvolved citizen, I'm beginning to see some light at the end of our tunnel. First, there's a seemingly off-the-radar Senate Hearing, conducted by a high-profile senator. Fagan wouldn't waste his time chairing the committee unless something big was at hand. We all know what a grandstander he is. Then, we have—as we now know for a fact from what you've just disclosed—an FBI man on the inside of the Elite organization that, for some strange reason, stages a fake assassination."

"And," Harry added, "from that, one can surmise that the FBI is totally immersed in this operation all around. They must be the 'good somebodies' protecting Fagan at his home. Who else would have been there seconds after his 'assassination', picking him up off the ground after his great performance of getting shot and killed?"

Pedamore looked surprised. "Really, Harry? And, how do you come to the conclusion that it's the FBI protecting Fagan?"

This time, it was Harry's turn to appear surprised. "Well, it's obvious, isn't it? Black SUV's, night suits, an undercover agent pretending to shoot a United States Senator. Who else would be watching his back while the senator follows through on such a ruse? I am a bit surprised that the feds would use such an elaborate scheme. If something went wrong and the senator had, in reality, been shot dead…" Harry let the comment hang in the air as if searching for, then considering what to say next, "…then the granddaddy of all cover-ups would have had to take place. I mean, who's going to let it get out that the Federal Bureau of Investigation let a senator get assassinated? And who would be the fall guy for such a major fuck-up?"

"Here we go," snapped Rockaway, "I knew you'd work in the conspiracy angle sooner or later."

"Me," said Brian, flatly. "I'm the fall guy, aren't I?"

Harry spread his arms as though taking a bow. "So, there you are. Sirhan Sirhan. Lee Harvey Oswald. Brian Braun." He sat back in his chair with a satisfied I-told-you-so look.

"Interesting," Pedamore retorted. "Any other grand assumptions you'd like to present, Counselor?"

"We talked to them," Brian added.

"Really? Who'd you talk to? When?" Pedamore asked, masking his concern about this new development.

"Fagan," answered Brian. "We called him when we were at The Shack. Just before we were herded outside."

"I'd like to know what was said, if you don't mind," Pedamore stated casually but firmly.

Brian shrugged. "Well, it was a bit confrontational, you might say."

"How so?"

"Well, to start with, I was angry. Angry about being set up. I told him to call off his dogs."

"What dogs? Who were you referring to?"

Rockaway finally jumped in the conversation. "The refrigerator that came to my office looking for Brian. He gave a total cock 'n' bull story about Brian and him having a meeting. I fed him a line of baloney about meeting Brian's asking me to meet him at the Fox and Hound, and he was welcome to join us. We basically just stood there and lied to each other toe to toe…and we both knew it. It was an interesting game of chicken, using bullshit instead of cars. Vet to vet made it even more interesting."

"So you think he was involved in the shooting at The Shack?" Pedamore asked.

"Maybe," inserted Brian. "I caught a glimpse of the shooter at the end of the sidewalk."

"Really," said Pedamore, surprised. "I didn't know you saw him. Did you recognize him?"

"No, it was just a fleeting glance, but it could've been the same guy who was looking for me at UTD. I don't know how he would have found us at The Shack, but I guess anything's possible."

"Okay. What else did Fagan say?" Pedamore returned to writing on his legal pad.

"Fagan? He said he'd prove that I was the Highland Park thief and have me sent to jail for life."

"Interesting tactic. What'd you say to that?"

"Uh, I told him to fuck-off."

Pedamore laughed aloud. "I'll give you this, Brian: You've got balls. Do you know how many people have wanted to tell that son-of-a-bitch to fuck-off to his face?"

Pedamore's face reddened, and he turned to Joanna with an embarrassed look. "I'm sorry, Ms. Johns. I apologize for my language. Still, the visual of the conversation is something to behold."

"No apology needed. I've heard it all before…believe me."

"Thanks." Pedamore said, returning to Brian. "Hell, Brian…that alone would make you a national hero."

"But you're not going to let that happen, are you, Special FBI Agent Pedamore? Let him go to jail, I mean," stated Harry. "That's why we're here, talking this out."

"When this all comes down, Harry, it is our intention that Senator Fagan be the one in the penniteniary for life. Trust me." Pedamore returned to his notes, then to Brian. "Okay, you told him about the pictures. He threatened you if you published them. Right?"

"Right."

"Any idea why he wanted you to take the pictures in the first place?"

"Insurance. Maybe blackmail. I really don't know."

"Did you talk to anyone else besides the senator?"

"No, but Harry did."

What the hell is going on, here? "Jeez, you guys get around, don't you?" Pedamore said, turning to Harry. "Okay, who'd you talk with, Harry?"

"Well, Brian wanted me, as his attorney, to initiate the call, which I did. I assumed it was someone from the FBI who initially answered."

"Did he identify himself as an agent?"

"No, he didn't, but he didn't deny it, either. He said he was an *aide*." Harry pointed at Pedamore. "But, I can tell you one thing for damn sure. The aide didn't know a damn thing about Brian taking pictures of the senator's assassination. Caught him completely by surprise."

Pedamore took a breath. "I can imagine it would. Interesting. All very interesting." He stared at Harry. "Pray continue."

"Okay," said Harry, letting loose with both conspiracy barrels, "Here's what I think: Fagan's in the pocket of a competitor of Elite's called Zeta. The ostensible purpose of the hearings was to bring Zeta to it's knees; however, what the two had secretly planned was to do a switch right during the hearings. In pubic. Fagan's plan was to bring down Elite in a scandal they couldn't possibly survive, one that was so much more damning than whatever Zeta had done to lose it's government contracts, in the wave of public outrage, Zeta would be left to retake over what they'd lost to Elite Security. That's why he set up the 'assassination'. I think that with Zeta's money, world-wide connections, assistance, and a bit of plastic surgery, Fagan was to 'disappear' off the face of the earth, leaving the pictures he asked Brian to take as evidence of his assassination. Everyone would assume his body had been disposed of elsewhere, and no amount of questioning could ever wrench it from Maxwell Edison, who wouldn't know anything about it. Maybe Fagan figured by using a professional photographer with a past, like Brian, he'd have more control over him. Maybe he planned on blaming the hit *and* the photographs both on Brian, the photos, supposed taken automatically with a concealed camera, being the proof to his employer, Maxwell Edison of Elite Security, of having done the job. Then Brian, under duress, took out Maxwell, the whole affair leaving the alleged cat-burgler-now-turned-killer flailing all alone against the public wind."

Pedamore smiled to himself as the attorney's conspiracy theory grew bolder and wilder.

"He misjudged Brian completely," said Joanna. "But, what I don't understand is that, pulling an assassination stunt as complex as this could end up biting him if anything went wrong. I don't think of Fagan as that kind of risk-taker or that big of a fool."

"Ego's a powerful thing, Joanna. And power tricks the mind into thinking that one can not be defeated or do wrong…" Harry began

"Or, get caught," added Brian.

"Or, get caught," agreed Pedamore. "Power comes with the insatiable need for more money and power, especially if you're in hock up to your eyeballs like Fagan is. Oh, you didn't know? Despite his 'percentage' from the tens of contracts worth hundreds of millions of dollars, Fagan was a senator with big aspirations. Elections these days cost not hundreds of thousands but millions."

Joanna, unsatisfied, continued to probe. "So what was so bad that Fagan felt desperate enough to take down a power house like Elite? I still don't understand him taking such an extreme risk."

"You have a reporters inquisitive mind, Miss Johns. For the moment, let's just call it murder and leave it at that."

Joanna started to ask another question anyway, but Pedamore cut her off. "Leave it there for now, Joanna. Please."

It was Rockaway's turn to jump into the fray. "To be honest, John Lee, I've been bored up to this point, but now things are starting to get interesting. So, this is how I see it. And correct me if I'm wrong, okay?"

"I'll do what I can."

"It's simple: Elite's probably got some goon squad knocking off important people in important places. Murder, as you say. Fagan finds out about it, but keeps it to himself. He sees himself as an American hero, fame, and dollar signs ahead in his future. Maybe even a run for President. There's no bigger power trip than being the leader of the free world. Brian's an afterthought that will be dead before the end of the day. Much simpler, and it might justify the risk. How am I doing so far?"

"Please continue," said Pedamore, neither confirming nor denying the professor's version.

"The feds are not involved…except to foil the plot with their own man, and bring down the senator for good."

"Wait," said Harry. "If that's the case, then who're the guys at the ranch with the senator?"

Rockaway pointed to Pedamore. "Ask him."

"Well?" Harry asked.

Pedamore once avoided answering a second time. "So Rockaway, what do you base your theory on? It sounds a bit out there to me."

"The competitors, the Zeta boys, I'm guessing. They're solidly behind Fagan…protecting their future asset."

Once again, Pedamore neither confirmed nor denied.

This time, it was Rockaway's time to smile. "So, bulls-eye! The whole damn thing is now out there, Mr. Pedamore…and you just confirmed my 'theory' with your non-answer."

"Exactly!" shouted Harry.

"I'll be damned," Joanna said softly.

"Pedamore?" Brian asked.

Pedamore nodded. *Smart man.* "You're all close. But let me put it this way for now: It's enough to say that your versions are close enough to the truth that I don't need to say anything more about it."

Rockaway stood up. "Good, then as far as I'm concerned this lavish bullshit session is over, and I'm going home."

Rocky looked at Brian. When Brian didn't speak up, he finished with a backhand invitation: "You got my keys, Brauny?"

Chapter 35

After Rock had made his declaration to leave, the other three, following his lead, got to their feet. Pedamore was the only one who remained seated, and he didn't appear alarmed by the Fab Four's intended exit. Brian looked at Rockaway with a mild what-are-you-talking-about look, thinking at the same time, *Shit. Don't mess this up, Rock.*

By then, Rockaway had caught his blunder. Brian was sure Pedamore did, too.

"Oh...that's right," said Rockaway calmly, digging in his front pocket and pulling out a set of keys. "That's right, you gave them back."

Pedamore calmly motioned for them to be seated. "Just a few more questions, and you're outta here."

"You're not holding us against our wills are you, Mr. Pedamore?" Harry asked. "We've answered your questions, and, I'll admit you've disclosed what you promised at least up to a point. So now we're free to go, right?"

"Of course, Counselor, but not until we're finished, if you don't mind. There are just a few final things I need to clear up. Call it professional curiosity on my part, if you like. Please..." he motioned them down again.

It was obvious Pedamore held all the cards, no matter how much *bravado* Brian or his friends showed. They would be allowed to leave when Pedamore allowed them.

Brian sat down first. The others reluctantly followed suit. "Ask away," Brian stated flatly.

Pedamore scanned his notes. "I'm curious that you mention keys, Rockaway." He looked up from his pad and looked each of the Fab Four in turn in the eyes he spoke. "We've impounded only three cars from the Mockingbird scene: Harry's Mercedes, Joanna's Chevy, and Brian's Jeep." Pedamore remained staring at Rockaway, who looked like a cat waiting to catch a canary.

"Where's your Road Runner?"

With an indignant and genuine look of surprise, Rock answered, "You don't know? How could you not know? Brauny parked it behind the restaurant. Shouldn't be too hard to spot."

Pedamore shrugged. "Yes, well, Hatfield spotted your car when he arrived at the restaurant. He called in the license number and we got your name from the DMV. It was parked, as you said, behind the restaurant immediately after the shooting, exactly where Hatfield spotted it earlier. It was late into the night before we had your cars brought in. Hard to see how we missed it." He turned to Harry, Joanna, and Brian. "Your cars, at least, are all safe in our garage. It's not the best neighborhood, and we didn't want anyone to grab them." Pedamore's stare continued boring into Rockaway. "But your car was definitely missing when the tow-trucks got there. Any ideas?"

Rockaway shook his head, obviously angered after being told his car had gone missing. "No, but you better find it. That's all I've got to say." He held up his keys. "I've got the keys. Brauny gave them to me…" he let it hang a few seconds, "at The Shack."

"Well," said Pedamore calmly, "since you've got the keys, it obviously must have been jacked somehow. I'll put out an APB for it."

"You damn well better."

Pedamore remained undisturbed by Rock's display of outrage.

"Can we go now?" Brian asked. His mind was jumping. He knew Pedamore wasn't buying the stolen car story.

"Almost done. Brian…one final question, then I'll fill all of you in about today's plans. Earlier, I mentioned professional curiosity and remember…"

Harry jumped in. "I'm not sure where you're going with this Mr. Pedamore, but off the record or not, I'm not letting my client answer anything more that's self-incriminating."

Pedamore nodded. "Understood." Then, he twisted his body in his seat to where he was eyeball to eyeball with Brian. "What led you to become a thief?"

"Don't answer, Brian. This interview is over!" Harry wasn't going to allow this go any further.

Pedamore is just reminding me of who's in charge. "What life of crime would you be referring to, Mr. Pedamore?" he asked coldly.

Pedamore smiled and conceded with a nod. "That's fine, never mind." Then he continued as promised. "Here's the plan. Since your lives are in danger, we'd like to keep you in a safe place for at least one or two more days. It'd be irresponsible on our part to allow you to go out and get shot at again, maybe even killed this next time."

"Exactly who are we in danger from?" Brian asked.

Pedamore shrugged. "Who was taking pot shots at you at The Shack? Elite's goons? Someone in Fagan's pocket? Zeta? There might be another entity out there we're not yet aware of. In the meantime, you're each vulnerable."

"Who do *you* think was shooting at us?" Brian probed.

Pedamore hesitated,. then decided to be up front. "I believe it was an Elite man. The one who visited UTD. But we don't know if he was after you, or Edison, or this Rogers person, or one or all of you. At least, not yet. He may try again. Alternatively, others could be shooting for you too."

"A cheery thought," Rockaway insinuated. "If he's an assassin, he's a pretty lousy shot. That's all I have to say. Do you have a line on him at all?"

"Hatfield's on it right now. He's running down some leads. If anyone can find out who the shooter was, it's Agent Hatfield."

"Look," Brian said, "we can take care of ourselves. I've got friends who can help us. Think about it. Time is crucial. Based on what you've said today, you're going to be moving in on Fagan soon anyway. You can't afford for this to go on any longer and get further out of hand. The sooner you lock it down, the quicker it's over."

Pedamore nodded his agreement. "That's my argument, exactly. Forty-eight hours under my care. Then you're free to run with it."

"That'll never happen," stated Harry. "All three of my clients and myself refuse your 'hospitality'." He motioned the other three to close in about him. "We've committed no crimes and we cannot be held against our wills."

This time, Pedamore stood. "Well, Counselor, Mr. Rockaway killed a man. If you insist, we could..."

Harry frowned. "As you've mentioned several times, this is an information gathering meeting. Are we to assume your word was worthless? That you're using entrapment to extract information from us under duress? Besides, the shooting should fall under the jurisdiction of the local police, not the federal government."

Pedamore smiled. "I could argue that point with you, Counselor, but, as I said, my word is my bond. I promised not to press any criminal charges. On the other hand, I could without a doubt hold you on national security issues. If you refuse my offer of a safe, warm, comfortable house for each of you, then I could be forced to invoke national security issues and lock you up here in our overnight facilities. They're not as comfortable, of course..."

"This isn't a national security issue and you know it," said Harry. "It's a national embarrassment issue. The only people with their asses hanging out in the wind are you guys."

Joanna joined Harry: "We had a deal, Mr. Pedamore. I told you I'd hold back printing the full story, and I did. Now you're threatening to put a muzzle on the press. I don't appreciate it. I have work to do, and obviously, I can't do it from here or a safe house."

Brian decided to toss in his two-bits: "You can't keep us locked up forever. Two days turns into three, and on and on. When this story eventually gets out, and it will, you're handling of us could put quite a spin on it.."

"Brian's right," Joanna added. "Wouldn't you agree that it'd be better to have the press on your side than against you? The potential damage to the FBI and whatever other government agencies that are involved is monumental. You could come out as heroes." She smiled. "Defender of the little guy, or…"

Brian could tell Joanna'd struck a nerve with Pedamore. It appeared that the power of the press might prevail.

Pedamore picked up his notes from the coffee table and went through the pretense of scanning them one last time. Finally, he looked up and said, "I see we've arrived at an impasse. Reluctantly, I'm going to give in to your wishes."

Pedamore crossed the office to his desk, grabbed a stack of cards, and handed one to each. "My office and cell numbers are on these. You can reach me day or night at either of those numbers. Use them. If you get in a bind, wish to share information…"

"Need a shoulder to cry on?" Rockaway added.

Pedamore grinned. "That, too. Give me a call." He gave Rockaway a pat on the arm. "And don't worry. We'll find your Road Runner."

"Screw Fagan. Find my car," Rockaway replied without a grin.

"We'll do both. I'll arrange for an agent in the lobby to take you to your respective cars. But, be careful." Pedamore warned, as he shook hands with each of them. When the group arrived in the lobby, an agent was waiting to take them to the garage.

"How can he do that so fast?" Brian whispered to Rockaway.

Rockaway shrugged. "I guess they know what we're thinking before we do."

As soon as Pedamore was sure they'd cleared the office, he picked up his phone, dialed a number, and waited for the answer at the other end. "Are the men in place?"

"Yes sir," answered Dairy Queen. "It'll be a circus until they all go their separate ways, but we'll pull it off."

"Twenty-four hours. Around the clock. If you need more manpower, call. I'm pulling all the stops on this one. Each has a big red bullseye on his or her back, and the fatal shot could come from anywhere. Has Hatfield called in?"

"Not yet."

"Any word from Jail Bird, yet?"

"No Sir," answered Dairy Queen. "And that concerns me. Fagan's a loose cannon at this point, and we don't know what the hell's going through that desperate politician-mind of his. I've marked the signal-site for him. It's a waiting game, now."

"Time always seems to be our biggest enemy. Keep me informed." Pedamore hung up and dialed another number.

"I was wondering when you'd call, John Lee," the person at the other end of the line answered.

"You know how it is, Chief Fouts. I had to put out as many fires as I could first. You ready for me to take the monkey off your back?"

The Chief of the Dallas Police Department laughed softly. "You mean the shooting at The Shack last night? Hell, it's all yours for the asking, John Lee. I'll end up with a homicide detective chompin' at the bit, though. He didn't like getting brushed off when your guys got there, and he won't like being taken off the case, either."

"Believe me, Randy, you don't want any part of this. We're at a crucial point in an undercover sting that's been going on over a year."

Pedamore let a few seconds of silence lapse, then continued. "We can talk, right?"

"Of course," answered Chief Fouts.

"I'm afraid there could be more collateral damage before this is all over, and if there is, I'm gonna have a lot of work to do in order to cover somebody's ass. I'm just giving you a heads up."

The silence lingered at the other end this time. "Just keep me abreast of happenings, John Lee. And what about Edison? Have you identified the shooter?"

"It was a clear-cut case of self-defense, you have my word on that. Who was the detective who got pushed off last night?"

Chief Fouts gave a short laugh. "You'll love this…it was Luther Megs."

"Shit. You mean, Bulldog?" whined Pedamore. "Why did we have to piss off your number one go-to guy? He really mad?"

"Livid. You want to call him and tell him why he can't continue with the case?"

"No, you're the chief, Randy. You get that the pleasure, but for God's sake, keep him on a very short leash. I can't afford having him digging into this. If you have to, tell him the feds already have the killer and it's a closed case. Just keep the Bulldog at bay."

"Will do. Anything else?"

"Not for now, and I promise to keep you up to date when I can."

"See you in the papers," quipped Chief Fouts.

"I'm afraid you will, Chief. I'm afraid you will."

Chapter 36

Senator Fagan and Mark Freeman, the leader of Zeta's special "tiger-team" unit, stood across from each other at the ranch house kitchen bar. Freeman, who strove to remain emotionally detached from his clients, was finding neutrality a difficult position to maintain with the senator. The man personified everything that was wrong with politics. The greed, the back-room deals, and the life or death ruination of innocent people decided on a whim, all seemed to be the norm instead of the exception. Not that Freeman was a choirboy, by any means, but he'd never killed anyone who didn't have it coming. He gave the senator a flat stare, refusing to blink, caring less and less if the bullets had been real instead of blanks at the barn. "There's good news and bad news, Senator," Freeman began.

Fagan scowled. "Of course there's bad news. There always is. Okay, feed it to me. The bad news first."

Freeman started, "I've had to call in old favors on this one, Senator, and even burned some bridges along the..."

Fagan interrupted, waving him off with annoyance, "I don't give a rat's ass about what you've called in or burned. There's no time. Just the facts, Freeman."

The Zeta agent shrugged with indifference. "As I was about to say," he continued, "I've had teams out scraping up everything they can about the whereabouts of Braun, Johns, and Morgan. There's a fourth man, a professor from UTD. The word is that he's the one who shot Edison."

"I should give the son-of-a-bitch a medal," Fagan injected. "And? Tell me something I don't know."

"The four were holed up in a FBI safe house last night."

"Shit."

"Exactly. And, they were taken to the feds home office just this morning. They were certain to have been thoroughly debriefed."

"By who, do you think? I wonder if that prick, Pedamore was in on it?"

Freeman shrugged. "If it was me, I'd have used one maybe two of my top interrogators. Depends on what they wanted, what they knew, and the cooperation level of Braun's group. They'd probably go at them soft at first. That would be Pedamore's style. There's no reason why Pedamore wouldn't be there for the debriefing."

"I hate that pompous asshole. You said there was good news. Is it approaching the horizon any time soon?" Fagan spat.

Freeman ignored the vindictiveness in his client's voice. "I've got three teams out there keeping track of things. The reporter and the attorney left the Dallas FBI building separately in their own cars. Braun and the professor left together in Braun's Jeep. Actually, I'm surprised the feds let them out of the nest. That's not standard operating procedure for them. The four are now once again vulnerable. Anyway, they're being tailed by feds, and we're tailing the feds."

"You think that's why the feds cut them loose, so we'd make a move and expose ourselves?

"Of course," said Freeman. "But it nonetheless presents a definite opportunity. Trust me, Senator, we've got this one all worked out. The wheels are turning, and things are already in motion. As you so like to say, shit *will* hit the fan by the end of the day."

Fagan placed both hands on the bar and leaned forward. "Frankly, it sounds like things are getting worse to me. I'm still waiting for the good news, Mr. Freeman. "

Freeman finally broke into a small, reluctant smile. "I've already started execution of a plan that'll get us the photos, eliminate the principals, and clean up the shit-hole you dug for yourself."

"Let's hear it," said Fagan.

Freeman shook his head. "There're some conditions, first. Then there's the matter of the bonuses for my team."

"Of course, of course, there are always conditions and bonuses. You want to sweeten the pot for yourselves, huh?" said the senator with a thin smile. "Fine, Freeman, but if you and your goons don't handle this, and handle it well and soon…then I'll begin making my own arrangements."

"We've all seen what you can do, Senator. That's why we're in this fix. Don't forget, my man was the one that gave us the heads up about the hit on you in the first place, and if it wasn't for me you'd be one dead fucker." Freeman's eyes narrowed. "So, in order for all of us to keep sucking air," Freeman pointed at the senator, "you just do your part, and let me take care of mine."

Shutterbug

Chapter 37

In the garage, an agent stressed the importance of limited travel and minimum exposure. "This isn't over, you know, and, by leaving on your own, you're severely compromising the protection we would normally afford..." The four ignored what sounded like the required, canned warning and got into their three cars.

As they drove through Dallas, the caravan of cars leaving the FBI offices looked more like a presidential procession than a covert protection detail. The agents tailing Joanna took no precautions to remain unseen, and, frankly, that was fine with her. Even though she had put up a vigorous fight to be on her own and not coddled in the FBI offices, knowing that agents were close behind gave her a sense of comfort. Brian and Rockaway had cautioned her just before they all left about being out and about too long, and instructed her to stay in regular contact. Joanna said she would be heading home after a brief stop-off at the paper. Harry said he was going directly home to a shower and bed. Just before boarding their cars, it was decided to meet later as a group. Rockaway joked about meeting again at The Shack, but the suggestion was shot down immediately. For now, their rendezvous time and place would remain up in the air.

Shutterbug

Joanna was concerned about Brian. Ever since they'd left Pedamore, a subtle change had come over him. Something in his eyes, his demeanor. He was edgy. Not nervous. Not scared. Just edgy. It was something she'd never seen in him during the five years she'd known him. More concerning, Brian had said he wasn't going to wait for Fagan, Zeta, or the FBI to make their move. That especially worried her. She knew that professional killers, men trained to track their prey and eliminate them, were out there waiting, stalking them somewhere. She also knew that Brian, the former gentleman thief, was more than capable of taking care of himself. Still, there was a dark side to him that lay just below the surface of his gentleman-thief façade, that she'd never been able to connect with. Even so, she knew it was there. What she didn't know was what it meant, given Brian's statement and edginess.

Her trip to the newspaper proved surreal, even unnerving. Her two assigned agents followed her into the parking garage and waited for her to park. When she climbed out of her Chevy Malibu, the nearer agent exited his car and waited beside her while the other one parked the company car to rejoin them.

"Aren't we taking this a little too far, boys?" She said, exasperated by all the drama.

The older of the two agents stuck out his hand to shake hers. "Ms. Johns, I'm Agent Quach," he said, and then pointed to his partner. "This is Agent Tate." Tate stuck out his hand after she'd finished shaking Quach's. "Our orders are to protect you, at all costs, and that's what we intend to do. We're sorry for the inconvenience, and we'll do our best to stay out of your way and respect your privacy. But…"

"But you're our personal responsibility, Ms. Johns," finished Tate.

Joanna nodded. "Thanks, boys, but I need a little space, okay?"

"A little, ma'am," relied Quach.

"*Very* little, I'm afraid," added Tate.

"This should prove interesting. Okay, let's go, but don't expect high fives from the denizens as we walk through the newsroom," she quipped.

"We don't expect any, ma'am," said Quach.

"None at all, ma'am," said Tate.

When Joanna and her entourage stepped off the elevator, she immediately attempted to put some distance between herself and the agents by weaving her way through the big newsroom. Her pedigree watchdogs followed as if in tow. Heads lifted from desks, the otherwise constant clatter of keyboards hesitated momentarily, and all eyes followed them to the editor's door. Joanna saw Durrett through the glass windows of his office getting up from his desk, grinning to high heaven. *The twirp is actually enjoying this,* she thought. "Stay," she said to the agents, not waiting for Durrett to invite her in.

"Got you on a short leash, do they?" chuckled Durrett. He pointed to a chair. His face abruptly changed from jovial to serious. "Sit."

Joanna did as she was told, and then jerked a thumb over her shoulder in the agents' direction. "You think they'll cramp my style as a reporter?"

"Nothing to cramp for now, Joanna. I told you I wanted you off the grid until it's safer. With you, it took the FBI to do it. I figured they'd keep you in protective custody a couple days. All kidding aside, Jo…I'm glad you're here. The story's got our readers hooked. For now, the suspense will only sell more papers. For now, I'd rather you stay alive long enough to finish it."

Joanna nodded. "I know. Waiting's frustrating." Then she smiled. "But oh-how-good it's going to get. You've no idea what Fagan is up to!"

"Tell me what you can," said Durrett, walking behind his desk and sitting.

"Can't. New rules as of this morning. But I can assure you it'll be worth the wait, which shouldn't be long. For now, my new friends waiting for me outside your door and I are going back to my place. I'm going to clean up and get some of that much-needed rest everyone keeps talking about. I'll meet again with the group later. Safety in numbers."

Durrett frowned. "I can't believe the feds allowed you leave. It's almost like…"

"All four of us insisted," Joanna cut in. "And you know how insistant I can be when I want to."

"I'd rather you hang around here, Joanna. You'd be surrounded by reporters. Too much could go wrong with all you're caught up in out there. You and your 'group' are too close to everything."

Joanna stood and walked over to him. "Sorry, James, this isn't a debate. Don't worry, I'll be safe." She bent over and gave him a tight goodbye hug, then turned to the door.

"Keep in touch," her worried editor said as she exited his office.

"Gentlemen?" she said to Quach and Tate outside the editor's door, "Shall we?" and hooked her arms through those of the agents on either side. This time, she let herself enjoy the attention as the three marched their way back through the newsroom. She even saw a momentary grin crease Quach's face.

On the way home in her car, Joanna received a phone call from Brian. He gave her a new phone number where he could be reached and a new one for Rockaway. He cautioned her that from now on they should all use "burn phones." There was no question in her mind about what that signaled.

Shutterbug

Chapter 38

Brian wanted to put as much distance as possible between him and their tail, no matter how well-intentioned it might be. Brian whipped his Jeep into the Wal-Mart parking lot, taking the first and only empty space available for quite a distance. There wasn't anywhere for the federal boys. When Brian smugly looked back over his shoulder, he saw, however, this wasn't the first dance these boys had been to. One agent jumped out from the passenger side of the agency car while it was passing. The agent was standing, arms folded, waiting by the rear bumper before Brian could kill the engine and get out.

Ignoring their guard, Brian and Rockaway got out and started jogging towards a store at the outer boundaries of the parking lot. The agent at the bumper gave them about a five-yard head start, and then began jogging behind them, while the tail car shot up in front of the store and waited for the three to arrive.

Rockaway glanced over his shoulder and called out to the agent behind them, "What's your name?"

"Zahn," he said between breaths. "Agent Zahn."

"Why don't you join us, Agent Zahn? We don't bite, you know."

Brian glanced back and noticed Zahn scanning the parking lot.

225

He's experienced, without a doubt. Zahn seemed to note every pedestrian, every car, every driver and passenger within their vicinity.

"I'm not sure about the biting part, Mr. Rockaway," said Zahn, keeping his distance. "But I can observe better from back here. I appreciate the offer, though."

"What're you doing, Rock?" Brian whispered. "I want to keep these guys at bay, not make friends with them."

"Ah, so you've decided to talk again. That's the first thing you've said since we left the garage. Something's brewing in that head of yours...I can sense it." The two slowed their pace to allow an automatic door in front of them to slid open. They walked leisurely into the store, Agent Zahn trailing. "And it means trouble. I feel that in my bones. You're in 'old days' mode, my friend."

"Maybe," Brian said. "We need to seize control of the situation before someone starts shooting at us again." Brian pointed to the rear of the store. "Back there, that's where we're going."

In the electronics department, Brian scooped up four T-Mobile pay-as-you-go phones and a compact recorder, paying cash for them. Agent Zahn hung back, observing any customers who came close to his two charges. If Zahn knew what the two were up to, his face never indicated such. At least there'd be no way for anyone, friend or foe, to monitor the phones or figure out who they were talking to. And with the calls Brian needed to make, he didn't want anyone eavesdropping.

"I thought you didn't know anything about those," said Rockaway, pointing at their purchase. "That's what you said when you sent me out from my office on that fool's errand."

"I lied," Brian answered curtly.

Back at the Jeep, Brian tossed the recorder in his camera bag and then peeled two of the phones from their nearly human-proof plastic encasements. "Shit, I need the internet to activate them," he said reading the back of one of the packages. "I've got to return to the store and..."

"Use this," Rockaway said, sliding a hand into the inside pocket of his jacket and handing him his Blackberry. "You can activate them on that."

Brian looked at it, dumbfounded, and then back at Rock.

"What's this?

"What's it look like? It's my Blackberry. Don't you have one?"

"You've been playing me all along, haven't you?" Brian asked with indignation.

"No more than you," he replied matter-of-factly.

Using Rock's Blackberry, Brian activated the phones, giving one to Rock. "That one is yours," he said, handing back the Blackberry at the same time. "And for God's sake, use it rather than your personal cell phone!" Brian immediately called Joanna and gave her the new phone numbers. She was headed to her house, agents in tow.

"Keep them in sight, Joanna. No games, you hear me?"

Brian ended the call and sat for a minute. The sun was shining, bright and clear, but there was a palpable chill in the air. Memories of his time in the barn loft flashed by. He turned on the heater fan, but it didn't take away the chill. He wasn't ready to leave.

"We're going to sit here a bit, Rock; I've got some more calls to make. If that's not okay with you, I can drop you somewhere first?"

"You little turd, you. So now you think you're my babysitter?"

"No, I..."

Rockaway's voice mimicked Brian's, but with the tone of a little, spoiled girl. "No. I don't want you to drop me off." Then, his tone returned to normal. "I want you to pull your head out of your ass and tell me what's going on inside of it. I'm in this up to my eyeballs with you, Brauny. What? You're afraid you're going to hurt my feelings, or I might not approve of your little plan?"

"No, I…"

"You think you're the only one with a plan?"

Brian tried again to get a word in. "No, I..."

"Well, one thing for fucking sure: I'm the only one in the car who killed somebody over Labor Day Weekend." Rock folded his arms across his chest, then looked at Brian with a sly grin. "So is that what you were trying to pry out of me, or were you wanting something different? More whining, maybe? Or that I don't wanna play with you anymore?"

"Just testing," Brian finally got in and laughed. "The fun's about to begin, and people are probably going to get hurt. I had to be sure."

"Fuck you, Brauny." He returned and grinned wider. "Well, we've got a good start on the 'getting hurt' part, so let's just do it."

"Then, you're going to love this next call." Brian punched in a number from memory that only a handful of people were privy to.

"Yes?" The voice at the other end of the line sounded cautious.

"Sensabaugh. How the hell are you?" Brian asked, pleased with the look of surprise on Rock's face when he recognized Brian's old fence's name.

"Well, Brian! Well. And how the hell are you?"

228

"Okay for the moment. Listen, is the pawn shop open? I need some things. I'm going to put you on speaker phone I have a new friend for you."

"Fine. A friend of yours...as the saying goes. Are you back in business again? I thought you were laying low."

Brian hit the speaker button and laid the phone on the console. "Let's just say I'm being forced out of retirement. My new guest is... Mickey. I'd appreciate you extending the same courtesies to him as you do for me."

Rockaway winced at the use of his first name.

"I can and will do that simply on your word. You know that. Now, can I play in this game, too?" Sensabaugh asked.

"You already are, Harvey. I'm on a tight string, so here we go." Brian glanced at Rock, who shook his head in disbelief.

"Go, then."

"Simple things first: I need a dye pack and some roadside flares."

"You've been out of the racket too long, Brian. You can go to Wal-Mart and get them."

"I don't think the two FBI agents on my tail would understand. They might want to start asking questions. Know what I mean?"

"Oh, this is getting more interesting by the minute. Okay, done. What else?"

Brian turned to Rockaway. "You need a gun...Mick?"

He nodded. "Yeah, that'd be nice. For some reason, the feebies didn't return my forty-five."

"That what you want, then?" Brian questioned. "Harvey can get whatever you want."

"A forty-five automatic will be fine, Brauny."

"A forty-five automatic," Brian echoed, "and a Beretta 92FS nine millimeter for me. And extra clips."

Rock's eyebrows rose in surprise.

"Hm-m-m. Stepping out are you? Okay, what else?" Sensabaugh asked, as though Brian was asking him to get milk and bread from the nearest grocery store.

"A fast car. And a discreet secondary."

"That sounds fun. Anything in particular?"

"A Dodge Challenger would be nice for the primary. You pick the secondary."

"Okay. You should enjoy that. A particularly fast one I presume. With current plates. Racing stripes?"

"Yeah, why not?"

"When do you need all this, Brian."

"Two hours."

"Usual parking garage?"

"Yeah."

"You want valet parking?"

"Yes. And five grand in cash, a new ID, and insurance papers on the secondary." Brian added as an afterthought. "I may have some pay-offs to make."

"Got it. Under what name? Something catchy?"

Brian thought a second. "Eddy Ross. I've used it before."

"Boy, that was a wild time. Remember? "

Brian ignored him. "I also need a nice black velvet or leather container, like a new watch box or something. It has to be big enough to hold the dye pack. Tight. Something nice."

"My, you are planning to have some fun. You sure I can't play a little more in this one? Like in the Seattle job."

Brian laughed, avoiding an answer. "That was a good one, wasn't it?"

"I haven't needed to work since. Now I only work when I want to. These days I play around at the shop, you know, to make it all look legit," Sensabaugh said.

Brian wanted to give his former accomplice at least a partial heads up on what he had planned for the man's own protection. "I may need some more help down the road, but listen, Harv, you need to make sure you're completely clean on this. This one goes very high up, my friend."

"You know me, Brian. Clean as a whistle," Sensabaugh confirmed, adding, "How high?"

"You know about the shooting at The Shack yesterday?"

"Yeah, that was some nasty business, but Edison was a prick. No hurt feelings from anyone I've talked to about it. That what this is about? You gonna need a safe place?"

"Maybe later. I just wanted you to know it's nasty business, and the fingerprints on this go all the way up to D. C., my friend."

Sensabaugh whistled. "This is more than monetary then, isn't it?"

"Money has nothing to do with it."

"Okay. Two hours. Nice to meet you , Mickey," said the voice. The line died with a click.

Rockaway stared at the phone on the console, and then turned toward Brian. "Why is it I now have the feeling you're more than a former jewel thief, Brauny?"

"You really want to know, Rock?"

Rockaway refolded his arms across his chest and stared out through the front windshield. "I'd like to go beyond some of the mystery, voodoo shit for once. Past and present."

Brian stared out through the same windshield, probably looking in the distance at the same blank space. It was time to lay the truth out for his old friend. Some of it, anyway. He deserved it.

"So, what do you want to know?"

"Seattle? What's so fucking great about Seattle, other than it's a great place for ducks?"

"I figured that'd be your first question. Let me ask you this, Rock. Who's easily the number one employer in Seattle?"

Rockaway slowly shook his head. "Should've known better. Answering questions with questions. Fine," he said. "Let's play Trivial Pursuit: I'd say—Microsoft. Bill Gates."

"I ripped them off."

"Ripped them off?"

"Let's just say they had something that a competitor coveted."

"Coveted. Nice word. Are we talking about a bite from the original *apple*?"

Brian smiled. "Nicely put. Sensabaugh was the middle man, before you ask."

Rock frowned. "Then, why risk everything on a bunch of second-rate burglaries in Highland Park? That's idiotic…"

Brian shrugged. "The thrill, Rock. Old habits are hard to break. Keeps me tuned up for the bigger jobs. It's hard to explain. You ever want to go back into the fire, Rock? Get back in the middle of a good juicy civil war instead of teaching deadheads how to take a picture?"

"Sometimes," he mused.

"One of my competitors was jealous about the Microsoft heist and was getting ready to squeal on me. Probably could have made it stick with the D. A., too. That's when Harv and I put our heads together. He wants to retire while he can still enjoy the fruits of his labors.

"He was careful to give them just enough to be 'useful' but never enough to hang anything on me. He gets 'burned' and out of the fencing business. Nobody'd touch him with a ten-foot pole after that, except his highest-end clients."

Brian thought back to those days. "I get out with just enough name recognition to make a straight living, and a little notoriety to help things along. I stay clean for a few years working on a coffee table book, and eventually disappear into obscurity on an island somewhere."

Rock laughed. "Shit, this is better than cable. Who'd a thought?"

"What about Joanna? She in on it? The Highland Park stuff? She sure went to bat for you."

"Nah, but I used her at the time. Fed her enough tidbits to turn the tables against the D. A. The feelings between us developed naturally. Best thing that came out of the whole deal, really."

Silence filled the Jeep.

"Can I come?" Rock finally asked. "To the island?"

"If you bring your own date."

He smiled. "At least I can do that without going to jail, Brauny. Okay, here's another question: Where's my fucking Road Runner?"

This one made Brian smile. "It's safe. It's the safest thing in this whole mess. Louise has it. That's why I panicked when you asked for the keys back in front of Pedamore's."

"Louise? What the hell is she doing with it? You don't think she'd let that psycho, Sam, drive it do you?" His tone was one of genuine worry.

"I doubt it. I slipped her the keys when we were being herded outside by Edison and Cowboy. I didn't say anything. Didn't have to. She understood."

"And your reasoning behind that stroke of genius?"

Brian shrugged. "I don't know about the genius part. It was just a reaction. The same spur of the moment, knee-jerk reaction I had when I also handed her the memory card from my camera."

Brian paused. Then, he watched his friend erupt like an overdue volcano. It was the first time he'd ever seen Rockaway belly-laugh. The laugh developed into a smoker's cough. Next, came the rubbing of his watery eyes. Then, finally, the slow painful process of bringing it all together. Brian enjoyed every minute of it. He was just hoping Rockaway didn't have a coronary in the process.

Rockaway gave one last guttural, nasal snort. "You're a real piece of work, Braun. That was fucking genius. It'd take a whole Marine division to pry the card from her. Absolute genius."

Brian shrugged again. "What can I say?"

"Let her keep it, is my suggestion. Fagan, Zeta, the FBI. They're all going crazy looking for that thing, and here it is in the possession of a barmaid."

"I've no intention of getting it, at least for now. Are we done with the Twenty Questions, yet? We've got things to do."

"One more," he said. "So what's with dye packets, road flares and fast cars?"

Brian turned to face his old mentor and shook his finger at him. "Ah, now. That, my friend, you'll have to wait to find out."

Shutterbug

Chapter 39

Harry parked his Mercedes in the secured underground garage of his high rise condo located on Turtle Creek. Like Joanna, he didn't mind the two watchdogs on his tail. His battleground was the courtroom, not the streets. He wasn't Brian, who was well versed and blessed with natural survival instincts, or Rockaway, who'd spent the better part of his adulthood in firefights in what seemed like every hellhole conceivable. Harry's world was one of Italian suits and silk ties, not black zip-suits and rubber sneakers, or camouflage and combat books. In the last twenty-four hours, he'd had a gun poked in his ribs, his face rubbed into an asphalt parking lot, and cringed while hundreds of bullets streaked over his head like a West Texas hail storm. Hell, he'd let the agents get in the shower with him if they guaranteed his safety. Of course in public, he tried to evoke bravado, shout down the federal oppression of the masses, blah, blah, blah. He had the rhetoric down. For now, though, what he wanted more than anything else was a proverbial dry martini, shaken, not stirred, a shower, and ten hours of unbroken sleep. Then he'd be ready to, once again, conquer the world on the flip side.

One agent greeted Harry while still exiting the car; the other drove off to park the agency car under the covered driveway leading to the front entrance. "We haven't met," Harry said, holding out his hand, "I'm Morgan. Harry Morgan."

"Agent Smith," returned the young agent. "Nice to meet you, Mr. Morgan. Nice place," he added, looking around a garage that was nothing less than bright, clean and *haute couture. I could live comfortably in such a garage if I were so lucky,* Smith thought to himself.

"Hell, if you're impressed with this, you should see my living quarters," Harry joked. "This way, Agent Smith. We'll take the elevator up to the lobby."

The second agent was waiting for them next to the lobby elevator. "If he's Agent Smith then you must be Agent Jones," said Harry, noting the waiting man's telltale dark suit and sunglasses.

"Yes sir," said the waiting agent.

"Really?" Harry said, surprised. "I said it as a joke. You know, Smith and Jones? Butch and Sundance?"

"Gee, Mr. Morgan, neither of us ever heard *that* one before. That's so original," Jones deadpanned.

Harry laughed and lightly slapped the agent on his upper arm. "A fed with a dry sense of humor. I like it. I like it, Agent Jones. Or are you, Smith?" Harry motioned for the two to follow him into the opening elevator.

"We'll remain here, Mr. Morgan," answered Jones. "A team checked out your premises ahead of time."

"I need to get upstairs and rest in peace awhile."

Smith nodded, completely understanding that sentiment, and

handed Harry a cell phone.

"Take this with you and keep it at hand at all times."

Harry took the phone.

"Just press this button," the agent said pointing, "and it's a direct connect to us. Got it?"

"Got it," Harry said with a lazy half-salute. "So I'll see you boys in about twelve hours," as the elevator doors closed about him.

Stepping at last into his own apartment, fatigue engulfed Harry's mind and body like a Saharan dust storm, and he decided to forego the martini. Until after the shower. He dropped the emergency phone given to him by the agent on the nightstand next to his bed, and left a path of discarded clothes behind him on the way to the master bathroom. In the shower, he let the hot water, as hot as he could stand, mercilessly pummel his aching body.

After standing like a statue in the biting shower for several minutes, he felt the built-up fear and terror from yesterday's shooting begin to burst through his skin as if through a puncture wound. His body shook as though engulfed by a freezing winter chill, and his mind started replaying the ordeal over and over. He'd just finished deciding to stay locked in his apartment until the whole terrifying debacle was done, when he remembered the Fab Four agreeing to get back together later in the afternoon; holding tightly onto that thought, his neck and shoulders began to relax.

Harry stepped out of the shower, grabbed a towel and partially dried off. He left the bathroom, towel in hand, and upon entering the master bedroom, stopped in mid-stride on the deep-piled carpet, feeling the fibers between his toes. He felt alive, and was about to burst into song, when the damp towel dropped soundlessly from his hand. Before him stood an expressionless man in his mid-20's. His skin was light olive, his hair jet black, gelled straight back. He was dressed in a black pin-striped suit, a heavily starched white shirt, and a bright yellow tie with a diamond stick pin piercing it's center. *Funny the details one notices when he's about to die*, Harry wanted to say but could only think.

The stranger, standing less than ten feet away, was pointing a silenced revolver at Harry's chest.

Harry's mind continued rolling like a silent movie, and he thought about how embarrassing it was going to be to be found by Smith and Jones laying stark naked on his own blood-stained carpet. Tomorrow's headlines flashed in his head: PROMINENT ATTORNEY FOUND NAKED, SHOT DEAD. "Can I at least put my pants on?" Harry finally said, in a voice stronger than he anticipated.

"No." The stranger's voice was direct, cold, and calculating.

Harry heard a soft puff, felt a sliver of hot metal rip through his flesh and fell, as he imagined, face first to the floor. Just before he slipped into unconsciousness, he thought about his three best friends and hoped they wouldn't meet the same end.

Chapter 40

Duvall watched a silver Toyota Camry pull out from the FBI building. *Now, who would tail the FBI while they were tailing the reporter?* He'd spotted the tail-on-tail immediately after the caravan left. In fact, *two* cars appeared to be running the box: a white Ford Fiesta *and* the Camry. Whoever was driving knew what they were doing—the feds could spot anything less than a perfect tail job from a mile away. Duvall, for his part, inched out well behind the group, choosing to follow the Camry when the group split. Pulling to the curb a block behind the Camry when the car pulled up a block from the *Dallas Morning News* offices, Duvall settled for another wait.

Twenty minutes later the Camry took off following a car following the reporter, the scattered line motoring down Interstate-30, leaving Dallas for Garland, and left the freeway a mile from Lake Ray Hubbard, with Duvall once again carefully following. That was the easy part. Once everyone exited the interstate, the road changed to double-lane residential, winding through a quiet suburb, then crossing the bridge over the lake and into Rowlett, a town that fifty-years-ago had a population of five hundred and one stop sign. Now, it hosted fifty thousand and a fast food restaurant at every intersection.

Despite the distance, Duvall noticed Johns turn into a driveway, and the FBI's Crown Vic pull to the curb across the street before he turned off her street. The Camry tailing the feds had left the scene as soon as the driver ascertained Johns' destination. From the modest rise where he had stopped, Duvall watched the Camry continue a half block further, then coast into the alley behind the reporter's house. He was about to follow, when he noticed a nondescript white van parked tight up against the reporter's six-foot wooden alley fence, half on the easement, half in the alley. This wasn't good.

Joanna pulled into her double-car garage, got out, and walked out into the front yard to pick up the newspapers that'd been neglected for the past two days. While bending over, she waved to the agents. "You coming in?"

The window on the driver's side rolled down. "The house was checked out before we arrived, Miss Johns. A K-9 unit was on their way here as an extra precaution, but was called away on an emergency at the last minute. We were about to recheck the house until my partner, Agent Tate, mentioned you might enjoy a few minutes of privacy before we invade your house," answered Agent Quach as Joanna approached their car.

She stopped beside the driver's door and frowned, but gave the agent a slight grin. "Don't you need a warrant for that kind of thing?"

"No, ma'am, a warrant's only necessary for evidence or an arrest. We need your consent, however. We can accompany you, if you want us to recheck everything," said Quach with a smile. "Otherwise, we'll wait here for your signal."

"Did the agency folks who checked out my house clean it up

while they were at it? I'm sure it was a mess."

Quach smiled again. "I wouldn't count on it."

"Well, you're welcome to come in after I've freshened up." Joanna went back through the garage, hit the closer, and waited for the door to shut down completely before entering the house. She looked forward to soaking in a hot bubble bath, letting the heat soften the knots in her aching muscles and the bubbles reinvigorate her mind.

Using her house key, she unlocked the door from the garage into the utility room, let herself in and flipped on the lights. She kicked off her shoes and walked barefoot one step into the kitchen, where, from behind, a strong arm wrapped around her chest, a large hand holding a damp cloth clamped over her nose and mouth, and she was jerked backwards. In her panic, she inhaled deeply. It was then that she noticed the sweet smell of chloroform, her last thought before total blackness closed in around her.

Shutterbug

Chapter 41

Parking his Taurus behind a trash dumpster in the reporter's alley, Duvall had just the right combination of cover and visibility he needed to keep an eye on the silver Camry, and especially the white van. His instincts told him something dangerous was afoot. The reporter who lived here had been involved in a high profile shooting, held by the FBI, released, and now had a van and car parked inconspicuously along her back fence gate—highly suspicious. Once again he watched and waited.

He'd already had to ditch his original plan, and several subsequent ones, because of unexpected events like this. His intention was to use Johns's profession as a reporter to his advantage. She was the conduit to the completion and success of his overall mission to get revenge against his adversaries. He wanted no tell-tale evidence left behind of his involvement. An alternate plan was already coming to light in his head. It was time to choose whether to cross the bridge or burn it. Duvall chose to burn this one.

With the windows of his car rolled down, and his close proximity to the back of Johns' house, Duvall easily heard a sliding glass door opening to his right. It was showtime.

He removed the keys from the ignition, then stealthily opened the driver's side door, closing it just enough so it didn't latch, then he crouched next to the fence. Looking through the cracks of the aging planks, he saw a tall, well-built man in his mid-thirties, dressed in black with what he assumed was Joanna Johns' body slung slack over his left shoulder like a sack of potatoes.

She wasn't struggling, so she had to be out. He didn't see any blood, so he assumed she wasn't dead. Duvall moved up close behind the dumpster and peered between it and the fence, watching the man easily drop Johns' body into the van. The kidnapper appeared to be in no hurry as he crossed in front of the van making his way to the driver's side.

Duvall dug into his jacket pocket and fingered the leather slapper —what used to be called a "blackjack"—and poised, ready to take advantage of the right moment when it presented. The time to move was the second the driver got into the van, with his attention on inserting the car key, just before he closed the door. Duvall bolted abruptly forward, narrowing the space between himself and pulling the weapon from his jacket. Seeing Duvall suddenly appear next to him, the driver froze, a look of total surprise painted across his eyes, his mouth open as if wanting to say something. Duvall didn't wait. He slammed the slapper upside the driver's temple. The man in black collapsed like a deflated balloon, his upper body falling sideways across the console and onto the empty passenger seat.

Duvall left the passenger door open, raced around between the van and the fence, and slid the side door open. As he leaned into the van to check on Johns, he caught a whiff of the sweet fumes of chloroform.

Her breathing was regular and pulse strong.

This wouldn't be the optimal time for the fed watchdogs out front to get curious and do their job, Duvall thought. Leaving the door open, he ran back to his car and squealed back out the alley, turning left onto street and left again to drive in the opposite direction of Johns's house and the FBI.

While driving, Duvall unclipped the secondary Elite Security cell phone from his belt and dialed Hatfield's number.

When the call came, Hatfield was walking across the parking lot thinking that he'd just been played by one of the best. He flipped it open and read the name on the screen: *Duvall!*

"Michael?" the voice on the other end half-asked, half-stated.

"William?" Hatfield replied, returning Duvall's familiarity.

Duvall didn't rush; he wanted to make sure Hatfield got every word. He pulled up to a parking space in front of the South Garland Mail Depot just off Broadway, and stayed in the car while speaking to his former associate. "I don't have time for pleasantries, Hat, so listen closely and don't interrupt. Somebody just tried to kidnap the woman reporter, and I was able to interrupt. Contact your boys—at least I assume they're your boys—waiting out front of her house. Tell them to get off their asses in gear, and check the white van in the alley behind her house. She's been anesthetized, but looked okay. The kidnapper's taking a nap in the front seat, and will probably wake up tomorrow with a big knot upside his head. There's also two knuckle-heads sitting in a silver Camry at the end of the alley. They followed your boys to the reporter's place. Those two, and something that should reach you in the mail at your federal address are two gifts from me to you. When you get the mail, I ask that you forget all about me. After this job's over, I'm wanting to disappear. Completely. For good. Oh, and I threw in a bonus: a complete background resume and dossier on your friend Hasan Eldawoody. It's been good working with you, Agent Hatfield," he said, hesitating just long enough to let the "agent" moniker sink in, then said, "and thanks for not shooting me back at The Shack." With that, Duvall abruptly hung up.

Hatfield didn't know the names of the agents who had been assigned to Joanna Johns, but he knew the the name of agent in charge of the tailings. He punched in Charlie Logsdon's cell number.

Charlie picked up immediately, but Hatfield didn't waste time on greetings: "Your boys are asleep at the wheel at Joanna Johns's place, Charlie. I just got a tip that there was an attempted kidnapping. Have them check the alley behind her house. Now!"

"Shit!" Agent Logsdon growled. "How'd…"

"Doesn't matter. I trust the source. Call your men on Johns'. And who's on Morgan, the attorney?"

"Smith and Jones. I'll call them as soon as…"

"I've got Smith's number. You call Johns' agents. Keep in touch," Hatfield said, hanging up and scrolling through his zip-list for Agent Smith's number.

Smith also picked up immediately. "John, this is Hat. Michael Hatfield. Do you have a visual on Morgan?" Hatfield asked, his urgency clear in his voice.

Agent Smith picked up on Hatfield's tone. "No," Smith answered."Jones and I are in the lobby. He's upstairs sleeping. Why?"

"Someone attempted to kidnap the Johns girl. Whoever it is

behind the kidnapping may be trying for a triple play. Why don't you send Jones up and you continue to cover the lobby. Who's on Braun and Rockaway?"

"Zahn and Womack."

"You got their numbers, John?" Hatfield asked, talking faster with each second that went by. "I don't."

"Yeah, of course," Smith answered, "I'll send up Jones and call Zahn. What's your twenty?"

"I'm going your way until I hear otherwise. Call me," Hatfield said and snapped the cell phone shut.

Shutterbug

Chapter 42

"Let's have some fun, Rock," Brian said, starting the Jeep and buckling his seatbelt. Rockaway nodded and buckled his. Brian was backing out from their parking spot, when, out of the blue, their tail screeched to halt directly behind them.

"What the hell!" Brian yelled, slamming on the brakes.

Zahn and Womack jumped from their car, sprinting to either side of the jeep. Agent Zahn tapped on the driver's window, motioning for Brian to roll down window. Brian complied. The agent on the other side of the car pressed against Rockaway's window and door, but made no effort to communicate. His head was swiveling slowly back and forth, scanning the parking lot. It seemed as though he was using his body to shield Rockaway.

"What's going..." Brian began.

Agent Zahn cut him off. "Mr. Braun, Mr. Rockaway…you need to come with us. Now." His tone was way serious. "There's been…"

"As I said before, that's not gonna happen…" Brian started to fire back.

Zahn, however, paid no attention to what Brian was saying. Instead, his hand pulled back the right side of his jacket, and he rested it's heel on the butt of a holstered gun. He, too, was actively scanning the parking lot.

"Something's up," Brian said to Rockaway.

"No shit," Rocky replied.

Agent Zahn hit Brian's door with the force of his body this time, commanding Brian's attention. "Listen, Braun, I'm not fucking with you. There was an attempted kidnapping on Ms. Johns and Mr. Morgan's been shot. It looks like a coordinated effort at trying to take all of you out. Our asses are exposed out here in the open while you're play Mr. Tough. Get the fuck out of the car! Both of you! This instant!"

Brian and Rock grabbed their things and started moving towards the doors.

"Harry? Shot?" Brian said, stunned. "Is he dead?"

"No," Zahn answered curtly, grabbing Brian by the elbow, and shoving him towards the company car. Brian watched the other agent do the same to Rockaway, all the while continuing to shield him with his body. "Inside, first. I'll answer your questions when we're out of here." Zahn wasted no time getting out of the parking lot and onto the freeway.

Brian, ruffled and still in shock, was sitting up front with Zahn. Rock and his new "friend" were in the back. Both Brian and Rock opened their mouths to speak.

"How's Joanna?" Brian asked first.

"What do you mean she was kidnapped?" Rockaway followed.

The agent sitting next to Rockaway answered this time. "I'm Agent Womack, by the way. She's okay. She was dragged out of her house and into a van. She's at Lake Pointe Hospital. Evidently, she was chloroformed. An unknown stepped in and saved her."

"An 'unknown'? What the hell does that mean? Who saved her and where were *your* guys during all this?" Brian snapped.

"Out front, I think. Somebody was waiting for her inside. The agency checked the house before she got there and hadn't found anything untoward. Don't know any other details, yet. Don't know who saved her, either."

Brian cut immediately to his next question, dreading it. "Was she, uh…"

"No," answered Zahn immediately. "She wasn't molested, Mr. Braun. That much I do know. They'll be observing her awhile. She'll have a bad headache from the chloroform for a few hours."

"Ya'll don't seem to know much, do you?" Rockaway taunted from the back.

"You're unfortunately right, Mr. Rockaway," answered Womack with attitude. "You're sudden decision to split up left us at a distinct disadvantage. I got a call from the Special Agent in Charge as you and your friend here were once again preparing to break away, instructing us to get you back to headquarters, and that's exactly what we're doing."

"Where's Harry?" Brian asked.

"They took him to Medical City. He's in surgery," said Zahn.

"Then, that's where we're going," Brian commanded. "I know the way if you don't, Agent Zahn."

Zahn shook his head. "No way. We've got orders to take you in, and that's where we're going."

Brian turned to face Rock, who was already digging out his phone and the business card they'd each received before leaving Dallas FBI. "I've already got it, honey" Rockaway said, winking like Louise, as he punched in the numbers on the card and waited. "John Lee? Rockaway here." Rockaway stopped to listen to the other end. "Thank you, John Lee, for protecting us, but I need for you to instruct Agent Zahn here to take us to Medical City so we can be with Harry. We can, of course, find a way to get there, the hard way, if that's what you want."

Zahn looked in his rearview mirror at Rockaway.

"Appreciate that John Lee." Rockaway said, presenting the cell phone to Zahn. "This is what you get for calling me Mickey," Rockaway laughed. When Zahn didn't reach for it immediately, Rockaway continued. "It's for you. John Lee would like to talk to you."

Zahn took the phone, grim faced. "Yes sir?" he asked, a moment later answering, "Will do." He returned the phone to Rockaway. "Okay, Mickey. Medical City it is. He's going to meet us there."

The four rode to the hospital in silence, each lost in his own thoughts and concerns.

Chapter 43

Mark Freeman, acting chief of operations for Zeta Corporation at Senator Fagan's, assigned two of his best, Luis Diaz and Larry Little, to tail Braun and Rockaway. The two took separate vehicles, reasoning that it would be easier to tail their targets in tandem than as one. And, by regularly handing off the lead, there would be less chance of getting spotted by the targets or their federal tails. When Diaz saw Braun and the old hippie getting whisked away in the Crown Vic, leaving the Jeep behind, he knew something was up. *Shit. What now?*

Diaz u-turned the Buick, left the Wal-Mart parking lot, and fell in three cars behind the feds and their new passengers. Diaz checked his rearview mirror. Good. His partner was about to pass him and take the lead. Luis was about to decelerate and report to Freeman when his cell rang. It was Little.

"Just heard from the Chief," Larry said, "I told him we were on the move again."

"Good. You've saved me the call," Luis said. "Any idea on what's going on?"

"There's trouble," stated Little.

"Trouble? What kind of trouble are you talking about?"

"Well first, Morgan's still alive. That pussy, Carlo, shot the him in the chest instead of the head. He's in surgery," Little said, passing Diaz.

"What're you talking about? You mean that already went down? I thought that was scheduled for later tonight?

"Yup."

"Shit," Diaz cursed. "Well, that's another wop who can kiss his ass good-bye. Freeman'll have him eliminated before sundown for that fuck-up."

"There's more, and it get's worse."

"Everything seems to get fucking worse with this operation. What is it now?" Diaz asked.

"The kidnapping went south. Some fuckin' Samaritan came to her rescue. Hopper's in federal hands now."

Diaz was stunned. "What do you mean, kidnapping? The plan wasn't to fuckin' kidnap anyone. Junior was supposed to pop her in the head the way Carlo was supposed to do the lawyer. What's this about a fuckin' kidnapping?"

"Don't know," answered Little. "Another last minute change in plans, I guess."

"It's gotta be that fuckin' Freeman! You don't change plans without tellin' everyone! This whole thing's haywire, Larry, and I'm betting it's Freeman, overthinking everything again. He's always doin' that. Hell, I'm bailin' this motherfucker. This ship makes the Titanic look like the safest thing afloat."

"That's what Freeman said."

"Yeah, funny. Later," Diaz said cutting the line, immediately speed-dialing another number.

Chapter 44

Pedamore hadn't left the headquarters facility the entire weekend, and the pressure was wearing on him. Now, with the attacks on Morgan and Johns, the ante went up, and the need to bring this case to a close sooner than later was eminent. The repercussions he'd more than likely face from his decisions today could make him a civilian before the next weekend. In fact, the immediacy and viciousness of the attacks caught him by surprise. Everything was supposed to be settled, at least for the night. Somebody on the other side had clearly moved up his schedule.

Cutting loose the Fab Four had been a risk. When they'd insisted on going it on their own and in separate ways, he decided to offer them up as bait. He'd been careless, and now realized that he should have put more agents on, and more effort into each detail. He should've assigned a backup detachment immediately.

*Shoulda, shoulda, shoulda...*In the end, he felt for the four, but had no regrets. Complying with their "demands" justified the end results.

Joanna's kidnapper and the two thugs from the Camrey resisted their interrogators about thirty minutes, then cracked like a ripe walnut, and what the kidnapper had told them rocked his FBI interrogators to the core. The web, like a lethal cancer, had spread and was continuing to do so but at an ever accelerating pace. Pedamore would be required to stretch the limits of FBI protocol and ethics even more. Fagan, according to the kidnapper, was in an insane panic. Pedamore picked up the desk phone and punched in Hatfield's number.

"Yes, sir," Hat answered.

"Any luck?"

"The post office agreed to contact me as soon they got possession of the letters Braun mailed to Morgan and Johns. They were more than happy to cooperate."

"What about The Shack? Any luck with that Louise character?"

"She was cooperative. To a point. She gave me a pretty detailed synopsis of what happened inside, at least from her perspective. Rogers' first name is Gib, which I assume means Gibson. I'm having the Bureau run it down now. Louise's story fits with what the Fab Four told us this morning, but she's holding back something. Can't put my finger on it, but if we have any manpower left, I think we should put somebody on her. Just in case she makes a move."

Pedamore squinted his eyes and pinched the bridge of his nose. "Yeah, yeah, we can do that. But not now. Jail Bird called and, given the Morgan and Johns fiascos, we may need to start taking some drastic measures. We have to watch this carefully; things are beginning to spin out of control on all sides. Come back to the office. I want to chew over an alternative scenario with you. See what you think."

"On my way," Hatfield said, cutting the line.

Pedamore, however, didn't put his phone away. Instead, he immediately punched in some more numbers.

"Agent Quach?"

"Yes sir."

"How's the girl?"

"She's fine, sir. A bit groggy, a headache, and mad as hell. She's a spitfire, sir. We're taking her to Medical City now."

"Don't tell her anything. I'm about to make her even more pissed-off."

"Yes sir."

Pedamore cut the line to call a third person's personal cell phone. Pedamore waited several rings for him to pick up, then, "Chief Fouts? Are we having fun yet?"

Dallas Police Chief Randy Fouts chuckled, "Always, John Lee. And two conversations in the same day: Somebody must have you by the short-hairs."

Pedamore returned the laugh. "Damn near. You ready to turn the Bulldog loose?"

There was a brief hesitation at the other end then another chuckle. "We talking cooperation across federal and blue lines here, John Lee? You must really be in a pickle. I'm ready, he's ready, and I think I'm going to enjoy this. But..."

Pedamore grinned. "Always happy to make your day, Chief. But, what?"

"You know Lt. Megs isn't exactly the cooperative type. He pretty much does things his own way to get the results he wants."

"I know, that's why I want him in this. I'll give him a long leash, but when it's time to reel him in, it'll have to be immediate, Randy. No bullshit. No hot-dogging, either, or, I'll have to take him down, too."

Shutterbug

"My, my," crooned Fouts, "so what's going down, John Lee?"

So long reason, hello, rhyme. "Got a few minutes?"

Chapter 45

The L-shaped waiting room at Medical City Hospital had the usual amenities: a television posted hight up in one corner where no one could change the channel from CNN, and of course, a remote that was nowhere to be found. Neither were the ready-made coffee packets for the Mr. Coffee Maker, its fried, black flakes crusted on the bottom of the warm glass pot. The room had the look of a black suit and blacker ops convention, having been cleared of everyone that wasn't connected with the Fagan/Elite/Zeta/Fab Four case. Families and visitors, who were waiting on the news of their own loved ones in surgery or recovery, weren't too happy about being escorted out; however, the show of badges and grim, official looks stifled any potential complains. In the end, the civilians were happy to leave what appeared to be the beginnings of a national security event control center. And no one wanted to be anywhere near all the guns.

Zahn and Womack were joined by Harry's protective unit, Agents Smith and Jones. Pedamore, with Hatfield and Logsdon in tow, was informing Brian and Rockaway that Joanna and her unit, Agents Quach and Tate, were en-route. The word was, Joanna was more pissed-off than hurt or scared, and was audibly declaring that somebody's—

meaning Pedamore's—balls were on the chopping block.

After the quick update, Rockaway and Brian huddled quietly into a corner to wait. Everywhere else there were whisperings, finger-pointing, nodding, and shaking of heads. The authorities well-planned strategies had been blown out of the water by forces both known and unknown, and they appeared to Brian be in CYA—"cover your ass"—mode. Rockaway and Brian weren't privy to their conversations, but it didn't take much imagination to guess how embarrassing the situation must be for the FBI in general, and Pedamore in particular.

Brian checked his watch. They were scheduled to meet Sensabaugh in an hour, but he already knew that wasn't going to happen. No way was John Lee going to let him out of sight this time.

Harry, he reminded himself, was his and Rockaways immediate concern. Brian began asking white clad passersby of Harry's condition, but no one seemed certain of anything, good or bad. When he and Rockaway had first entered the room, a head nurse on duty brusquely informed them that all she was allowed to say at the time was that Harry'd been shot in the chest, lost a lot of blood, and was still in surgery. His chances? Fifty-fifty.

Swept up in the information vacuum, Brian shifted priorities. If he and Rockaway couldn't find out about Harry, then it was time to get in touch with Sensabaugh to let him know about the change in plans. Brian hadn't worked out the details of "Plan A" and was, but that shouldn't stop him from contacting Harv Sensabaugh and here he was texting his old fence the letter "B." Harv would know that "B" was Plan B, whatever that was, and know to hold back on the meeting until he heard further from him.

Rockaway tipped his head at the phone. "I don't get the fascination with that texting stuff. Why not just pick up the phone and talk, the old fashioned way?"

Brian didn't need to answer. Both could see Hatfield leaning against the opposite wall, staring at them.

Pedamore, noting Hat's stare, broke off conversing, and walked up beside Rockaway and Brian. He stopped and pointed to three empty chairs across from the elevators. "Let's go over there. We need to talk," and slumped into the one in the middle. "It's like this: We fucked up," he started, "and I can't think of a better way to put it. It was a bad decision on my part to let you go. I should have made you stay."

"'Fucked up' *is* a good way to put it," Brian agreed, "but if you remember, it was our condition to cooperate with you."

Pedamore dropped his eyes to his feet, waited a few seconds, then started back at Brian. "We had two separate teams sweep Miss Johns' place, and Harry's, too, before either arrived home. Harry's place was clean when they left. Turns out there was a vacant condo across the hall from Harry's. The shooter broke in. It took awhile, but one of my agents found traces of both doors having been jimmied. It was a professional job, though the fact that they left any traces at all suggests they were in a hurry."

That bothered Brian in several ways. Scared professionals didn't bode well. And what about what happened to Harry and Joanna? "Is that all this is about for you, Pedamore? Professional admiration and critique of wet work?"

Brian's words hit home. Pedamore straightened in his chair; he was talking much faster now. "Whoa! You took me wrong, Brian. What

I'm saying is, if Zeta is behind this—and that's what we suspect—they're employing their best: ex-Seals, Green Berets, Delta, Rangers, Marines, you name it. But these are so good at what they're doing, I have to assume they've been selected and further trained by Zeta itself. An elite assassination squad. If you want to get clinical, it was a well-executed, but surprisingly sloppy hit job. Why leave any signs of forced entry on the empty condo door when a third-rate burglar could have picked the locks? And Harry made it easy for them, as far as his own place was concerned. He didn't even set his alarm."

"Okay, go on," Brian said, not ready to argue the points with the man. He'd wanted to pique Pedamore just enough that the man would, in his anger, give away some more information.

"The assassin could've shot Harry in the head," Pedamore continued dryly, "and added a typical cleanup shot for good measure. But he didn't. Why would an elite professional, who knows better, not do the job right?"

"Maybe the guy was incompetent," tossed Brian, realizing more information was unlikely. "Zeta and Fagan are hooked at the hip. Maybe it was another entity?"

Pedamore hesitated. "There's no evidence of that. Yet. But that doesn't mean there's not another entity out there gunning for you four, or, at the least Harry Morgan and Joanna Johns."

Brian eyed him, then carefully changed direction, "Anything else on the break-in?"

Pedamore shrugged. "All the killer had to do was wait for Harry to return, break-in to his place and take the shot. Evidently Harry was taking a shower. That puzzles me a bit. He certainly would have heard the killer if he hadn't been taking a shower at just that moment."

"And I wonder why Harry didn't set his alarm?" added Brian.

Another shrug. "You'll have to ask Harry. Must not have thought he needed it. And how did the shooter make his getaway? The only person Smith and Jones spotted leaving the elevators after Harry went up was a tall, dark hispanic. Well-dressed. Otherwise nondescript. They questioned the front desk personnel, but the staff was unable to distinguish between him and the other hundred or so well-to-do hispanic tenants.

"Why didn't you send an agent up with him?"

"We didn't, so what does it matter? I'm not here to make excuses. Just to tell you what we know."

What you want me to know, Brian interjected in thought. "And Joanna's place?"

Pedamore's explanation continued in the same short, clipped sentences and flat, emotionless tone. "That was even more embarrassing, I'm afraid. The attic. After it was over, my agents nearly tripped over the draw-down ladder as they invesitaged the crime scene. The kidnapper slipped into the house, hid in the attic while my men made the first search, then descended the ladder and waited for his victim in the kitchen shadows near the garage-to-kitchen door. If the K-9's hadn't been called away, we would have nailed him. It was, again, clever but sloppy work.Somebody on our end is clearly going to fry for the K-9 blunder."

Brian continued to goad him. "And that someone is you?"

"Probably," Pedamore returned without humor. "The kidnapper was up there the whole time while my guys were checking out the place. The killer apparently knew about the first search team. Somebody could have been shot."

"Yeah, in the foot."

Pedamore ignored Brian's comeback. "She doesn't have an alarm system, so it was easy for a pro to get in. Easy to note her arrival home with a visual through the vents or upon hearing the automatic garage door opening. She parked her car inside, then went out to the front and picked up her newspapers in the yard. She even invited Quach and Tate to come inside after she had a chance to clean up. The guy had plenty of time to prepare. Clamped chloroform over her mouth when she stepped inside, and took her straight to his van in the alley. In, out, and gone in hardly a minute. Next thing she knew, she woke up in the back of an ambulance."

"A much more professional job, I'm guessing from the tone of your voice," Brian added.

"Up to the part where he got slapped upside the head."

"Yeah," Brian commiserated. "Zahn said somebody stopped him, and you've got the kidnapper. Who stopped him and who is the kidnapper? Is he part of Zeta?"

Pedamore shook his head. "For the moment, that's 'need to know', and you don't need to know. Just be glad it turned out the way it did."

Rockaway, who'd been quiet to now, humphed loudly. "So what happens next?" he asked.

"You're all going to remain here with us, under our custody." Pedamore's face turned darkly serious. "We'll take you each to a safe house, like we originally planned, where you'll be guarded 24/7 and have at least some creature comforts. Separate houses until we get this wrapped up. I'm not taking any more chances."

This bit of information, Brian didn't want to hear. While Pedamore was talking he had been working out Plan B. Brian's eyes met Rockaway's and both recognized that the other was on the same escape wavelength; Brian gave a slight nod in Pedamore's direction and immediately stood up.

"Enough of this for now," Rockaway said, standing, bending backwards and stretching out his arms as though working out the kinks. "I'm ready for a safe house and some good football. So, John Lee, just how bad do you think the Cowboys are going to kick the Steelers' asses next week? They're playing here in Dallas, you know," he asked as if acquiescing.

Pedamore chuckled, got up, and followed Rockaway. "Are you talking a wager, old man?"

While Rockaway engaged Pedamore, Brian blocked the banter, retrieved his phone, and ripped off another quick text to Sensabaugh: MED CITY, BLDG D, NOW. He didn't sense Hatfield's approach until the man took a seat in Rockaway's vacated chair. Brian snapped the phone shut and stuck it in his pocket, giving Hatfield a crooked grin.

"Hi."

Hatfield leaned forward, propping his elbows on his knees, and stared at the wall across the room, as though Brian wasn't there. Then, he asked, "Exactly how are you planning to get out of a room full of agents?

Brian, initially startled, shrugged a shoulder, as if indifferent to the suggestion.

"Anyone attempting something like that would need help,"

Hatfield said. "Professional help."

"I don't know what you're talking about, Agent Hatfield," Brian replied flatly. "For now, I'm not at all impressed with the way your group has 'helped' us so far." Hatfield continued staring at the far wall, so Brian joined him. "I mean, after all, here we are, sitting together in a hospital waiting room filled with agents whose sole purpose in life is to protect us, right?"

"Braun, I'm guessing you don't have much time for this kind of idle banter, so I'm…"

A commotion broke out near them, as the elevator doors opened and a suit, leading four uniformed officers of Dallas's finest, marched in. Brian saw Hatfield toss a quick glance in Pedamore's direction, as the suit passed by them and headed towards the crowd of FBI agents in the center of the room. Working his way into the middle, he snatched a badge from his belt and held it up over his head for everyone to see. All heads turned his way, more amused than surprised. All except Brian.

"My name is Detective Luther Megs," he announced loudly, "and I'm here to take Misters Brian Braun and Mickey Rockaway into custody for the murder of Maxwell Edison."

Chapter 46

Brian's eyes darted to the open elevator doors, less than ten feet away. *I can make it!* he thought, and was inches out of his seat when Hatfield gripped his left wrist in steel fingers, holding him in place. Brian tried but couldn't shake away the vice-like clamp. *Damn,* he thought, trying again to jerk away from Hatfield. Brian watched hopelessly while the elevator doors began to close, then, a most extraordinary thing happened: Hatfield stuffed his business card into Brian's shirt pocket.

"You're going to need it," he whispered. "Now go!"

Brian didn't wait to ask questions. He'd already lost to precious seconds, but he felt confident that if he moved this instant he could still make it to the elevator before the doors closed.

Halfway to the elevator doors, Hatfield boomed aloud, "Hey! He's getting away!" But Brian had reached the elevator, slipped in sideways and the doors closed soundlessly behind him. He punched LOBBY three times in quick succession, waiting for the elevator to begin its excruciating crawl down to the first floor, at the same time texting Sensabaugh: NOW.

Hatfield raced just ahead of the surge of blue uniforms heading for the elevator doors, and, once there, lurched forward and slapped the palm of his right hand flush against the up and down buttons, lighting both indicators. At the same time, Pedamore raised an arm a few inches from his side, halting his own agents from joining Detective Megs and his Blues in the fruitless melee.

Detective Megs pointed towards the adjoining hallway, "Two of you take the stairs! One up, one down!" He glared at the two lighted up/down buttons framed in the chrome plate and then at Hatfield. "What the fuck?" Megs' face turned beet red with anger. "What's this?" he said, pointing at the light indicators.

Hatfield calmly reached over and re-pressed just the DOWN button. "My bad, Detective."

Ignoring Hatfield, Megs pounded his fists on the metal doors. "Come on, come on!" Then he twisted around to face Pedamore and jabbed a threatening finger at him. "If this is your doing, Pedamore, I'll add my complaints to your rapidly growing list, and that you can count on!" The elevator dinged distantly, indicating its arrival on the second floor, going down.

The doors had barely opened before Megs and the two remaining uniforms squeezed their way in. The detective gave Hatfield a flying finger, while the agent stood idly by, arms to his side, watching the doors close.

Moving next to Pedamore, Rockaway stated, "I don't entirely understand what just happened, but I believe I may have underestimated you, John Lee."

"Happens a lot," he answered. "Think he'll make it?"

Rockaway chuckled. "Oh, yeah. He's probably halfway to Waco

by now."

Building D was on the backside of the sprawling Medical City Hospital complex with its own parking lot and entrance separate from the main building. The lobby there was medium sized, the ceilings two stories high, with an open waiting area cluttered with couches, cushioned chairs and strategically placed oversized coffee tables. There was a food court at the opposite end. Lucky for Brian, there were enough hospital patients, visitors and personnel milling around to provide good distraction and interference. He avoided the terminally slow revolving door and made for one of the alternate side emergency exit doors. Outside, parked one behind the other in the driveup, were two, identical, black Dodge Challenger SRT's with broad white stripes down the sides.

Behind him, Brian could hear Detective Megs shouting and cursing his way through the lobby trying to make a mad-dash to cut him off before he reached the outside. Too late. Brian imagined Megs looking venomously at the two vehicles out front, knowing that the black muscle cars were meant for Brian's getaway. Brian ran up to the first car with the profile of a man in the driver's seat wearing wrap-around sunglasses, tee-shirt, and baseball cap waiting expectantly inside.

He didn't enter the first, however. The second car's driver door was open, and, though no one was in it, the engine also idling. As Brian jumped in the second car and buckled the seatbelt, the tires of the lead car squealed, sending up a plume of acrid smoke. Brian noted the black athletic bag on the passenger seat, and jerked the gearshift back into drive, punched the gas pedal to the floor, and created his own scream of squealing tires and cloud of burning rubber. The acceleration pressed him to the seat, forcing his head against the headrest as the monster 5.7 liter, Hemi V8 fishtailed out of the driveway.

"I love this car!" Brian shouted to no one out loud.

He tailgated the car ahead of him, and they weaved their way through the parking lot. A final left turn, and the lead car crashed through a wooden exit arm. Brian was impressed, but the driver's next maneuver, an expert, high-speed right-hand turn, impressed him even more. Immediately out of the turn, the man purposely sideswiped an oncoming Mercedes, forcing the driver to veer to his right onto the curb, allowing Brian to exit the parking lot without inference.

On the road at last, Brian glanced quickly back at the parking lot to see what Megs and his officers were doing. In the distance above the rows of parked cars, lights flashed and sirens blared. Two blue and white DPD patrol cars, led by a gray-colored Chevy, appeared and began to wind their way to the shattered exit gate, speeding through. The Chevy and one patrol car latched onto Brian; the other turned right, ignoring the wrecked Mercedes, and pursued Brian's twin.

The street Brian took dead-ended a block away at Hillcrest, a four-lane street with a median. On approach, Brian glanced both ways, quickly calculated his odds of getting through the traffic, and knew he'd make it. Clenching his jaw and bracing himself, Brian blew through the stop sign and shot across the first lane of traffic going northward, then slipped between two cars, hit the brakes, and whipped the steering wheel to his left. The Challenger slid into a controlled sideways skid through the median, making a perfect left-hand turn well ahead of the next car in line going southward. Brian punched the accelerator, knowing he'd bought precious seconds with the maneuver and substantially increased the distance between him and his pursuers.

Two blocks ahead was another T-intersection, far busier than the last and with a traffic signal rather than a stop sign. This was his opportunity to lose his pursuers all together. If he could create enough traffic chaos, hopefully without anyone getting hurt, Megs and his troop would have to give up the chase. DPD, he knew, had a standing order regarding no high-speed pursuits. If and when they got through the mess he was about to make, they'd have to get special permission to pursue him further and perform a PIT maneuver—a pursuit tactic by which the pursuing vehicle forces the fleeing vehicle to abruptly turn, causing the driver to lose control and stop—if the opportunity even arose. Once again, Brian gauged the flow of traffic and estimated his chances of getting through the intersection on a red light without getting hit or hitting someone else.

Slim, but doable, he decided, and risked a glance in his rearview mirror. Lights and sirens continued to close in. *No choice.* He picked his opening, adjusted his speed down a notch, and watched an westbound pickup approaching from his left.

Brian lifted his foot from the accelerator just enough to create the needed timing hesitation, then stomped it to the floor, punching through the intersection, wreaking havoc all about him. Brakes squealed, cars swerved into each other causing several pile-ups that effectively blocked the lanes behind him. Within seconds, he heard more brakes, a loud smack, and the crunch of metal. The gray Chevy—Megs', he assumed—bought the farm. More brakes suddenly screeched, several more loud thuds echoed above the din, and horns began blaring from every direction.

Brian finished fishtailing through, and creating a secondary traffic snarl, forcing two cars, eastbound this time, to abruptly hit their brakes the cars behind rear-ending them.

Now that he'd foiled his pursuers, he needed a place to make some subtle, but noticeable changes to the Challenger, check out the contents of athletic bag on the seat next to him, and call Sensabaugh again. Continuing straight he eventually passed under the Central Expressway overpass, and he took the six-lane avenue east, checking his rearview every few seconds. There was no sign of pursuit.

After about a mile on, he topped a hill and spotted an apartment complex on the downside to his right, across from a Texas Instruments satellite facility. The car in front was signaling a right turn into the complex, so he decided to follow. Recessed back fifty feet from the street stood two black iron gates protecting the apartments from undesirables. And, as fate would have it, the annoying scream of distant sirens filling the air again.

The car in front of him pulled up to the gates, and Brian willed them to open. *Come on! Open!* Quickly. Before his pursuers saw him.

The driver before him didn't wait for the parting gates to completely open before entering, allowing Brian to follow. As the twin iron barriers closed behind him, he slowed to let the adrenaline rush from the past few minutes subside, and allow him to think through his next move. He found a spot next to a big green dumpster over-shadowed by trees located along the far eastern boundary. This would provide cover from the ground as well as the air.

He parked the Challenger facing towards a nearby exit, kept the engine running, got out, and pulled off the outer, velcro-attached license plates on front and rear bumpers. Next, he rushed to the front left fender and picked with his fingernail at the tip of the broad white stripe that ran along the side, quickly peeling it off. He repeated the process on the passenger side, wadding the sticky conglomeration together, and wrapping it along with the other stripe and old license plates in some old newspapers lying around. Then he trashed it. With new plates and no stripes, no one would be likely to look closer.

That done, Brian got back in the driver's seat and sat, closing his eyes. He was tired and hungry. He'd been wearing the same clothes for two days, and, more than anything, wanted to bring the ordeal to an end. He fought the thoughts of Harry and Joanna that kept trying to creep back into his head; he had to stay focused on the here and now.

Opening his eyes, Brian took a breath and checked the glove box for his new driver license and insurance papers. They were there along with his new identity. Then he started rummaging inside the bag on the passenger seat that Sensabaugh had left him.

The items Brian had requested earlier were all there. There was also a separate plastic sack containing additional goodies: a pair of wrap-around sunglasses, a cap, several bottles of water, numerous energy bars, a Buck knife, three new cell phones, and a fake Fu Manchu mustache. The last cracked him up. He adjusted the rearview and applied the mustache to his upper lip.

Grabbing his phone from the between-seat console, Brian called his accomplice.

"My man said you handle a car as good as him. He was impressed," Sensabaugh answered without a hello.

"My compliments to him, too," Brian added.

"Car okay?"

"Love it. I need one more thing, and I hope it's still there."

"Shoot."

"When we were picked up at Wal-mart and taken to the hospital, I left my Jeep in the parking lot. My camera bag and equipment are in the back floorboard on the driver's side. I really need it."

"If it's there, I'll get it. If it's not, then I'll get you a replacement. Any preference?"

Brian smiled. "Something automatic and expensive. All the bells and whistles." Brian didn't need to get specific with Sensabaugh. He'd know instinctively what to get. "And a tripod. Portable, but sturdy."

"Naturally," he replied. "You ready for your new car?"

"Yeah, something inconspicuous, I assume."

"Of course," he said. "I got you a ten-year-old white Toyota 4-Runner. Four-wheel-drive. This one's a stick, runs good, and dirty as hell on the outside. Where you want it waiting?"

Brian thought a minute. "The Toyota's good. This'll work close to the Wal-mart, too. In Mesquite, off the corner of Galloway and Town East Boulevard, there's a Texaco car wash."

"It'll be there. Keys in a magnetic box under the bumper on the driver's side. Anything else?"

"Yeah," Brian said. "They tried to kidnap Joanna, but it went awry She's okay. Probably the same folks who hit Harry. He's dicey, but still kicking. That's why I was at Medical City."

"Shit. Sorry, Brian. Anything I can do?"

"See what you can find out. That'll help. And what do you know about a Dallas dick in homicide named Luther Megs?"

"Shit, Brian. I'd rather have the FBI and the Purple Gang on my ass than 'Bulldog' Megs. You piss him off?"

"I'm not sure yet, but he's after me, Harv. Any suggestions?"

"Europe's too cold this time of year. He might not find you hidden behind a coconut tree in the Seychelles Islands."

"Thanks, I'll be in touch."

"Where you headed?" Sensabaugh asked. "Or is it better I not know?"

"East."

"Having fun yet?"

"Yeah…I am. It feels good to be doing what I do best."

Sensabaugh's tone lost some of its light-heartedness. "You know what you're doing here, right Brian?"

"Yeah, Dad. I've got this. Don't worry. I learned from the best."

"Okay, thirty minutes at the car wash," Sensabaugh said. "Break a leg."

Brian decided to wait ten more minutes at the complex before leaving. It'd only take fifteen minutes to drive to the car wash. He munched on an energy bar and washed it down with water, and then took a better inventory of the athletic bag. Flares, the dye pack, his Berreta, Rockaway's .45, and three extra clips for each were on top. Brian moved things around, spotted the black velvet box with ROLEX printed in gold lettering across the lid, and grabbed it and the dye pack together. He pried opened the box and checked to make certain the dye pack would fit inside. Just right. Leaving the pack in the box, he returned it to the bag. He'd wire it later. Next to the extra phones was a fat, crumpled paper bag. Brian took it out, and opened it, knowing exactly what was there: five thousand dollars worth of hundreds and twenties neatly wrapped in bundles with rubber bands.

"Guess I'm good to go," Brian mumbled, tossing the sack back into the bag.

Back on Forest Lane, no sirens or speeding patrol cars were anywhere to be found. Brian drove the speed limit and kept his eyes busy, scanning every passing vehicle, every parking lot entrance and exit, preparing for the unexpected.

Within minutes, he'd jumped onto the LBJ Freeway heading south towards Mesquite. If nothing untoward happened, he'd be at the car wash in five or ten minutes. Traffic was light, but the minutes dragged by excruciatingly slow until he reached Town East Boulevard and turned left.

The car wash was busy, as usual at this time of day, which worked in Brian's favor. He parked the Challenger in line, and, though reluctant to give it up, got out, and walked up to the man taking wash orders. Brian gave him the keys and a ten dollar tip on top of the price of the wash.

The Toyota was parked nearby in the rear parking lot, along side other dirty cars waiting their turn. Brian retrieved the keys, and noted the camera bag and a sleeping bag wrapped around a pillow in the front floor board.

He was more at ease now that he was out of the muscle car and had changed his appearance. He drove into a Burger Street a few blocks down from the car wash, and got a double cheese burger, curly fries, and a large cherry Coke.

When he was done wolfing it down, he pulled the crumpled business card from his shirt pocket and examined it. *Hatfield, huh?* He turned it over, out of habit, and saw a name written on the back.

Brian stuck it back in his pocket, wondering who the hell the person was. *Welcome to the circus, whoever you are.*

Shutterbug

Chapter 47

Detective Luther Megs sat fuming back in Pedamore's waiting room. He'd been cooling his heels for nearly thirty minutes, and with every minute that passed, his hatred for the federal boys increased exponentially. He hated the contemporary furniture with the perfectly stacked magazines on the coffee table. He hated the scenic view from the plate-glass windows. He especially hated how pristine it all looked and felt. Worst of all, he hated how his time was being wasted.

Fuck it; I've got work to do, he concluded and tossed the unread magazine in his hands back onto the coffee table, intentionally hitting the stack it came from, then stood. In the most sarcastic voice he could manage, he waved to get the secretary sitting behind the desk and said, "Excu-se me. Would you kindly tell Agent-in-Charge Pedamore or whatever else you call him, to *kiss my ass*," the detective said, his voice emphasizing the last three words. "He called a meeting. I'm here; he's not. Fuck him! I'm canceling the meeting." He pointed to the door. "Don't stand, I'll let myself out."

"Elevator's to the right," she said, without looking up.

Megs opened the door to exit Pedamore's office only to be greeted by an agent standing across the hall pointing towards the elevator.

"Agent Ferguson's waiting for you on the first floor, sir, and will escort you to your car. Have a nice day," he said too politely.

Megs ignored him, marched to the elevators and grumbled just loud enough for the hallway agent to hear. "Fucking feds. I *hate* 'em."

The secretary's voice piped through Pedamore's desk intercom while he stood gazing out of his office window. "He's gone, sir."

"Very well, and thank you. That'll be all," Pedamore said, remaining still, hands folded behind his back.

Well, there's your extra time, Braun. Now let's see what you can do. Fishing, he reminded himself, hardly ever works out for the bait, but he had a feeling that this time…

Rockaway and Joanna were in Pedamore's FBI command center office in the hospital, waiting for his return. He'd told them to have a seat, and that he'd be right back, and then had disappeared.

"What's going on, Rock?" Joanna asked. "My two guard dogs whisked me here like the world was about to end. Now, nobody will tell me anything. I think I'm going nuts."

"I'm not sure," he said. "Did you know that Brian escaped from here earlier with Detective Megs hot on his tail?"

She grabbed his arm in alarm. "No! What are you talking about?"

"There's this detective from Dallas PD named Megs. He charged in here with four blue boys in tow and announced that he was arresting Brian and me for murdering Edison. Brian was sitting by the elevators and bolted. The cops took off after him, leaving me here, thankfully, and Pedamore ordered me to wait, then left. I've been sitting beside my own watchdogs ever since as you can see. 'Now here we are, the two of us…'" Rockaway crooned.

Joanna looked shocked. "Do you know if Brian got away? Where could he have gone? Have you heard from him?"

Rockaway shook his head. "No, no, and no, kiddo. Don't know, not sure, and haven't heard from him."

The elevator doors opened and both of them automatically clammed up.

"Water?" Pedamore asked, stepping casually forward, holding out bottles to each of them.

They each took a bottle and Pedamore sat down on a free chair. "Okay, I'll cut straight to the chase. I'll tell you everything I can."

Rockaway leaned forward. "You know, John Lee, I'm really tired of your, *I'll tell you what I can bullshit.* Just tell us. I mean, who the hell are we gonna tell, held under guard like this? You're definitely not planning to cut us loose, am I right?"

"You are right," Pedamore agreed. "I can't afford for you to shoot anybody else, Rockaway. Or to lose our key newswoman, Joanna. Most important, somebody may still want to harm the two of you. I'm afraid you're with me for a while. And, by the way, I heard on my way up that Harry's doing fine, at least for now. He's not completely out of the woods, but the surgeon said everything looks good. If the bullet had been another centimeter to the left, however, we'd be notifying his next of kin, I'm afraid."

"Thank God for that, at least. Okay, tell us what you can, then," Joanna said sternly. "What's going on?"

Pedamore leaned back and toyed with the cap to his water bottle, as though contemplating his next words. "Okay, but you're not going to like it."

"That's a given," said Joanna, "I haven't liked any of this since I met you."

Pedamore smiled wanly. "I'm sure. Well here it is: The whole thing here at the hospital was a setup." He held up a hand to stop the verbal reaction he expected from them. "But, it worked. Brian reacted exactly the way I hoped he would. I…"

"What?" Exclaimed Joanna.

The agent held his hand higher. "Just listen a sec, Joanna." He then focused on the professor. "Rockaway, think a minute. Exactly where were we sitting when the detective, 'Bull' Megs rushed in?"

"By the elevators," he answered.

"Who led you there?"

Rockaway thought for a second. "You did."

"That's right. An easy exit, wouldn't you say? I'm the one who turned Megs loose. Brian escaped him, by the way, if that's what you're wondering. I didn't doubt that he would." Pedamore leaned forward closer to the pair. "Most of what we have on Fagan is still circumstantial, except one thing we think we can now hang on him for sure."

"Which you're not going to tell us about, right?" Joanna said sarcastically.

Pedamore nodded. "Can't right now, but when I can, you'll be the first to know. We could have eventually gotten a conviction on him down the road, I think, but it would take years, and the man is smart. He has more connections than the President of the United States. For all I know, he could be the President of the United States by then. As a federal agency, we can only do so much. Hatfield's going undercover was a help, but we have rules, lines we can't cross. There are no such lines as far as Brian is concerned."

"So you throw him to the wolves? Put his life at risk? Is that what you're doing?" Joanna retorted loudly. "I thought you did that once before and learned your lesson! Or is it that you can't be held strictly accountable for a wildman? How noble of you, Mr. Pedamore."

Pedamore remained patient, expecting the comeback. "I didn't say that, Joanna. You and I both know that Brian wasn't going to be held back, no matter what I did to 'protect' him. One way or another he was going after Fagan. He has his own score to settle with the man, and was going to eventually do it his way, and you know it. Brian was up to something when he left here. Right, Rockaway?"

"Maybe," Rockaway offered cautiously.

"Listen, I have nothing to hold him on, so he could cut loose whenever and wherever he wanted, but, you got to admit this way was dramatic. I'm guessing he's already figured things out on his own, too. He's now free to operate on his own without constraints." Pedamore gave a sly grin before continuing. "Believe it or not, he's infinitely better protected being on his own. I couldn't just cut him loose and say, 'Go do your thing with my blessings.' I had to create the…opportunity."

"By calling in the cops?" Rockaway asked, dumbfounded.

"Exactly," answered Pedamore. "He had to be 'on the run'. 'Out from under our thumb'. Believe me, Fagan knows, somehow, what just happened. He knows that Brian's on his own and on the loose."

"And you think you know what Brian's up to?" Rockaway asked, skeptically.

"Of course, I do. Don't you? What would you do, Rock? You've had a lot of experience with this kind of thing."

Joanna turned to Rockaway, confused. The professor appeared surprised, then smiled assuredly. "So you called in some favors, did you, John Lee?"

"Called some and burned a number of debts people owed me, as a matter of fact, and still didn't get squat for it. That told me a lot in itself."

"What's he talking about, Rock?" Joanna asked.

Rockaway patted her arm. "Nothing, kiddo. It's all in the past." Then he turned back to Pedamore. "I'd go straight to the horse's mouth. I'd go to Fagan for a showdown. On my terms."

"Exactly," said Pedamore.

"But you couldn't order him to do it. Deniability," stated Rockaway frankly.

"Exactly."

"I like it," said Rockaway, a faraway look in his eyes.

"What?" exclaimed Joanna. "You mean you agree with this madness? Are you crazy, Rock?"

Rockaway took her hand and cradled it in his. "Joanna, I don't know how to explain this to you, but trust me, Brian can do this. Matter of fact, if I had to choose between the FBI and Brian on getting the goods on Fagan, I'd definitely put my money on Brian." He glanced at Pedamore. "No offense intended, John Lee."

Pedamore nodded. "None taken, We're together all the way. That's why I did it."

Joanna shook her head. "I still don't understand all this. What's he doing? Is he in danger?"

"Of course he's in danger, Joanna," Rockaway said, "but danger is his element."

"Joanna, we're not abandoning him, we're letting him do what he does best," said Pedamore.

"And what's that, Mr. Pedamore?" she asked dryly.

"Well," Pedamore said, "he's a crook and a thief. A master manipulator. And he has the necessary brilliant mind to fully complement those talents." He snapped his fingers as an afterthought. "And, oh yeah, he's also a damn good photographer."

Rockaway slumped in his chair. "Couldn't have said it better myself, John Lee."

"And now it's time for me and my men to escort you two back to my office," Pedamore concluded. "There's nothing more to do here."

Shutterbug

Chapter 48

The problem with being on the road alone at night on a long stretch of Texas highway is the inordinate amount of time it leaves one to think. In Brian's case, there were still too many things to sort through. Overload, that's where he was. However, the time gave him the chance to realize how insanely stupid he could be when he set his mind to it.

Back at the hospital, when Detective Megs stormed in with his goons to announce his arrest for killing Maxwell Edison—well, Brian knew he couldn't wait any longer and let that happen. First of all, he was innocent. Given time, he could prove that. Second, he knew that regardless of how many times he proclaimed his innocence and how many times Rockaway confessed to the shooting, he was going to end up in jail, and that wouldn't work. He had a plan in operation that needed to be executed, and being behind bars would have definitely put a damper on that. His original had been a damn good one, but had since been blown to the wind. His plan was to trap the honorable Senator Jimmy Fagan red-handed, but on Brian's turf, not the senator's. Then, when that flatfoot stormed by him in that waiting room and he saw those open elevator doors summoning him...well, he just couldn't help

289

himself.

Plan B, or was it Plan C, now...was less well formed and definitely crazier. Chance of getting caught? Probable. Chance of not getting caught? Possible. Chance of something going wrong? Most likely. Brian hadn't yet thought through a viable exit plan. Everything he was about to do felt wrong, but that damn senator was beginning to piss him off, big time. And, Hatfield's last words at the hospital still hung in the back of his mind, creating the glimmer of hope he was counting on.

One of the first rules of operating outside the law for a living was to keep all emotions in check and not move for revenge or payback. But now, he was clearly operating outside his own rules on just instinct and guts. Everything he'd experienced these last hours screamed that if he didn't do something, the situation would only get worse. What would've happened if Fagan had been successful in killing Harry and kidnapping Joanna? If he's crazy enough to go to those extremes, what chance did Brian have if he was depending on rules?

Pedamore had made it sound like he had plenty on the senator, yet, he still hadn't made a move. The FBI hadn't arrested Fagan, and rather than end this strange and dangerous game, seemed to be unsuccessful players in it. And, Hatfield's behavior at the hospital just before Brian's escape simply didn't add up. Brian thought through the strange events.

So, now he wants to be my friend? He'd said, 'You're going to need this, now go!' *Yeah, right.*

Brian retrieved the card and turned it over, looking at the name on the back again. *Is it the name of yet another person 'keeping an eye on me'? And, if so, why tell me?* Brian just wasn't at all sure. Furthermore, he wasn't sure if Hatfield, or his boss, Pedamore, were really that smart or that devious.

Did he know Megs was coming to get me? If so, why all the drama? Why not just let me go do my thing? He had to know I was up to something. Think. Think! Brian examined the card closer, hoping a closer inspection would reveal it's meaning and purpose, but all he saw was a card with a name hand-written on its reverse. Then it came to him: *Hatfield must have known I was going to run!* He had written the name on the card before everything with the detective had played out.

Then, if that was true, was his sitting in front of the elevators more than a convenient coincidence? Was Hatfield's suddenly 'friendly' gesture the signal meant as a signal for Brian to run? From their first meeting, there had been no love lost between him and Hatfield. So, once again, why be so buddy-buddy all of a sudden? Was he there to run interference? Is that why there were no cops stationed outside when he made his break from the hospital?

Brian tried to clear his head. This conjecturing was interesting, but it did nothing to help prepare him for the grim reality that lay immediately ahead. And, if Pedamore and Hatfield were so damn smart, then good. He could always use backup. At this point, however, he couldn't let anything change. That'd make things even more dangerous. He had to proceed as though the two agents were clueless. Right now, he was counting on Fagan being a creature of habit. The rest would be…improvisation.

It was about 10:00 p.m. when Brian hit the city limits of Tyler. He had a long night ahead of him and he needed a good meal to tide him over. One thing he had, for now at least, was more time. He spotted a

Cheddar's restaurant to his right, parked around back, grabbed his camera bag, and went inside. The crowd was light and, when asked about seating, Brian pointed to a booth that would give him a good view of the entrance. After ordering his meal, he made the pretense of searching for the restrooms to scope out an alternative exit in case he needed a quick way out. On the opposite wall was a door leading to a patio where a few brave customers were braving the night chill. Satisfied, he returned to the booth, enjoyed a pre-meal Bud, and then stuffed himself on a chicken fried steak the size of Oklahoma, accompanied by mashed potatoes, and red beans.

Back in his 4-Runner, he felt, at last, ready to roll. The food had helped immensely; his spirits were high, even optimistic. He turned right off the loop at the mall and onto the rolling hills blacktop of U.S. Highway 69, his destination, Rusk. Another hour and a half and he'd be there. Brian kept his speed at a consistent 65 mph, figuring the locals and the Texas Highway Patrol units would both be out in full force. He wasn't disappointed. By journey's end, he'd passed one Sheriff squad car and two Texas State Trooper black and whites waiting to bust the first careless driver that passed.

A little after midnight, he finally approached Rusk city limits, and once again, was reminded of the dark blanket that typically engulfed the countryside at night in this part of the country. The glow of city lights on the horizon didn't afford the same comfort they had when he cruised into this little town the first time.

Was that really yesterday?

His body said yes but his mind refused to believe it. He slowed as he drove through town, spotting two local cops parked side by side at the downtown square, chatting across open windows. No pursuit. Not even a second look. Soon after, Brian drove onto FM 23 and took off on the dark, roller coaster ride provided by the two-lane road headed for Senator Fagan's ranch.

Destiny. Brian had never thought much about destiny before. He'd always taken life one week at a time, but now he wondered if he had a future beyond the upcoming morning. Traveling the same country road again after less than thirty-six hours reminded him of one of his favorite classic movies, V*anishing Point.* The main character met his destiny driving at break-neck speed, running from the cops on the same highway he'd travelled on twenty-four hours earlier.

Will I meet my destiny on FM 23?

In the movie, Barry Newman knew he was going to die and accepted it. Brian didn't and wouldn't. No, his destiny wouldn't be marked by the same road he'd came on. It would be marked by the one he left by.

The old schoolhouse and the turn off across from it were easier for Brian to locate the second time around, and instead of walking the dirt road to the barn that bordered the senator's property, he drove it. *No following Fagan's asinine instructions. No deserted mobile home. No pretending to be drunk. No sneaking out the back door. Now we do it my way.* Having measured a quarter mile from the odometer, he found a place he could back into and parked facing the road. He grabbed his camera bag off the front seat, and trekked the remainder of the way to his old friend, the barn. Upon entering, the smell of hay, stock animals, feed, and manure combined and, for a moment, flashed him back. Brian climbed the ladder, making his way back to the spot where he'd taken the ominous photos, and opened wide the loft doors.

He squatted down cross-legged on the hay mattress and stared out into darkness, barely able to make out the shadowy tree line of the surrounding woods. The night sky was lit by the billions of stars that shone like sparklers in an ever-expansive galaxy; it was profoundly beautiful. He wanted to take a picture. *Maybe another time.*

Using his night-light, Brian rummaged through his camera bag, took out his tripod, mounted the camera and placed the unit judiciously, adjusting the camera angle towards the spot where he figured Fagan would stop for his morning run.

Then, he closed and braced the loft doors just far enough to leave about six guaranteed inches of space between for the camera and leaned back on the hay interlocking his fingers behind his head. He needed a couple of hours of shut-eye. He set the alarm on one of the purchased cell phones for 5:00 a.m., then dropped it into his shirt pocket, letting the sounds of the woods, the varied smells of the barn, and the hypnotizing sparkles of the stars lull him to sleep.

Outside, in the tree line, Hatfield whispered to one of his partners, "Song Bird Two? One, here. You in place?"

Agent Womack answered, "Yeah, One. Got the house covered."

"Three?"

"Positioned at the edge of the woods, hoping I don't get eaten alive by a night carnivore," complained Agent Zahn.

"Okay, the canary's in the nest," Hatfield said. "Now we sit tight till morning."

Shutterbug

DAY 3

Monday, September 7, 2009

Shutterbug

Chapter 49

Behind Brian and the barn, the red glow of dawn crested over the tips of the tree line. Before him, a heavy coat of dew blanketed the pasture's grass creating sporadic sparkles and glints from the rising sun's rays. The forest was coming alive with sounds of nature's beasts. A beautiful morning, totally contradictory to the chaos Brian anticipated was about to take place. He rechecked his camera angles for the hundredth time and his watch for the thousandth, then reassuringly touched the handle of the Baretta stuffed down the front of his jeans.

In the tree line, unseen agents assumed their positions, alert and ready.

"Song Bird One, this is two. The fox is headed your way in his pickup with three escorts following in a single black SUV."

"Got it, Two," Hatfield answered. "Good work. Now shag up here as quick as you can. I've got no idea what's about to go down, but you can bet it's going to be interesting."

"On my way. Two out."

"Three? You set?" Hatfield asked.

"Yeah. As soon as the guests arrive at the party, I'll let you know what shots I've got."

Hatfield nodded to himself. "I'll do the same. Be ready. I figure this'll go down fast. I don't anticipate much glad-handing. Not Braun's style."

Breaking into the open pasture on the dirt, rutted road, Fagan's pickup emerged slowly from the surrounding woods followed by a black SUV. Hidden in the barn, Brian eyeballed their approach through the crack he'd arranged in the wooden loft doors. When the senator's truck finally came to rest about fifty feet from him, he sighted the camera a final time, and cradled the remote shutter release in his hand. Taking Hatfield's earlier cue he waited for the senator to light his cigar before making his move. The senator got out of his truck, looked around as though admiring his fiefdom, then pulled a cigar from his jacket pocket and lit it, blowing out a thick grey stream of smoke.

It was time to start the ball rolling.

Brian activated the remote and the Nikon D3X started silently ticking off multiple pictures every second.

Climbing down from the loft, Brian slammed both hands against the barn's ten-foot, double doors and passed through the opening at a brisk pace. The look on Senator Fagan's face alone was priceless. Brian caught himself hoping the camera captured Fagan's mouth when it dropped open as wide as the barn doors. The three men from the SUV immediately formed a quick, protective semi-circle around the senator. All grabbed for either a hip or shoulder holster, ready to draw in an instant. Brian slowly outstretched his arms showing the senator and his protective entourage the black velvet Rolex box he held in his right hand.

"Sorry to not call first, Senator Fagan," he called out as casually as possible, "but I figured you'd be here about this time. Just like a couple days ago...remember?"

Mark Freeman, the biggest of the three guards, stepped between Brian and Fagan, hand still resting nervously on his hip sidearm. "Stay where you are, Braun. Keep your hands in front of you, and get down on your knees. Now!"

Still no drawn guns. Good. Defying the order, Brian walked forward at a slow, but deliberate pace, keeping both hands outstretched and in sight. "I'm here to see the Senator." Brian waved the Rolex box. "I brought the memory card and pictures from Saturday morning's melodrama."

Fagan instantly raised an arm and whispered something to Freeman out of the side of his mouth. Big Guy stood down and moved cautiously to the senator's side.

Fagan summoned Brian towards him with a wave. "Come, Brian. Let's work this whole thing out here and now, son."

Click, click, click, click...

"Move," echoed Freeman, with obvious displeasure, "but keep your hands in front of you. Don't make any sudden moves. Walk *real* slow."

Brian slowed his pace further, but continued forward. He had to get closer to the senator in order for his plan to work. "I'm tired of all this, senator. I want to bring this whole affair to an end. You get your pictures, and agree to leave me and my friends alone," he said, knowing that wasn't the way it was going to end.

"That's all I ever wanted, Brian. No need for all the animosity. No need for it, at all."

"Keep 'em where I can see them," the Freeman reiterated, as Brian stopped next to the senator. Then, Freeman frisked Brian: first his outstretched arms, then slowly down his torso. When he got to Brian's belt-line, he removed the Beretta from Brian's waistband. Big Guy held the weapon by it's stock between two fingers for the senator to see. "Now that was real stupid, Braun. What'd you think you were going to do with this? Shoot us all while the senator inspected the box?" He snorted a short laugh. Stuffing the weapon in his jacket pocket, Freeman reached for the Rolex box in Brian's hand.

"It's for the senator," Brian said, nodding in Fagan's direction.

"I'll take that," Fagan replied, grabbing it greedily.

Closely watching the scene from his new position behind the front corner of the barn, Hatfield whispered. "Three? Do you have a clear shot on the big one? Braun's blocking my view of him."

"I'm good to go. Just tell me when and how many you want taken down."

"Jesus, I can't believe Braun brought a gun!" Hatfield exclaimed.

"And was carrying it on him where it could be so easily found!" replied Three. Hatfield hadn't expected such cavalierness from an experienced professional like Brian. He tightened his grip on his binoculars.

Brian took one step backwards, slowly raising his hands above his head.

Click, click, click, click…

"Nice little box you brought me, Brian boy. Is there a Rolex in there, too?" Fagan bounced the box on the palm of his hand. "It's heavy enough, all right. Shit, it feels like a Rolex," he said, smiling, and brought it up to his face, opened the box lid a fraction, and peered through the crack like a little boy opening his first present at Christmas. His eyes shifted back at Brian as he opened the lid the rest of the way.

Click, click, click, click...

Brian, the Senator, and the three Zeta agents all reacted at the same time, jumping back from the explosion of compacted ink that covered every exposed inch of Senator Fagan's face, hair, and clothes.

Hatfield? Brian prayed. *If you're out there somewhere, now is the time to intervene.*

Fagan looked like the Red Demon on Halloween night, hopping around, screaming and rubbing his face and eyes with the back of his red hands, which did nothing but spread the ink and increase the irritation. He coughed and spit red phlegm from his mouth. "Braun!" he yelled. "Where is he? I'll kill him!" Fagan rubbed a red-soaked sleeve across his brow, his eyelids fluttering in a hopeless attempt to open.

The three bodyguards stood frozen, hands on their still-holstered weapons, unsure whether to shoot the unarmed man with his hands above his head, or laugh at the senator's embarrassing antics. Brian made no move to escape, though he did glide another step back and slowly drop his arms to his sides.

"Freeman!" Fagan screamed. "Do something! Kill the bastard!"

Fagan groped blindly forward, eventually finding Big Guy, and grabbed the team leader by the shoulder. To everyone's surprise, Fagan tore manically at the jacket until his hands located what he was looking for. Ripping Brian's Beretta from Freeman's pocket, he leveled it in the direction where he supposed Brian to be.

The reaction from the three Zeta employees was simultaneous, smooth, and practiced. Each unholstered his weapon and drew a bead… on Fagan. Brian took another full step backwards.

Click, click, click, click…

Luis Diaz yelled, "Drop the weapon, Senator! Now!" but Fagan ignored him.

"Fuck you, Diaz!" he growled. "I'm taking this fucker out!"

Diaz? Isn't that the name on the card Hatfield gave me?

Click, click, click, click...

Freeman acted before Fagan had the chance to pull the trigger, lunging to the side, twisting the gun out of the senator's hand, and throwing it on the ground behind the senator next to the pickup.

Brian remained still, waiting for events to continue playing out.

Freeman went berserk. "You crazy old fool! I ought to shoot you myself. You've done nothing but fuck things up from the beginning. Now, look at you! How the hell are you going to explain what you've just done? That's the same permanent ink that banks use! You're gonna look like a clown when you go back to D. C. and how, in heaven's name, are you going to explain?"

In a move that shocked everyone, Freeman back-handed the senator full in the chest, knocking the elder statesman to the ground. The senator, blind and screaming, scrambled backwards, arms and legs in motion, scooting on his butt like a crab. The left rear tire of the truck stopped his progress.

Red streams of spittle dripped in strings from his bottom lip as he spat out, "*Nobody* lays a hand on me, you fuckin' cocksucker! You understand that, boy? I'm a United States Senator! I'm one of the most powerful men in the world, and I can do things to you and your family that'll make those ragheads in the Middle East seem like Mickey and Minnie Mouse!" He groped the ground beside him, and, out of nowhere, the Beretta appeared in his hand. The senator aimed it in the general direction of the Big Guy's voice, and was spot on. "Say goodbye, you prick!" Fagan yelled, and pulled the trigger three times in quick succession. The only sounds that came from the automatic, however, were three loud, dry clicks. "What the hell?" he sputtered.

Freeman breathed a sigh of relief and aimed his gun at the senator. "As you said, I think it's time for us all to say goodbye, asshole."

Brian backed up another step. At that instant, Diaz turned his weapon on Freeman, yelling, "Drop the weapon, Mark! I'm FBI, and I'll drop you dead right where you stand if you don't! Drop it! Now!"

Brian took yet another step back, effectively removing himself from the stage.

Swinging his gun from the senator to Diaz, Freeman barked, "You motherfucker! So, *you're* the fuckin' inside mole Edison was worried about? I should of known..." But, before he could complete the swing, a shot rang out. At the report, birds emptied the trees surrounding the pasture in a raucous mass exodus. Everybody instinctively ducked except Freeman. His gun dropped from his limp hand, and he staggered backwards a few steps, a look of disbelief and awe on his face. He stared down at a spreading red spot on the left side his chest, touched it lightly with a finger, and then stared at his bloody fingertip as if mesmerized. Then, his knees buckled and he collapsed like a deflated balloon to the ground.

Click, click, click, click...

Diaz didn't wait to watch the show, though. Brian had never seen

305

such quick reflexes. As the shot was ringing out, Diaz, a two-handed grip on his drawn automatic, squatted, twisted, and centered it on the third agent.

"Drop the weapon, Larry, and lay on the ground, face down!"

Larry did exactly as told. Brian could tell by the look on his face that he wasn't happy about it, but he sure as hell didn't look like he was going to argue anytime soon.

Across from Diaz, Senator Jimmy Fagan leaned with his back against the tire, slack-jawed, drooling, and mumbling, "No, no, no, no..."

Click, click, click, click...

Chapter 50

It was a matter of seconds before agents Hatfield, Zahn, and Womack were on the scene. The sudden rush of men from the wooded area and the barn caught Brian by surprise at first, but then again, it was getting to the point where nothing about the whole affair really shocked him anymore. Fagan and the Zeta agent, Larry Little, were stretched out, face down on the ground, with their hands handcuffed behind them. Fagan kept rambling on about how everyone was going to pay for the atrocious treatment and that heads were going to roll. Brian tried to remain in the background and out of the way as much as possible, but he could see Agent Hatfield wasn't going to let that happen. Hatfield spotted Brian off to the side and motioned to him with his finger.

Hatfield looked both impatient and pissed at the same time. "You okay, Braun? Not hurt, are you?"

"I appreciate your concern about my well-being, Agent Hatfield. I'm okay. I was able to successfully stay out of the line of fire."

"You've got me wrong, Braun. I'm trained to say that, it has nothing to do with caring. And I'll tell you what's pissing me off, if you want to hear it."

I need to get to the camera. "Uh, sure, make my day."

Hatfield pointed out the scene around them. It looked like a battleground: one dead body on the ground, two handcuffed, FBI agents talking on their phones, taking notes, and collecting evidence. "This," he said. "You caused all this," he reiterated, waving his arm around. "You could've gotten Agent Diaz killed…and a United States Senator."

"Who was trying to kill me," Brian added. "By the way, I didn't hear any gunshots when he pointed the gun at me. I'm not going to apologize for anything, if that's what you're fishing for. The senator tried to kill me, damn near killing a close friend of mine, and kidnapping another. He got what he had coming, as far as I'm concerned."

Hatfield shrugged, ignoring Brian's commentary. "In the end, Freeman saved your ass, you know. I'd have shot him if Agent Zahn hadn't first, but I must remind you, you're the one that brought a gun. What the hell were you thinking, Braun?"

"Well, for one thing, it wasn't loaded," Brian said in defense. "I figured if somebody was going to shoot me, I'd make sure they used my unloaded gun to do it. Your cryptic card with 'Diaz' scribbled on the back helped, thank you, but only after I figured out the meaning. I didn't know who or what 'Diaz' meant until the senator called one of his henchmen by that name, and even then, it wasn't until the man taken action that I knew for sure he was on my side so to speak. In the end, it turned the odds decidedly more in my favor."

"What the hell kind of reasoning is that?" asked Hatfield. "I still don't know what your 'plan' was, and it's all over. You come to a gunfight with blanks in your gun? Hell, not even blanks, an empty magazine! What if one of them had checked? What would you have done if Diaz and my men hadn't been here?"

Brian shrugged. "Wasn't sure. I normally don't operate like this. Much was spur of the moment," he said. "But, you *were* here. Besides, I kinda thought you'd put it all together and rescue me if I kept it simple. After all, you're the one that let me escape. Where else could I go? Ya'll blew my plan to have Fagan come to me when you put that Megs character on me. Who the hell is he, anyway? I can't afford to have a bloodhound hanging 'round, you know."

Hatfield shook his head. "I don't believe you, Braun. You jump from one frying pan directly into another. And I don't know about Megs, though I think you two might deserve each other. You'll have to talk to Mr. Pedamore about that."

"You're a hard man, Hatfield."

Hatfield shrugged. "That's a good thing in my line of work. So, you figured that out, too, on your own, did you? Yes, I let you escape."

"It took a while, but when I did, I counted on you, Hatfield. Thanks for the help. I'd probably be on the ground with a bullet in me instead of Freeman if you hadn't been here. Things got even more dicey than I expected when that dye-pack went off. Funny as hell, though, you've got to admit."

No reaction registered from the agent.

"Uh, listen, I've got a camera up in the barn taking pictures as we speak. I need to go get it."

A devious grin creased the agent's lips. "Really? Let's go together," he said, motioning towards the barn. The two men strolled leisurely, side by side, as though they'd always been best friends. Which they weren't.

"I did like the dye-pack thing, by the way. Nice diversion. Might use it myself someday."

"Yeah? Well, you're welcome to it. Consider it a gift."

"I will. You know, Braun, in the end, you're not that hard to figure out. I knew exactly where you were going, I just didn't know how wild things would get. Why'd you do it? Risk your life, I mean. It wasn't necessary, you know. Seems out of character, in my opinion."

"Not really, if you knew me as well as you say you do. Listen, can we drop the gloves for a minute, and I ask you something that's been bothering me ever since I got dragged deeper into all this by Fagan."

"You can ask."

"Okay. How did Fagan know that Edison was planning to bump him off?"

Hatfield remained silent while they continued their stroll towards the barn.

Just when Brian thought Hatfield was going to answer, that he had decided to maintain his stoic, mouth-shut routine, he found himself pleasantly surprised.

"I guess there's no harm in saying, after all you've been through. I'll give you the condensed, simple version and let Pedamore fill in the holes if he wants to: It was all very complex bringing things together. It actually goes back over a year. The FBI got wind that Elite Security was doing more than private duty. Hit squads. I managed to infiltrate the organization. I had to impress them to get in deeper, so we arranged a show for them down in Argentina. Made it look like I took out some bad guys and their boss. The whole thing was a setup, of course." He tapped Brian's arm as they walked. "It went hell of a lot smoother than this deal."

"I'm sure it did, *Songbird*."

"Since you seem to like aliases so well, Diaz—we called him Jail Bird—was imbedded in Zeta because they also had some shady dealings going on, several indictments from their actions in Iraq. It was pure luck that they hooked onto Fagan's shirttails at the time. Anyway, once I found out what Edison was up to, so Diaz and I got together with Pedamore and put the whole thing together. Diaz dropped the word to Freeman that he had inside info about what Elite was up to, namely, a hit on the senator, and that fell in perfect with Fagan's mania about Elite. He had them targeted in his mind from the beginning, anyway. This second phase has been in operation about six months. Then, you showed up, and you know the rest."

Listening to Hatfield's abbreviated version, Brian was amazed at how it had all come together. "So, Fagan was already breaking the law before I showed up, right?"

"Oh yeah. We had him dead in our sights. He really screwed the pooch when he called you in, though." Hatfield removed his cap and vigorously scrubbed his burred scalp. "I need a bath. Bad. We never did figure out why he called you. He could've pulled this all off with none of the drama."

"Pedamore said it was power," Brian offered. "I think he planned on everything working smooth as glass, then he would flash my pictures of his fake assassination across television screens everywhere. He didn't know you were FBI. From what you said, he thought you were in cahoots with Diaz and Zeta."

Hatfield just shrugged.

Just inside the barn, Brian stopped him from going any further. "You think I'm pretty self-centered, don't you, Hatfield? I just want you to know, it's not all about me, all the time. I count my friends on one hand and still have fingers to spare. If Fagan hadn't gone after Joanna and Harry…I might have bowed out earlier."

"I doubt it," Hatfield replied.

"Well, I guess we both used each other to get what we wanted in the end. Why else let me go? I got my piece of hide from Fagan, and you get to put him behind bars." Brian started for the loft ladder.

"Just never figured you for a hero, Braun," he said, pointing at the ladder, "Go ahead, you first, I'm right behind you."

After making it through the floor opening, Brian stepped aside out of the agent's sight, and slipped a decoy memory card from his watch pocket and palmed it.

Hatfield's head popped up through the opening, "Wait a second, will you?" he ordered.

Brian waited until Hatfield had climbed off the ladder and then moved to the still clicking Nikon. He remotely switched off the shutter, and proceeded to remove the camera from the tripod.

"I'll take that," Hatfield said, holding out his hand.

"Shit, Hatfield. I thought we were friends? You can have the memory card, but the camera's mine," Brian shot back, tugging it to his chest. "I'm not letting the FBI confiscate this. It's how I make an honest living."

"Yeah, right. Okay, the card then," he said, his hand still

outstretched.

"Fine." Brian popped out the memory card, palmed it, made the switch, and handed the decoy to the agent.

"Happy?" Brian snapped.

"No, just surprised. No argument? No fuss? It's not like you to let something as valuable as this go so easily."

"You really think you know me, don't you, Hatfield? But in this case, there was no need. I knew you'd want it, and that you'll give it back when you're done."

"Yeah, like you think you know *me*," Hatfield retorted. "That was a good attempt, but I can't make any promises there. You'll have to negotiate returns with with Pedamore. I'm just collecting evidence. You're not as smart as you think you are, Braun. Speaking of which, how'd you come up with 'Eddy Ross'?"

Brian shrugged nonchalantly, wondering how Hatfield had come across one of his several identity names, in the case, the one he'd resurrected to making the car arrangements with Harvey Sensabaugh.

Hatfield gave Brian a sly smile, then switched subjects. "And while we're on the subject of memory cards, what about the first one? From Saturday?"

"Don't get greedy, Hatfield." Brian said, moving to the loft door and gazing out over the scene below. "Here comes the cavalry," he said, spotting an ambulance and a long line of SUV's, and cop cars bouncing along the pasture road. "So Fagan will go down hard?"

Hatfield walked up beside Brian to view the caravan. "I need to be down there," he said, and turned back towards the ladder. "Oh yeah, at the very least, he tried to shoot you today. That's attempted murder, but since you have a tendency to piss off people, I'm not sure that one will stick." He smirked at his own joke. "He put out a contract on Mr. Morgan, that's capital murder. There's the kidnapping of Miss Johns, and we can probably hang an 'engaging in organized criminal activity' charge on him, since he was in cahoots with the Zeta boys. I would imagine it's safe to say he'll never again see the light of day, starting tonight."

"Good," Brian nodded. "Then, it was worth it."

"Not a bad day's work, Braun."

"By the way, who shot Freeman? You?"

Hatfield shook his head. "No. Agent Zahn took the shot. His first. He'll be dealing with that for a while."

"But, he saved another's life."

"Doesn't make it any easier, Braun. This wasn't Hollywood. It was the real deal."

"Well, then, thank him for me, if I don't get a chance to do it on my own."

"I will. But you should make a point to tell him yourself if you're so concerned about him."

Brian shrugged, undecided. "Since you're wrapping things up here, can I go home, now?"

"Not yet, I've got more business to take care of here, first. Make sure Freeman's body is picked up, and get Fagan and Little into custody and booked. After that we can."

"We? Why can't I just go now? I've got a four-wheeler waiting for me on the back road."

"It's stolen, Braun. Don't you have enough explaining to do

without getting caught driving a stolen vehicle, too?"

Brian started packing up his equipment for the ride home. "Then, you go and do what you need to. I think I'll just wait awhile and watch from up here," he said, and flopped down, dangling his feet outside the loft door. He reached into his bag, and dug out a couple of peanut butter energy bars and a bottle of water. He offered one of the bars to Hatfield. "Energy bar?"

Shutterbug

DAY 4
Tuesday, September 8, 2009

Shutterbug

Chapter 51

Rockaway was sitting in the same booth at The Shack they'd occupied on the fateful day of the shootout, holding a half empty pitcher of beer, a full frosted mug in front of him, an empty one next to it for his longtime student-photographer friend. He waved Brian over.

"Long time, no see, Brauny. Take a seat," he said, motioning Brian to the booth.

"Need some help with that pitcher or you working both mugs all alone?"

"Actually, I'm just startin'." He poured Brian a glass. "Sit down."

They shook hands and Brian took a seat. Brian could see right off that Rock wasn't his usual cocky self. Something was on his mind.

"How are you, Brauny? You doing okay?"

"Yeah, sure. Nothing a little sleep won't cure. And you? You look like shit."

Rockaway finally cracked a smile. "To be frank, my friend, I've never been better." He held up his mug and saluted his young friend. "Here's to more good times."

"Speaking of good times," Brian said, "what's the word on Harry? Last I heard he was doing better every day. I'm going by to see him when we finish here. You want to go with me?"

"Nah, you go ahead," Rockaway said. "I went this morning. They moved him out of ICU. He's got his own room now. He's already grabbing at nurses' asses. The guy's got no class. That conspiracy maniac will milk this thing to the end and beyond. He's such an asshole."

"Yeah, I know how you feel about him. That's why you're up there day and night since he was shot. Yeah, he's a real asshole." Brian clinked his mug to Rock's and continued: "Where's Louise? You order anything to eat or are you drinking your lunch today?"

"She'll be back in a minute. She's out back. Two rib plates are on their way here. So, I understand you had some excitement yesterday. Fill me in."

For what seemed the hundredth time, Brian regurgitated his tale, except he included the details he couldn't divulged to anyone else. He told him about his escape, and how Sensabaugh helped. He described the chase from the hospital, the successful car switch. He described in minute detail how he felt waiting for Fagan in the barn, and how strange it was that he felt no fear when he approached the man and the three Zeta boys out in the open. He got a good laugh from Rockaway, when he described Fagan opening up the watch box and the dye-pack exploding all over him.

Rockaway stopped him to catch his breath while holding onto a side-stitch. "I was curious as hell about that, ever since I heard it was on your grocery list to Sensabaugh. What was that all about, really?"

Brian shrugged. "I wanted him marked. Humiliated."

Rockaway took a drink. "I was pretty pissed, buddy-boy, when you ran out on me in the hospital and left me in the middle of all those feds." He took another sip of beer. "But I got to know John Lee better. He's not such a bad sort for somebody on the wrong side of the law, you know."

"Didn't have time to think, Rock. Instinct, survival maybe. I don't know." Brian continued how the whole thing was a setup orchestrated by Pedamore and Hatfield, which Rocky seemed to already know. "Yeah, I had the same time later with Hatfield that you did with Pedamore. We never kissed and made up," Brian said, with a grin. "I think we just ended up agreeing to disagree and left it at that. And Pedamore's not too happy about the memory card I switched on Freeman at the barn with pictures of my senior prom. But we'll work something out. I don't need him doggin' my trail every minute, trying to get the original back."

"Well! If it ain't Mr. Brian Braun! I swear!" Louise called out, appearing as if out of nowhere.

Brian got up and gave her a big hug and a kiss on the cheek. "You're my girl, Louise. Don't know what I've done without you."

"Get your skinny ass shot off, that's what! Now, sit down, Honey. Food's on the way." She slapped the palm of her hand flat on the table. The sound of metal against wood resounded. "You're waitin' on these, I expect. Right, Honey?" She lifted her hand away and exposed the keys to the Road Runner and the memory card from Brian's first trip to the barn. She waved at Brian and Rockaway on her way out. "I can tell ya'll got a lot to talk about. I'll get the food and be back."

"That's some woman," laughed Rockaway.

Brian scooped the memory card off the table, put it in his watch pocket. Then he pushed the keys across to Rockaway. "Even the FBI couldn't find it. There you go, the keys to your baby."

Louise returned almost immediately with their plates. "Another pitcher?" She asked. Rockaway nodded in the affirmative.

"So you planning on just sitting here getting shit-faced, Rock? That's not like you," Brian offered.

Rockaway picked at his potato salad for a second and then gave Brian his serious look, indicating something big was up. "I went by school this morning."

"Get your parking spot back?" Brian probed, biting into a rib.

"Don't need it anymore. I resigned."

Brian stopped in mid-chew. "You what?"

"Resigned." Rockaway said, propping his elbows on the table and leaning in. "Let me ask you something, Brauny. How did you feel out there this weekend? I mean, really. Runnin' from the cops. Facing down Fagan, guns drawn, all that shit."

Brian copied Rockaway and leaned in, too. "Jazzed. What about you, Rock?"

He nodded "Yeah. Fuckin' jazzed, Brauny boy. I'm not proud of what I did to Maxwell, but he started it. Still, I'm tired. Tired as hell of teaching these little preppie college pricks how to put a camera up to their noses and push a button. Everything's 'stick it in a machine and bingo, it's printed'. No more dark rooms, sniffing chemicals. I'm telling you, the good ol' days of photography are gone, Brauny."

"So? What's next?"

Rockaway smiled big this time. "I've been on the horn with Reuters, Associated Press, *The Times*. I'm going back to war, Brauny.

322

I'm hitting the hot spots again. Hurricanes and earthquakes are the rage for now, but I'm sure I can locate a good war somewhere in between. I've got enough money stashed away to pay my own way until I'm either too old to keep going or get my ass shot off. One of the two."

"Rock, are you crazy?" Brian asked. Then, he stopped and thought about what further to say. Given his own life-choices, what right did he have to question his friend's. Brian reached across the table and grasped Rock's hand, then released it. "You old fucker, you. Need an assistant? I know one."

"Nah, you'd slow me down." He reached in his shirt pocket and pulled out a piece of paper, laid it on the table next to the Road Runner keys. He pushed them both across the table.

"What's this?" Brian asked.

"What do you think it is? You think I can drive the Road Runner through the jungles in South America? Here's the title, I've already signed it over, and the keys."

Brian shook his head. "Takin' this all a little far, aren't we, Rock? I mean..."

"Shut up, Brauny. Don't look a gift horse in the mouth." He took a swig of beer and wiped the foam from his mustache. "I'm not dead or dyin' kid, not yet, anyway. I'm gonna be all over the place. It'd be a waste to put such a beauty in storage for two or three years. She's like a wild horse. Needs the range. Needs to be driven...ah shit, it's only a piece of damn metal, Brauny. Take it."

"Okay," Brian said, reaching for the keys, "I'm tired of driving that ratty old Jeep anyway. Just don't come crying back here in six months wanting it back, 'cause it ain't gonna happen."

Rockaway smiled. "Good. Now, what's on *your* mind? What're you going to do with yourself?"

"I'm going to Canada." Brian waited for a reaction, but all Rockaway did was take another swig of beer and grab a rib.

Finally, Rockaway said, "Vacation?"

"Work."

"Taking pictures of senators getting shot?"

"Not unless it's over my shoulder while somebody's chasing me down, taking pot shots at me."

Rockaway stopped eating. "You're going back in the business, aren't you, Brauny? Damnation. I knew it."

Brian shrugged. "Same bug that bit you bit me. Sensabaugh and I already have a sweet deal in the works. We talked this morning. It seems I'm developing a certain notoriety..." Brian paused to take a drink. "Rock, I'm dying taking pictures of things that sit still and don't do anything."

Then Rockaway asked the question Brian didn't want to hear. "What about Joanna?"

Brian looked down into his plate for an answer. "I talked to her earlier today. She's been receiving phone calls and emails from every major national and international media organization around the world since the story broke. And, she received a Fedex package from an unknown sender that contains enough mind-blowing information to create a second shit storm of even greater proportion. She said it will blow wide open all of that Elite has been up to for years. It'll create a feeding frenzy for the Washington crowd. I think she's going to be very busy. We both hit that big fork in the road: I'm going back to my old career while hers is about to blast off into space. I can't bring her crashing down as a result of my dealings. Guilt by association, you know. Like you, for me the straight life sucks. Been there and sampled it, at least."

Rockaway's reached his hand across the table palm up.

"Then give me back the keys."

Shutterbug

About the Author

Buz Sawyers resides in Rowlett, Texas, where he taught English in the Garland Independent School district for twenty years. He graduated from the University of Texas at Dallas with a BA in Literary Studies and an MA in Creative Writing. He currently teaches English and writing at Argosy University in Dallas. He has four published books under his belt: "No Point in Dying Now" (PublishAmerica 2003), an historical novel of the Civil War; "A Debt Unpaid" (PublishAmerica 2005), a post-Civil War sequel; "Decades in Anadar" (PublishAmerica 2006), a collection of short stories; and "Murder: Shaken, Not Stirred" (PublishAmerica 2009), a murder mystery circa 1969.

Buz can be contacted via his author website at www.bsawyers.com

If you enjoyed *Shutterbug,* consider these other fine books from Savant Books and Publications:

Essay, Essay, Essay by Yasuo Kobachi
Aloha from Coffee Island by Walter Miyanari
Footprints, Smiles and Little White Lies by Daniel S. Janik
The Illustrated Middle Earth by Daniel S. Janik
Last and Final Harvest by Daniel S. Janik
A Whale's Tale by Daniel S. Janik
Tropic of California by R. Page Kaufman
Tropic of California (the companion music CD) by R. Page Kaufman
The Village Curtain by Tony Tame
Dare to Love in Oz by William Maltese
The Interzone by Tatsuyuki Kobayashi
Today I Am a Man by Larry Rodness
The Bahrain Conspiracy by Bentley Gates
Called Home by Gloria Schumann
Kanaka Blues by Mike Farris
First Breath edited by Z. M. Oliver
Poor Rich by Jean Blasiar
The Jumper Chronicles by W. C. Peever
William Maltese's Flicker by William Maltese
My Unborn Child by Orest Stocco
Last Song of the Whales by Four Arrows
Perilous Panacea by Ronald Klueh
Falling but Fulfilled by Zachary M. Oliver
Mythical Voyage by Robin Ymer
Hello, Norma Jean by Sue Dolleris
Richer by Jean Blasiar
Manifest Intent by Mike Farris
Charlie No Face by David B. Seaburn
Number One Bestseller by Brian Morley
My Two Wives and Three Husbands by S. Stanley Gordon
In Dire Straits by Jim Currie
Wretched Land by Mila Komarnisky
Chan Kim by Ilan Herman

Who's Killing All the Lawyers? by A. G. Hayes
Ammon's Horn by G. Amati
Wavelengths edited by Zachary M. Oliver
Almost Paradise by Laurie Hanan
Communion by Jean Blasiar and Jonathan Marcantoni
The Oil Man by Leon Puissegur
Random Views of Asia from the Mid-Pacific by William E. Sharp
The Isla Vista Crucible by Reilly Ridgell
Blood Money by Scott Mastro
In the Himalayan Nights by Anoop Chandola
On My Behalf by Helen Doan
Traveler's Rest by Jonathan Marcantoni
Keys in the River by Tendai Mwanaka
Chimney Bluffs by David B. Seaburn
The Loons by Sue Dolleris
Light Surfer by David Allan Williams
The Judas List by A. G. Hayes
Path of the Templar - Book 2 of The Jumper Chronicles by W. C. Peever
The Desperate Cycle by Tony Tame

Soon To be Released:
Blessed are the Peacekeepers by Tom Donnelly and Mike Munger
The Lazarus Conspiracies by Richard Rose
The Hanging of Dr. Hanson by Bentley Gates

http://www.savantbooksandpublications.com

329